To the memory of Gary Salt, fine friend, esteemed literary agent,
West Coast pillar of strength, an ally for 22 years,
dead of cancer at 53. I call that too young.
Goodbye, Gary.

Corkscrew

Corkscrew

Donald E. Westlake

ROBERT HALE · LONDON

© Donald E. Westlake 2000
First published in Great Britain 2000

ISBN 0 7090 6757 7

Robert Hale Limited
Clerkenwell House
Clerkenwell Green
London EC1R 0HT

The right of Donald E. Westlake to be identified as
author of this work has been asserted by him
in accordance with the Copyright, Designs and
Patents Act 1988.

2 4 6 8 10 9 7 5 3 1

Typeset by
Derek Doyle & Associates, Liverpool.
Printed in Great Britain by
St Edmundsbury Press, Bury St Edmunds, Suffolk.
Bound by Woolnough Bookbinding Ltd.

One

Bryce wrote: 'Kyrgyzstan. Mineral wealth includes gold. 95% within Tien Shan mountain range. Capital: Bishkek.' Then he put his pen on the pad and turned pages in the book open before him on the table, looking for more about the Tien Shan mountain range. It sounded rugged, a good setting.

Around him in this research section in the Mid-Manhattan Library were dozens of other solitaries, studying books, making notes. It felt comforting to be among them.

A whisper at his ear: 'Mr Proctorr?'

Oh, well, he thought. Duty calls. He looked up and there he was, young, mid-twenties probably, skinny and pale, his face too small for those big eyeglasses, his smile tentative, afraid of rebuff: 'You *are* Bryce Proctorr, aren't you?'

Bryce nodded. 'That's me.'

'I *love* your books, Mr Proctorr,' the fan said. 'I don't want to interrupt—'

'That's okay.'

The fan's lined notebook and ballpoint pen were extended: 'Would you—? I'll tape it into my copy of *Double in Diamonds* when I get home.'

'Well, fine, you do that,' Bryce said. He took the pad and pen. 'What's your name?'

'Gene.'

They agreed on a spelling, and Bryce wrote, 'To Gene, All The Best, Bryce Proctorr.'

'Thank you, sir, thank you.'

'My pleasure.' He felt as though he were asleep through this, watching through closed transparent eyelids. Gene went away, and Bryce tried to search again for the Tien Shan mountain range, but he couldn't. He couldn't *care* about the Tien Shan mountain range.

This wasn't working. He knew he was spinning his wheels, but he'd thought, to do some research, even to do some pretend work, would be better than to just sit in the apartment, watch old video-tapes, certainly better than to go back to the empty house in Connecticut on a weekday. But he couldn't feel himself, he was here but he wasn't here, this crap he was doing was crap. There was no *story* in this.

He felt restless, a little lonely, as he moved through the library toward the exit, and then his eye was snagged by something famil-iar. Someone familiar, a familiar face, in profile, bent over a thick book, seated before a thick book, copying addresses into a small memo pad. A familiar face, out of the past. Bryce slowed, and the name came: Wayne Prentice.

He almost walked on by, but then he thought, Wayne. Whatever happened to Wayne Prentice? Twenty-five-year-old memories riffled, like a book of postcards, always groups, at parties, crowded into cars, at Jones Beach, in bars, the small living rooms of small underfurnished apartments. They were never close, but always friends, and then there was a day they didn't happen to meet, and now it's twenty years, more than twenty years, and whatever happened to Wayne Prentice? Didn't he publish some books?

Wayne's hair was thinner and neater than Bryce remembered, his face in profile fleshier; but I've aged, too, he thought. Both men were in chinos, Wayne's tan, Bryce's black, Bryce in scuffed big sneakers, Wayne in shabby brown loafers. Wayne's windbreaker was dull green cotton, Bryce's buff suede. We look like old friends, he thought.

Bryce veered toward the other man, his pen in his left inside pocket, notepad left outside pocket, smile on his face. Now that he was famous, recognized almost everywhere, he found it easy to approach people; they thought they already knew him. And of course Wayne already did.

'Wayne?'

He looked up, and his expression was haggard, eyes morose. He was what? Forty-four, Bryce's age? Around there, but he looked older.

And of course he recognized Bryce at once, and his expression lifted, film lifting from his eyes, eager smile on his face as he jumped to his feet, losing his place in the book. 'Bryce! My God, where did you come from? What are you doing *here*?'

'Same as you,' Bryce said with an easy grin, hoping this wasn't a mistake. What if he asks me for money? 'Library research. I keep telling my editor, I got into the fiction racket so I could make it all up, but no, everybody wants the details right.' Gesturing at the now-closed reference book in front of Wayne, he said, 'You know what I mean.'

'Sure,' Wayne said, but he looked faintly doubtful.

He won't ask me for money, Bryce decided, and if he does I'll give him some and see the back of him. 'Want to take a break?'

'Absolutely,' Wayne said.

'Let's go have a drink.'

The bar was old-fashioned looking, with heavy dark maroon banquettes and fake Tiffany lamps turned low, as though the place had been designed for adulterers, but the dozen people in here at four in the afternoon on a Tuesday were all tourists speaking languages other than English. The waiter was an older man, heavyset, sour, who didn't seem right in the job; as though he'd lost a more suitable position and this was all he could find. Bryce told him, 'A Bloody Mary,' and explained to Wayne, 'It's a food.'

'Then I'll have one, too,' Wayne decided.

The waiter went away, and Bryce said, 'God, it's been years.'

'I've been trying to think how many.'

'At least twenty. I think you'd just sold a novel.'

Wayne nodded. 'Probably. I took that money and went to Italy for a year, to Milan, research for the next one. Lost touch with a lot of people, then.'

Their Bloody Marys came, they toasted one another, and Bryce said, 'You don't write any more?' Then, at the twisted expression on Wayne's face, knew he'd been terribly stupid. 'I'm sorry, did I—'

But Wayne was shaking his head. 'No, no, don't worry about it. It's a good question. *Am* I writing any more?'

Bryce wasn't used to feeling awkward, and was regretting this reunion. 'I just, I don't think I've seen your name for a while.'

'No, you haven't.' Suddenly, Wayne gave him a beaming smile, as though the sun had come out. 'By God,' he said, 'I can tell you the truth! For the first time, I can tell the truth.'

Bryce's regret grew more acute. 'I don't follow.'

'This won't take long,' Wayne promised. 'I didn't write one novel, I wrote seven. The first one, *The Pollux Perspective*, did—'

'*That's* right! I've been trying to remember the title.' And the subject; that part hadn't come back yet.

'Well, it did better than anybody expected,' Wayne said. 'So then I got a two-book deal at a *much* better advance, and both of those books did great.'

'This is all fine so far,' Bryce said, and wondered what the disaster would be. Drink? A bad marriage?

Wayne said, 'Let me tell you the world we live in now. It's the world of the computer.'

'Well, that's true.'

'People don't make decisions any more, the computer makes the decisions.' Wayne leaned closer. 'Let me tell you what's happening to writers.'

'Wayne,' Bryce said gently, 'I am a writer.'

'You've made it,' Wayne told him. 'You're above the tide, this shit doesn't affect you. It affects the mid-list guys, like me. The big chain bookstores, they've each got the computer, and the computer says, we took five thousand of his last book, but we only sold thirty-one hundred, so don't order more than thirty-five hundred. So there's thinner distribution, and you sell twenty-seven hundred, so the next time they order three thousand.'

Bryce said, 'There's only one way for that to go.'

'You know it. As the sales go down, the advances go down. My eighth book, the publisher offered twenty thousand dollars.'

'Down from?'

'My third contract was the best,' Wayne said. 'Books four and five. I got seventy-five thousand each, with ad-promo money and a little publicity tour, Boston and Washington and the West Coast. But then the sales started down . . .'

'Because of the computer.'

'That's right.' Wayne tasted his Bloody Mary. 'My editor still believed in me,' he said, 'so he pushed through an almost-as-good contract next time, sixty for the sixth book and seventy-five for the seventh, but no promos, no tours. And down went the sales, and the next time, twenty grand. For one book only. No more multi-book contracts.'

Bryce could comprehend all that, as something that might have happened to him, but had not. 'Jesus, Wayne,' he said. 'What did you do?'

'What other people already did,' Wayne told him, with a glint of remembered anger. 'I got out of their fucking computer.'

'You got out? How?'

'I'll tell you a secret,' Wayne said. 'All over this town, people are writing their first novel *again*.'

It took Bryce a second to figure that one out, and then he grinned and said, 'A pen name.'

'A protected pen name. It's no good if the publisher knows. Only the agent knows it's me.' Wayne had a little more of his Bloody Mary and shook his head. 'It's a complicated life,' he said. 'Since I did spend that one year in Italy, the story is, I'm an expatriate American living in Milan, and I travel around Europe a lot, I'm an antiques appraiser, so all communication is through the agent. If I have to write to my editor, or send in changes, it's all done by E-mail.'

'As though it's E-mail from Milan.'

'Nothing could be easier.'

Bryce laughed. 'They think they're E-mailing you all the way to Italy, and you're . . .'

'Down in Greenwich Village.'

Bryce shook his head, appreciating that as though it were a story gimmick. Then he said, 'It's worth it?'

'Well, you know,' Wayne said, 'there's got to be a downside. I can't promote the book or go on tour or do interviews. I can't develop any kind of personal relationship with my editor, which can be a drag.'

'Sure.'

'But there's an upside, too,' Wayne told him. 'I took that eighth book, the one my first publisher would only offer twenty thousand for, I switched it around enough so it wouldn't be recognized, my agent sent it out, a different publisher offered sixty thousand.'

'Because it was a first novel.'

'Because it was *good*,' Wayne insisted. 'It was an exciting story, and the writer didn't have any miserable track record in the computers. So they could look at the *book*, and not at a lot of old sales figures.'

Bryce grinned. 'I love a scheme that works,' he said.

'For a while, it went fine,' Wayne said. 'One-book deals, because I wasn't a pro, I was some antiques expert off in Italy. But the second book went up to seventy-five, the third to eighty-five. Sales on the third were slower, the fourth we went back down to seventy-five.'

'It's happening faster,' Bryce said.

'Three weeks ago, the publisher rejected book number five. No deal at any price.'

Bryce could sympathize with that pain, though nothing quite like it had ever happened to him. 'Oh, Wayne,' he said, 'that's a bitch.'

'My agent made some phone calls,' Wayne said, 'but everybody knows everybody's track record, and everybody has to sell through the same computers. Nobody wants Tim Fleet.'

'That's you?'

'It used to be.'

'Wait a minute,' Bryce said. '*The Doppler Effect*?'

'That was the third one.'

'Your publisher sent me the galleys,' Bryce said, and offered a sheepish shrug. 'I don't think I gave you a quote.'

'Doesn't matter.' Wayne looked past Bryce at nothing and said, 'I'm not sure anything matters.'

'Well, what's going to happen with the new book?'

'Nothing. I said to my agent, why don't I put my real name on it, see what happens, and he said, the computer still remembers me, nobody's in a hurry to bring Wayne Prentice back, and besides that I've been gone for seven years. The computer will remember me, but the readers won't.'

'Jesus Christ, Wayne, what a shitty situation.'

'I'm well aware of that,' Wayne said. 'Shall we do another round?'

'Not another Bloody Mary.'

'Beer is also a food.'

'You're right.'

They called the waiter over and decided on two Beck's, and then Bryce said, 'What are you going to do?'

'I made a resumé,' Wayne told him. 'I'm gonna try to get a teaching job somewhere. That's what I was doing in the library, getting addresses of colleges.'

'Well, at least it'll keep you going for a while.'

'I suppose.'

The beers were brought, and they sipped, and Bryce looked at Wayne's unhappy face. He doesn't want to teach in some college, he thought. He wants to be a writer, the poor bastard. He is a writer, and they've shot it out from under him.

What a stupid joke, to meet him at this point, when *I'm* not even a writer any more, when it's dried up and I'm—

And he thought of it. He thought of the story, he thought of it *as* a story. For the first time in over a year, he thought in terms of *story*.

That had been the first element in his love for and fascination with the work of the novelist, that slow but unstoppable movement through the story, *finding* the story, finding each turn in it, each step forward. It was a maze, a labyrinth, every time, that you constructed and solved in the same instant, finding *this* turn, finding *this* turn, finding *this* turn.

That's what had been missing from his brain for the last year, more than a year, the tracking through the story, discovering the route, surprised and delighted by himself at every new vista, every new completed step forward. His life had been frustrating and boring and interminable the last year and a half because that, the motor of his existence, had been missing from it. He hadn't had that pleasure for such a long time, and now, just this instant, it had come back.

But not exactly a story, not something he would go home and write. Something else.

Wayne was looking at him, curious. 'Bryce? What is it?'

'Hold it a minute,' Bryce said. 'Let me think about this, let me think this through.'

Wayne waited, his brow furrowed, a little worried on Bryce's behalf, and Bryce thought it through. Could he suggest it? Could it work? Was it the answer?

He thought yes.

'Bryce? You okay?'

'Wayne, listen,' Bryce said. 'You know how you— You know, you're working along in a book, you're trying to figure out the story, but where's the hook, the narrative hook, what *moves* this story, and you can't get it and you can't get it and you *can't* get it, and then all of a sudden there it *is*! You know?'

'Sure,' Wayne said. 'It has to come, or where are you?'

'And sometimes not at all what you expected, or thought you were looking for.'

'Those are the best,' Wayne said.

'I just found my hook,' Bryce told him.

'What, in the book you're working on?'

'No, the life I'm working on. Wayne, the truth is, I haven't been able to write in almost a year and a half.'

Wayne stared at him in disbelief. 'You?'

'That's how long I've been involved in this shitty shitty divorce. I should never have left my first wife,' he said, and shook his head. 'I know how stupid that sounds, believe me, Ellen was Mother Teresa compared to Lucie. Lucie's out to get everything, everything, it's wearing me down, lawyers, depositions, accountants. She has half the copyright on everything I published during the marriage, and she wants a hell of a lot more, and it just won't come to an end.'

'That's awful,' Wayne said. '*There* I've been lucky. Susan and I are still together, no problem. I've known other people got into that kind of thing, and I really think it's usually more the spite and the bad feelings than the money.'

'With Lucie, it's the money,' Bryce assured him. 'It's the spite and the bad feelings, all right, but it is goddam well the money.'

'I'm sorry, man.'

'Thank you. I'm almost a year past my deadline on the next book, the editor's calling me, little gentle hints, I'm lying to him, it's coming along, wanna be sure it's right. And meantime the lawyers and all the rest of it are eating up what money I have, and I don't get the next big chunk until I deliver a manuscript.'

'You've got to have some kind of cushion.'

Bryce grinned at him. 'You think so? Three kids in college at the same time, none of them with Lucie, thank God, plus the lawyers and the accountants and the alimony to Ellen and the house in Connecticut and the apartment in the city and the maintenance *she* gets every month.'

'Well, every divorce has to end sooner or later,' Wayne said. 'This is only temporary.'

'Well, it *seems* permanent,' Bryce told him. 'But now I've got my hook, my narrative hook. All of a sudden, I've figured it out. I know how to get past this place. And *you're* getting past it, too.'

Wayne shook his head. 'What do you mean?'

'You have a book and no publisher,' Bryce reminded him. 'I have a publisher and I don't have a book.'

'What?' Wayne half-grinned, saying, 'You're joking, you're putting me on.'

'I am not. I remember *The Doppler Effect*, it was good, I remember thinking, this guy writes kind of like me. Suspense, action, but with the big picture. This manuscript of yours, what's the story?'

'There's a businessman,' Wayne said, 'he's had some dealings with a senator. Nothing shady, nothing important. But now a special prosecutor is investigating the senator, and his staff keep sniffing around the businessman, thinking he has something for them. He doesn't, but he does have shady stuff elsewhere, environmental shit he's pulling, and he doesn't want them to find that when all they need is the goods on the senator, which he doesn't have. He has to make the investigation go away.'

'So what does he do?'

'He kills the senator,' Wayne said.

Bryce shook his head. 'That's a short story.'

'It's the first hundred pages. There's a lot more, a lot about Washington, about deep-sea pollution, and Wall Street. Your book *Two of a Kind*, if you described the setup on that, anybody would say it's just a short story.'

Bryce smiled. He knew it was going to be all right. 'You see? We can make it work.'

'No,' Wayne said. 'You aren't serious about this.'

'Of course I am. Who's seen your manuscript?'

'My wife and my agent and my former editor.'

'Send it to me,' Bryce said. 'I'll give you my card. Send it to me, and if it's what I think it is, I'll fiddle it around a little, send it in as *my* next book. Wayne, my advance is a million one.'

Wayne looked impressed, but nodded and said, 'I thought it was in that area.'

'I split it with you,' Bryce said. 'Before commissions and taxes and all that, we'll work out all those details, that's five hundred fifty thousand for each of us. That's seven times what you would have gotten if your publisher had stuck with you.'

Wayne said, 'Bryce, this is crazy.'

'No, it isn't. Wayne, what does it matter to you what name goes on the book? You were never gonna be able to claim it anyway, it was gonna be Tim Fleet.'

'Yes, but—'

'This way, we both get a breather, we both have money in the bank, we both have time to organize our lives.'

'You'd have a book out there,' Wayne told him, 'with your name on it, that you didn't do.'

'I don't give a shit,' Bryce said. 'It wouldn't be the first time in the history of publishing that happened, and it won't be the last, and I don't give a shit.'

Wayne sat frowning, trying to find objections. 'If anybody ever found out . . .'

'That's my worry, not yours.'

'I suppose, I suppose you could . . .' Wayne frowned and frowned, then shook his head and gave Bryce a quizzical grin as he said, 'It could work, couldn't it?'

'It'll save my bacon. It'll save your bacon.'

Thoughtfully, Wayne said, 'I was never gonna be a good college teacher.'

'You'll send me the book.'

Wayne nodded. 'I'll mail it in the morning.'

'And we have a deal.'

'We have a deal.'

'With one condition,' Bryce said.

Wayne looked at him. 'There's a condition?'

'Just one.'

'Sure. What is it?'

This was it, now. Bryce looked levelly into Wayne's eyes. 'My wife must be dead,' he said.

Two

Susan wasn't home yet, which was just as well. Wayne wanted to think some before he told her about today. He wanted a clear head. He wasn't used to a Bloody Mary and a bottle of beer in the middle of the afternoon, it left him buzzy, with a vaguely upset stomach. And he also wasn't used to offers like the one from Bryce Proctorr.

Did I like him, in the old days? He could barely remember the Bryce of back then, because of course he'd been so aware of the changing Bryce over the years. Book after book on the best-seller list, interviews on television, op-ed pieces in the *New York Times*. He'd done a magazine ad for BMW. So it was hard to remember back twenty years when they'd both been young writers in New York, scuffling, hanging out with similar friends, all of them in that soft world before the triumphs and the defeats.

Wayne hadn't wanted to say so, but he'd read about Bryce's marriage trouble in *People*, about eight months ago. There was a picture in the magazine of Bryce and Lucie 'in happier times' sprawled grinning together on a red velvet chaise set out on the green lawn in front of their big white-columned Connecticut home. He'd thought then that Lucie, a narrow-faced blonde, looked beautiful but dangerous, as though she might be slightly unbalanced.

Wayne sometimes talked to himself out loud in the apartment, because Susan worked away and he worked at home, so he was alone a lot in these rooms, wandering around them when not at the computer, saying his thoughts aloud, sometimes surprised to hear what he was thinking, often not even bothering to listen. Now, walking through the apartment toward the kitchen, hoping there was some buttermilk left, thinking buttermilk would ease the jumpy stomach and help clear away the buzziness in his head, he said, 'It takes a rich man to think that way. He's a rich man now. And if you're a rich man, you find somebody to do your dirty work.'

There was a third of a carton of buttermilk in the refrigerator; he drank it straight from the carton, standing in the middle of the kitchen. It was a large kitchen for Manhattan, in a rather large six-room apartment on Perry Street in Greenwich Village. Susan couldn't have children, so it was really too big an apartment for them, but it was rent stabilized. If they went anywhere else, they'd pay more. And they liked having the space, having one room that was the equivalent of an attic, another rarity in Manhattan. When times were good, they saw no reason to move to a better place, and when times were bad – were they bad now? or not? – they hung on to this nice inexpensive roomy cave in the city.

Standing in the kitchen, holding the empty carton, looking at the neat array of spice bottles and boxes on the open shelf near the stove, alphabetized by Susan, Wayne said, 'Why does he think *I'd* do a thing like that? He doesn't even *know* me. I've never so much as *hurt* anybody, I don't— When was the last time I even had a fight? Grade school, must be. I'm not the person for this! It's *insulting!*'

He threw the carton away, in the bag under the sink, and when he straightened he saw himself in the window there. The kitchen and second bath were the only interior rooms in the apartment, both with windows onto the airshaft, six stories from roof to ground, they on the fourth floor of this walkup. By day, what they saw out this window was grimy black bricks and the window of another kitchen, that one always with its yellowish shade drawn. By night, they either saw the yellow light of that window or, if that other kitchen was dark, they saw themselves, reflected in the glass.

It was just dark outside, no one home in the apartment across the way, and Wayne saw himself. He looked frightened, like someone who's been almost hit by a car. Or doesn't know if there's another car coming.

He turned away from that image. He never spoke aloud when he could see his reflection. Now, his back to the sink, he said, 'He doesn't know he's insulting me. He doesn't know or care anything about me. I'm just a tool he might use. What the rich man might use. Five hundred and fifty thousand dollars.'

He shook his head and left the kitchen and moved on to his office, the smallest of the bedrooms, what the families in apartments like this called the nursery. He liked its snugness, the array of pictures and cartoons and notes and book jackets and oddments on its walls, the desk he'd made years ago out of two low metal filing cabinets and a solid door from the lumber yard.

He sat at his desk, and did nothing at first, simply absorbed the sense of the room. Then he switched everything on, and rested his fingers on the keys.

My wife must be dead.

What? What do you mean?

In order for this to work, Wayne, Lucie has to die. If she doesn't die, the deal's off.

Are you asking me—

Wayne, Wayne, no, I'm not asking or suggesting *anything*. But just this is the situation, Wayne. The divorce isn't done yet, we're still married. If I turn in this book, she'll want half. The law says she gets half. And I'm giving you half. What does that leave *me*?

But— Why did you suggest it if you— If you can't *do* it!

We can do it, Wayne. We *can* do it. There's just one simple thing. Lucie has to go.

You want me to—

Wayne, I don't *want* you to do anything but send me the manuscript. Then we'll see if it's possible to work something out, like I suggested.

But not if your wife's alive.

There's no point in it, Wayne, you can see that yourself.

(silence – long silence – Bryce looks at Wayne – Wayne tries not to look at anything)

I have to meet her. I have to talk with her.

Wayne? About what?

The weather. Connecticut. Anything.

Not to say, You know, Lucie, your husband just put a price on your head.

No, no, that's not what I was thinking at all.

Then what were you thinking?

You say she's a bad person, spiteful and greedy.

Oh, trust me, Wayne.

Well, no, I don't want to. I want to know she really is as bad as you say.

You mean, if she's the witch I think she is, it'd be easier.

Bryce, I don't even know if it's possible.

No, neither of us does. I understand this is a brand new thought for both of us, it isn't easy.

I have to meet her.

I don't think that's a good idea.

Why not?

She's everything I said, every bit the bitch I say she is, but she can come on like something else. Wayne, reflect a minute. I fell in love with her once. Maybe you'll fall in love with her.

No.

How can you be so sure?

Susan.

You've never—

Not for a second.

Not even thought about it?

What for? Were you catting around? While you were married to Lucie?

No, I wasn't. But the instant she left, boy...

Susan isn't leaving me.

You've been married, how long?

Nineteen years.

Kids?

No.

Just the two of you.

That's all we need.

That's wonderful, Wayne, I envy you that.

Thanks.

That's what I want, next time. Do it right at last.

I wish you the best.

Thank you. I'll figure out some way for you to meet her.

Good.

And send me the book.

Oh, I will.

Wayne read the dialogue over and over. Sometimes he read parts of it out loud, both his lines and Bryce's. He made Bryce sound insinuating, manipulative. He made himself sound innocent, vulnerable. When he heard Susan's key in the front door, he looked at the wall clock to the left of his desk. Six-fifteen. He'd been in here an hour and ten minutes. He moved the cursor to the X in the upper right corner of the screen, clicked. The boxed message appeared: 'Do you want to save changes to Document 1?' Cursor to *No*: click.

All gone.

Susan worked for UniCare, a kind of umbrella organization for charities, funded mostly by New York State and partly by the tobacco companies. Not a charity itself, its job was to move the available funds around, to match resources with needs. The people with the money were for the most part soulless bureaucrats, who had no real interest in what they were doing, while the people running the charities were for the most part sentimentalists with their hearts on their sleeves, forever on the brink of tears at the thought of their 'clients.' These two groups could not possibly talk to one another under any circumstances. Susan, who could talk to both sides without losing her temper, was invaluable. She'd started with UniCare as a secretary fourteen years ago, and was now assistant director; that invaluable.

She was also invaluable to Wayne. He knew that his life was devoted to fiction, to the unreal, and he thought sometimes, if it hadn't been for Susan's solid linkage to the factual, he wouldn't have survived this long. He believed that might be the reason so many writers fell into drink or drugs; at the end of the day, they just didn't want to have to go back to that drabber world where everybody else had to live.

'Hi, honey,' he said, appreciating her lithe slenderness as she came down the hall in her office jacket and skirt, fawn-brown hair bobbing at her cheeks.

'Sweetie,' Susan said, and paused in the hallway for a quick peck of a kiss. Her lips were always so soft, so much softer than they looked, that it always took him by surprise. Every day he kissed her, more than once, and every day he was surprised.

He followed her into the kitchen. Even though she had the job outside the house and he was in here all day long, she was responsible for dinner. They'd both grown up in traditional families, where women did the cooking and men famously didn't know the first thing about cooking indoors but did all the cooking outside. There was no outside connected to a Greenwich Village apartment, so whatever alfresco culinary talents Wayne might have picked up from older male relatives around Hartford had certainly atrophied by now, and he had no interior chef talents at all. Susan too thought of cooking in a gender way, and after a few failed efforts on Wayne's part, several years ago, to put together something that could look like the evening meal, she'd assured him she didn't mind taking the responsibility, and apparently she didn't.

What this meant, in practical terms, was that during the week she would bring home a meal already prepared by somebody else, which only required heating. Fortunately, in the Village there were a number of specialty shops that could provide meals a thousand times better than supermarket frozen foods, so they didn't have to dumb down their taste buds to get through life. And frequently, on weekends, particularly if they were having friends over, Susan would actually cook, and was very good at it.

Now he followed her as she carried her white and green

Balducci's shopping bag into the kitchen and put it on the counter. Looking at the wall clock, she said, 'Dinner after the news?'

'Sure,' he said.

'I'll put it in during the first commercial.'

He also looked at the clock. The network news would be on in twelve minutes. He'd come into the kitchen with her in order to tell her about the meeting with Bryce Proctorr, the strange proposition he had to think about, but could they cover all that in twelve minutes? He wanted her undivided attention, because he really needed her thoughts on this. I should forget this craziness right now, he told himself, and I know I should, but I won't be able to until Susan says so.

I'll tell her after the news, he decided, which was a relief, because in fact he hadn't figured out how he would tell her. How lead into it? What spin to put on it? I'll figure all that out during the news, he thought, and then tell her.

In fact, he told her over tonight's cod fillets in cream sauce and broccoli and scalloped potatoes and Corbett Canyon chardonnay in the dining room, another rarity in this neighborhood. Candles were on the table, and only reflected electric light spilled in from the kitchen. 'You won't believe who I ran into today,' he began.

'Mmm?'

'I went to the library,' he explained, 'to get college addresses. You know, for the resumés.'

'Mmm,' she said, without looking at him. He knew she wasn't happy about that idea. She didn't think a college campus was the right place for him, and she certainly didn't want to have to give up her job and her home to go live in some small college town in Pennsylvania or Ohio. She'd let him know her feelings on the subject, as she always did, but she'd also let him know she understood he'd only go through with it if he absolutely had to, so whatever happened, she'd go along with him. But she wouldn't get into animated conversation with him about college addresses and resumés.

He said, 'Bryce Proctorr.'

She looked up. 'The writer?'

'The famous writer. I used to know him years ago, before I met you. Before I went to Italy. Then I came back from Italy, and there was you.'

He grinned at her, still delighted that she'd entered his life. She knew what he was thinking, and grinned back.

That was such a lascivious grin, which no one would ever see but him. He felt himself stirring, but he still had his story to tell, and the thought of the story deflected him entirely.

He said, 'Anyway, he was in the library, doing some research. He saw me first and came over and said hello and we went for a drink together.'

'So he's a regular guy.'

'I suppose. But he's rich now, you know. He told me he gets a million one per book.'

'He told you.'

'Well, he had a reason.'

'Does he know about your problem?'

'I told him, yeah.'

'And he told you he gets a million one. Rubbed your nose in it.'

'It wasn't like that, Susan. Let me tell you what happened.'

He described their drink together, and how he went first, telling Proctorr his problems, and then Proctorr telling him how his second marriage was ending in a very messy protracted divorce. 'There was something about it in *People* months ago, remember?'

'Not really,' she said. 'But you used to know him, so you'd have been interested.'

'He offered me a deal,' Wayne said. His heart was pounding now, and his stomach muscles were clenched. The food from Balducci's was good, as it always was, but he couldn't possibly swallow.

'A deal? What do you mean, a deal?'

'He's been so emotionally caught up in this divorce thing, he hasn't been able to work for a year and a half. He owes a book, and he doesn't have one, and he needs the money. He wants to publish *The Domino Doublet* under his name. If,' he added quickly, 'he thinks it's good enough.'

Susan put down her fork and cocked her head, to hear him more plainly. 'He wants to take *your* book? As though it's his?'

'It's a kind of a compliment, in a funny kind of way,' Wayne told her. 'I mean, he already knows my work. He's read *The Doppler Effect*, some of the others.'

'But Wayne, why would you want to do that?'

'For five hundred fifty thousand dollars.'

She sat back. 'Oh.'

'I'm supposed to mail him the manuscript,' Wayne said. 'If he thinks it's good enough, he'll put his name on it – his title, too, I suppose – and send it in as his, and we split the money. And nobody ever knows, not even his agent or his editor.'

'Oh, Wayne . . .'

'You know,' he said, '*The Domino Doublet* wasn't going to be by Wayne Prentice anyway, it was another Tim Fleet.'

'But it seems so . . . strange,' she said.

'Famous writers have been ghostwritten before,' Wayne assured her, 'when they had writer's block, or they were drunk, or whatever. Publishing is full of the rumors, always has been.'

'Yes, I know about those,' she said, since she'd been around the publishing world for years, through him.

'So this is just that again,' he said. 'I can't get *The Domino Doublet* published myself, under any name. This way, instead of not being worth a nickel, it's worth half a million dollars.'

'I guess . . . I guess you should say yes.'

'But there's one extra kicker to it,' he said.

She waited. 'Yes? What?'

'Something he wants.' It was very hard to actually say it in words.

'Something he wants?' That little leering smile again, and she said, 'What does he want, *droit de seigneur*?'

He laughed, suddenly realizing how tense he'd become, as rigid as crystal; tap me, and I'll shatter. 'No, that would be an easy one, I'd just tell him to go to hell.'

'Good,' she said, still smiling.

He didn't feel like smiling. He looked at his uneaten dinner in the candlelight, pale cod, pale potatoes, acid-green broccoli. 'He wants me to kill his wife.'

'What?'

Now he looked at her astounded, disbelieving face. 'Essentially, what it is, that way, I'd be getting her half of the money.'

'Wayne, what are you *talking* about?'

'If she's alive, she gets half his advance for the book. If I get the other half, there's nothing for Bryce, no reason for him to do it.'

'He's paying you to kill his wife.'

'Yes.' Wayne shook his head. '*And* for a book.'

They were both silent, neither eating, she frowning at him, he miserably looking everywhere around the candlelit room except at her. The wall clock in the kitchen was battery-operated, and the minute hand *clicked* at every second's jerk forward, a sound they almost never heard, but which both could hear now, as loud as a metal spoon being tapped on the table between them.

'What did you tell him?' Said so softly he barely heard it, above the ticks.

'I said I had to meet her.'

That surprised her. 'Meet her? Why?'

'Well, he was describing how awful she was, greedy, nasty, a real bitch. If she was that bad . . .'

'It would be a little easier. Oh, Wayne.'

'I know, I know. But the point is, he agreed. He's going to figure out a way for me to meet her. In the meantime, I'm supposed to send him the manuscript. Tomorrow.' He shook his head. 'I'll send out some of those resumés at the same time, might as well get back to reality a little bit.'

'No.'

He looked at her. 'No? What do you mean, no?'

'Don't send out any resumés,' she said. 'Not yet.'

'Why not?'

She didn't say anything. He watched her, waiting, and she said, 'Wait till you've met her.'

His breath stopped. They gazed at each other, both unblinking, and he thought, she wants me to do it! He'd been so sure she would pull him back from the brink, sure of her solidity, her disdain for fantasy. They stared at each other, and he read the grim set of her jaw, and he said, 'And if it turns out he's wrong? She's a decent woman, someone we'd like?'

'Then you send the resumés,' she said, and looked away from him, and said, 'You're not eating your dinner.'

'Neither are you. Susan, why do you want me to wait?'

She nodded, still looking away, then faced him again to say, 'I've been feeling awful about this college idea.'

'I know you have. I have, too.'

'Wayne, it's the end of the marriage, I know it is, but what could I say? What was the alternative? You can't live on *me*. Of course, you *could*, but you can't. The life you had for twenty years just dried up, and it isn't your fault, I know it isn't. The markets change, the rules of the game change, everybody knows that's true, nobody ever thinks the axe is going to come down on *him*. But it comes down on someone, and this time it was you.'

'Not the end of the marriage, Susan.'

'We'd hate each other in Fine Arts Gulch, sweetie, you know we would. We'd hate ourselves, and we'd hate each other, and one day I'd pack up and come home, and you wouldn't be able to.'

'But what we're talking about doing here, I mean, you know, this is—'

'You don't have to say the words, sweetie,' she said. 'We know what we're talking about.'

'Susan, I thought you'd—'

'I want *us*, Wayne. I want this apartment and this life. I want my job, I want what I *do*. I don't want the world to be able to kick us apart like some sand castle.'

He looked down at his plate. He picked up his fork, but didn't do anything with it. Then he looked up again, and Susan was watching him, impassive. He said, 'What if she turns out to be a nice person?'

Her eyes glittered. 'We'll see,' she said.

Three

The Ambien wasn't working. Bryce didn't want to open his eyes, didn't want to acknowledge that he was still awake, but finally boredom and exasperation and worry all combined in him with sufficient force to drive his eyelids up, and the red LED letters on the bedside clock read *4:19*. Oh, damn.

If Isabelle could have stayed over, surely he'd be asleep now. With her beside him, *somebody* beside him, a warm and companionable body, the insomnia would not come back. But Lucie had hired private detectives – he'd have known that even if lawyer Bob hadn't warned him about it – and there was only so much he dared do before the divorce was complete. He could date Isabelle, have dinner with Isabelle, but sleep alone, or *not* sleep, but alone, night after night.

Sometimes he got up and read, sometimes he got up and drank, sometimes he got up and watched a tape, but usually he just lay in bed and worried or raged or felt sorry for himself. Sometimes the sleeping pills worked, and then he would get up in the morning feeling fine, almost his old self. Sometimes they didn't work. Tonight it wasn't working.

And tonight he had a fresh worry to rasp and grate inside his brain, claw at him in the dark. What stupidity it had been to make that offer to Wayne Prentice! How could he have exposed himself that way, made himself so vulnerable to somebody he barely knew, didn't really know at all?

What if Prentice talks? What if he were to go to Lucie? What if he were to decide the way to kick his career back into life was with publicity, telling everybody in the world that Bryce Proctorr had offered him half a million dollars to kill his wife? The theory of rocketry: you go up by pushing down. Wayne Prentice goes up by pushing Bryce Proctorr down.

It was as though he'd been plotting a story, making something up he could use as part of a book; but not a very good book. Prentice must have thought he was insane, and maybe he was. This sudden little scheme pops into his head, and he acts as though it's *real*, for God's sake. Plays out a scene. Behaves as though fiction could ever be fact. Leave that stuff in your office, he told himself, but it was too late.

Could he deny it? If Prentice went public, could he say, 'What a stupid idea. I'd never make a suggestion like that, and certainly not to somebody I don't even know, haven't seen for over twenty years. The man's just a publicity hound, that's all, and if he repeats his accusations I'll have to make a complaint with the police.'

Be stern, be confident, be outraged. *I'm* the star, he told himself. Who is Wayne Prentice? Nobody. Less than nobody. Not even Tim Fleet any more.

When the clock read 5:04, he got up and roamed around the apartment, turning on all the lights. From the spacious living room, decorated by Lucie and Bloomingdale's, he could look out and down at Central Park, and the buildings of Fifth Avenue over on the other side. The dining room, at the south-east corner of the apartment, had the Central Park view as well, but also had the terrace on the south side of the building, fifteen stories up, looking down toward midtown.

He stepped out there, dressed only in his gray robe, barefoot, but there was a mean wind coming over from New Jersey, and tonight he didn't like the sense of height, the proximity of empty air hundreds of feet above the pavement. If I ever kill myself, he thought, I'll do it here, dive over that rail.

He wouldn't kill himself, he had no need to, he never would, but tonight he could feel that draw, almost tidal, the tugging on his arms, the gentle push in the middle of his back. You'd sleep, he found himself thinking, and went back inside.

It was very bad to be this alone, for this long. It made him afraid of himself on his own terrace, a place he normally loved. It made him blurt out foolishness to a stranger, leaving himself open to God knows what.

The 'study' was what he called the room that was part library and part entertainment center. His big-screen TV was hidden behind antique-looking mahogany doors, flanked by shelves of books, but the giveaway was the leather sofa against the opposite wall. Bryce wandered into the study, after coming in from the terrace, and opened the mahogany doors. Then he stood dull-eyed awhile, exhausted but not sleepy, looking at his dim reflection in the TV screen. Finally, he stooped to pull open one of the drawers under the TV where the tapes were hidden, and chose *Singin' in the Rain*.

Partway through, he fell asleep.

For two nights after his blunder with Wayne Prentice, the insomnia was worse than ever, so that he roamed around all day feeling logy and sapped of energy. These were the times when he felt, Give her everything, bring it to an end, sign anything, agree to anything, let her have it all, the past and the future, I'll start over with nothing, what do I care? But it couldn't work that way, the lawyers and the judges wouldn't let it work that way. The grindstone had to turn at its own slow pace.

Then, on the third day, he got two pieces of mail that changed his mood. The first was the manuscript, in a big manila envelope. Wayne had actually sent him the manuscript. Six hundred twenty-three pages, *The Domino Doublet*, by Tim Fleet. Dedication page: For Susan. That would be the wife. And an unheeded unsigned note on a blank sheet of typewriter paper:

I have to meet her.

He's going to do it.

Bryce sat at the dining room table with his mail, sunlight on the terrace to his left, which had lost its menace. He's going to do it, he thought, and saw that he had been astute, he'd chosen his man well, he'd made a brilliant move.

The other piece of mail that mattered was an invitation to the première of a play, off-Broadway, a little theater downtown on Grove Street. The play had been written by Jack Wagner, who was mostly a magazine journalist. He'd interviewed Bryce ten years ago, and they'd been casual friends ever since. This was Jack's first produced play, about which he was very excited, though it was unlikely that so many as a thousand people would ever see it, and there was certainly no profit to be had from it, not for Jack and probably not for the theater either. But Bryce understood Jack's pleasure and pride; profit wasn't why you did it.

It was nice to get this invitation, but Bryce didn't at first realize it was significant, nor that it was linked to the manuscript that had also come in today's mail. Then he noticed that, in addition to the phone number printed on the invitation with its request for an RSVP, there was a handwritten different phone number and note: 'Bryce, Please call me before you reply. Jack.'

Now, why would that be? The nearest phone was in the kitchen. He went in there, pulled one of the ash-blond stools over from the island, and made the call: 'Jack? It's Bryce.'

'Oh, good. Listen, I don't know if this is awkward or not, but I thought you ought to know.'

'Yeah?'

'Our director, Janet Higgins, is a friend of Lucie's.'

The idea that Lucie could have friends never ceased to amaze. Bryce said, 'Oh. You mean, she's invited.'

'I'm sorry, Bryce, you know I want you there. but if it's a problem . . .'

'Well, yeah, it is,' Bryce said. 'I'll come the second night, all right?'

'I'm sorry, I know what you're going through.'

No, you don't, he thought, but then he had another thought, and sat up straighter on the stool as he said, 'Wait. Jack? Will you wait a second? I have to go get something, I'll be right back.'

'Sure.'

Leaving the phone, he dashed next door into the dining room, grabbed the manila envelope the manuscript had come in, with its Priority Mail stickers on it, and carried it back to the kitchen.

'Jack?'

'Here.'

'There's a guy I'd like to see the play, I think he'd be interested in it. He doesn't know Lucie, so there's no problem there. Could I ask you to invite him instead of me?'

'Well, sure, if you want.'

'Not *instead* of me, I don't mean it like that. I'd just like you to invite him.'

'Fine. Who is he?'

'He's a writer, a novelist, named Wayne Prentice.' He read Jack the return address from the envelope.

Jack said, 'Do I know his work?'

'Maybe from some years ago. He's been blocked for a while, poor guy.'

'Ooh.'

'Maybe you'll inspire him.'

Jack laughed. 'You mean, he'll say, Christ, I can do better than *that*, and there he is, unblocked.'

'That's it. Thanks, Jack.'

'No problem.'

'And thanks for the warning.'

'May you have better days soon, Bryce.'

Bryce looked at that name and return address on the envelope. 'Maybe I will, Jack, thanks,' he said.

There was a Manhattan White Pages kept in the kitchen, under the phone. Wayne Prentice was in it, at the address on Perry Street. He dialed, listened to Wayne's voice on his answering machine, and after the beep he said, 'You'll meet her. Accept the invitation to *Low Fidelity*.'

That night, the pill worked. He slept through until morning.

Four

When Susan came home, Wayne kissed her, but he was distracted. 'I want you to hear something,' he said.

'What?'

She followed him into the kitchen, where they kept the answering machine, while he said, 'I went out to the deli to get some lunch, and when I brought it back there was one message.'

He pressed *Play*: 'You'll meet her. Accept the invitation to *Low Fidelity*.'

'That's Bryce Proctorr,' he told her. 'That's his voice.'

'Play it again.'

He did, and she listened with pursed lips, narrow eyes. 'He sounds arrogant,' she decided.

'He isn't arrogant,' Wayne said. 'He could be, with his success, but he isn't, not really. He's just sure of himself.'

'Play it again.'

After the third time, she said, 'It isn't arrogance, it's nervousness. He's tense, and trying to hide it.'

'He doesn't know if I'll do it or not. He should have *The Domino Doublet* by now, that'll tell him, at least, that I'm thinking about it.'

'What's *Low Fidelity*?'

'I looked it up in *New York*,' he said, and gestured at the magazine he'd left on the kitchen table, propped open with a carving knife. 'It hasn't opened yet, it's going to be in this neighborhood, over on Grove Street, opening next Thursday.'

She stood over the magazine to read the pre-opening notice. 'A new comedy. Never heard of Jack Wagner.'

'Around three-thirty,' he told her, 'I got a phone call from the theater. Nu-Arts, it's called.'

That surprised her. 'They *called* you?'

'I guess she was the cashier or a secretary, I don't know. She said I'd been added to the guest list for the opening night at the request of the author, and I'd be getting an invitation in the mail, but since time is short they wanted to be sure I knew about it.'

'Bryce Proctorr waves his magic wand, and you get invited to the opening of a play.'

'Off-Broadway.'

'Still.' She looked at the notice in the magazine again, then gave Wayne a quirky smile as she said, 'Do you suppose that's *his* pen name? Jack Wagner?'

'Who, Bryce?' Wayne laughed. 'No, why would he?'

'It sounds like a pen name.'

'Bryce Proctorr doesn't use a pen name,' Wayne said, certain of that. 'Besides, if it was something *he* wrote, *she* wouldn't be on the guest list.'

'I suppose.'

The pre-opening notice offered very little, no plot summary, no previous history of the author or anybody else connected with the play, but Susan kept going back to it, as though it contained the answer to a problem that was puzzling her. Wayne watched her, then gestured at the answering machine: 'Do you want to hear it again?'

'No. You'd better erase it.'

'Right.'

That was a strange feeling. You always pushed the *Delete* button to get rid of old messages, but this time it felt different, like being in a spy movie. Or a murder story, getting rid of the evidence.

Beep, said the machine: Your secrets are safe.

She was still frowning at the magazine, but after that beep she transferred her frown to him. 'It's so weird,' she said, 'that he can just do that. Reach out and pluck someone.'

'He knows people, that's all. Susan, we know people, too.'

'Well . . . You told her you're going.'

'We're going. The invitation's for the both of us, or, you know, I can bring a guest, so I said I would.'

'Oh, no,' she said. 'You do this on your own. Next Thursday? I'll have dinner with Jill.'

Jill was a longtime friend, now divorced, a sweet, rather vague woman, with many small unimportant problems. Whenever Wayne had to be away or wasn't available, Susan had dinner with Jill. Wayne's equivalent was a friend from college called Larry, who'd been a crotchety old bachelor from the day of his birth, but whose sardonic sense of humor made him fun to be with, in small doses. Wayne and Susan had kidded a few times about getting soft Jill and hard Larry together, and what a disaster *that* would be!

But Wayne didn't like the Jill idea now. 'Why?' he asked. 'Don't you want to see this famous Lucie?'

'Absolutely not,' she said. 'And I don't want to meet Bryce Proctorr, and I don't want to know any more details about what you're, what you're going to *do* than you absolutely have to tell me.'

'What is this, deniability?' he asked. He was grinning, but he wasn't amused.

'No, of course not,' she said. 'Wayne, this is *your* decision, because it's your burden, whichever way you choose. If I'm part of the decision, it isn't yours any more, and you'll never trust it. Years to come, you'll still have doubts.'

'But you *are* part of the decision. You say our marriage won't last if I take a teaching job at some college, and goddam it, you're probably right. So you are part of it.'

'Not the decision *making*,' Susan insisted. 'I'm not copping out, Wayne, but I don't want to have my own opinion of Lucie Proctorr, or whatever she calls herself. My opinion doesn't matter. My opinion could only complicate things for you, and if I go see her, you'll have to ask me what I think, and I'll have to tell you, and I don't want us in that position.'

He said, 'So you want me to go on my own.'

'You have to. In this, you are on your own.'

'But we do everything together, Susan.'

'Not everything,' she said.

Five

Early Friday afternoon, before leaving town for the weekend, Bryce stopped in to see his lawyer, having called for an appointment. Not lawyer Bob, the divorce man, but his real lawyer, Fred Silver. Fred and lawyer Bob – who thought of himself as Robert Jacoby – were both with the same firm, with offices in the Graybar Building, upstairs from Grand Central. Perfect for Bryce, who'd be taking Metro North into Connecticut.

Fred Silver's hair was silver, and everything about him seemed to flow from this conflux of name and hair. Smooth, gleaming, controlled, expensive. He gave Bryce the same smooth handshake as always, gestured with his clean plump hand at the leather chair where Bryce always sat, and took his seat across the desk from him to say, 'Bob tells me things are moving along.'

'Now ask me,' Bryce said.

Fred chuckled. 'The client always thinks these things take too long. Wait till it's over, you'll be glad Bob dotted the *i*'s.'

'What a lot of *i*'s you have, grandma,' Bryce said. 'But that isn't why I'm here.'

'No, of course not.'

'I need a contract written,' Bryce said. 'I need it as soon as possible, and I need it in absolute secrecy.'

Fred gave him a startled and curious look; Bryce Proctorr was not a client who normally came up with surprises. 'Whatever you tell me, you know,' he said, and waved a hand to suggest the rest of the sentence.

37

'Yes, naturally. Is private.' Bryce rubbed his left hand over his face, as though brushing away cobwebs. It was a gesture that had become frequent with him this last year, though he wasn't yet aware of it. 'You know,' he said, 'this divorce, all this dotting of *i*'s, it's been a real distraction.'

'Of course it has.'

'I haven't been able to work.'

'I know it's hard to concentrate with—'

'No, Fred, I haven't been able to work. Not at all.'

Once more, Fred was surprised. 'You haven't said anything.'

'I haven't exactly been lying,' Bryce said, 'but I haven't been admitting the truth either. Joe asks me – you know, my editor – how's the new book coming along, I say slow. Well, zero is slow, isn't it?'

'Zero? Bryce, honestly, you aren't working at *all*?'

'I don't like to go into the room with the computer,' Bryce told him. 'I'll let a week go by without even looking to see if I have any E-mail.'

Fred now looked very worried. 'Are you seeing anybody?'

'What do you mean, therapy? Fred, *I* know what the problem is. I have this buzzing in my ear and it's called divorce, and until it goes away I can't concentrate on anything else. All therapy would do is give me one more thing to be impatient about.'

Fred, who naturally believed there was a professional of some sort to be hired for every one of life's many problems, spread his hands, saying, with palpable doubt, 'You'll know best, Bryce.'

'I hope I do. Anyway, it can't go on. I owe a book, and I need money. So what I'm doing is, I'm taking on a collaborator.'

'You? Bryce, everything you say to me today is out of character.'

'I have to do *something*, Fred. This guy, I've known him a long time, he's a good writer in his own right, he's published some books, but he's hit on hard times. So he's gonna plot the new one with me, and write it with me, but it would be very bad news commercially if the word got out. So it has to be absolute secrecy.'

'And you can trust this other fellow.'

'Completely. He wants this as much as I do. And it wouldn't help *his* career if the word got around he was becoming a ghost. It would be like people finding out he was writing novelizations.'

'I don't know what that is,' Fred admitted.

'Oh, the paperback form of a movie, written from the screenplay.'

'And it's not considered a very high level of occupation, I take it.'

'Hackwork.'

'I understand.'

When Fred was getting down to business, he would lean forward and put both forearms on the desk, right hand near his pen and yellow pad, and that's what he did now. 'You've worked out the details of the agreement with him?'

'The contract will say he's being hired as an editorial consultant,' Bryce said, and paused while Fred wrote that down. 'It won't say anything about his doing any writing or plotting. It says his work is confidential, and that if he breaks confidentiality the contract is null and void and he doesn't get paid.'

'And if he does get paid?'

'Five hundred fifty thousand dollars, out of the first earnings of the new book.'

This time, Fred was absolutely astonished. 'That's an amazing amount of money, Bryce!'

'It's half the advance,' Bryce pointed out. 'I told you, it's a collaboration, so he has to get half. But after that, any future moneys, foreign sales, movie sales, anything like that, he gets a quarter.'

'Not half?'

'No, a quarter.'

'Will he agree to this?'

'I'm sure he will,' Bryce said, because he wanted to be sure. 'He'll understand, any additional income like that, it would all be coming in because of my name anyway, not because of any specific thing he might have put into the book.'

'I'm sure you're right.' Pen poised, Fred said, 'And what is this collaborator's name?'

'Tim Fleet. Like the street.'

Fred wrote it down. 'And who is representing him?'

'No one. This is just between the two of us.'

Fred put down his pen. 'Are you sure, Bryce? He really should have representation. If there are questions later—'

'There won't be questions,' Bryce assured him, knowing this was merely once again Fred's liking for everybody to be surrounded at all times by a magic circle of professionals. 'Tim and I worked it out,' he said, 'and we shook on it, and now we just need it done in proper legal format.'

'And what's the time frame?'

'As soon as possible. Some time next week?'

'No,' Fred said, 'I meant the term of the collaboration. Deadline, you call it?'

'Oh, no, we'll leave that open,' Bryce said. 'Neither of us wants to *add* pressure.' Grinning, he said, 'The book doesn't even have a title yet. It's just being worked on.'

It *was* being worked on, in fact, and so was the title. In the Danbury train, on the way to his stop, Bethel, the last before the end of the line, he found a dual seat to himself, since he was leaving early enough in the afternoon, ahead of the real rush, and settled down to read the book again, make notes, and think about titles.

The book was good, certainly good enough to become his own. This weekend, he'd scan it into his computer and start the rewrite. He'd keep the basic storyline, but there would have to be changes. There needed to be alterations in tone and mood, differences in language to make the book read like a Bryce Proctorr novel, and also a general tightening to increase the tension, since it seemed to him that one of Wayne's failings was a tendency to write flat, as though it were just a report he was making and not incidents ripe with drama.

Also, the main characters would have to be recast. The senator, for instance, who was our hero's main problem, would have to become someone else entirely. Wayne had written him sort of like a college dean, academic, tough but with gloves on, while Bryce would make him more of a movie director type, more obviously tough and self-assured, and a showboat as well. He'd be fun to write.

The first time through the manuscript, though, he'd concentrate on language. He noticed, for instance, whenever the characters reacted to something they didn't like, they 'winced.' 'Winced' wasn't a word he liked, nor would ever use, so an early order to the computer would be to change every 'winced' to 'twinged.'

The other question was the title. Even if he liked *The Domino Doublet*, which he didn't at all, he wouldn't be able to use it, because Wayne's agent and his former editor had both seen the work under that title. His own third book had been called *An Only Twin*, which would be perfect for this one, given the relationship between the businessman and the senator; too bad he'd already used it up.

A lot of people got off at the two Wilton stops, and then the countryside in the late afternoon light began to look more and more familiar, more and more comfortable. Isabelle would already be there, at the house, when he arrived, and they'd have the weekend.

He felt himself relaxing. He wasn't even thinking now about whether Wayne Prentice would do, he was only thinking about whether his novel would do, and the answer was yes.

Two Faces in the Mirror. He made a note.

Six

Wayne had been trying to work on a new novel. He had an idea about a man whose brother disappears in Central America, and he goes looking for him. The brother was supposedly a stockbroker in New York, but as the hero searches, more and more ambiguities arise. Was his brother really CIA? Was he a money launderer for the drug cartel? Was he involved with right-wing generals? Wayne hadn't decided yet, and felt the character of the hero would eventually lead him to the character of the missing brother. He was calling it *The Shadowed Other*, but he was having a hell of a time getting into it.

In the first place, what was it for? Who was it by? Would he spend all the time and research and effort, and then sell it to some minor house for five thousand dollars? Or to nobody at all? Would he try to create a *third* name? The effort seemed too much, and what good would it do?

Was he a hobbyist now? Was he one of those people who do their writing on weekends and spend ten years finishing a novel and then nobody cares? Even if . . .

Well. Even if he got the money from Bryce and *The Domino Doublet* was published under Bryce's name, what good would that do him in the long run? Bryce wouldn't be blocked forever, and wouldn't need a ghostwriter any more. Sooner or later, the money would be gone, and then what would Wayne do?

The money wasn't the point, anyway, the writing was the point. He wanted to sit at his computer, the same as ever, unreel the stories, but he didn't want it to be meaningless, spinning his wheels, a mockery. He didn't want to be foolish in his own eyes.

And the other problem, of course, was Lucie Proctorr. He started *The Shadowed Other* on Monday, but Thursday just kept looming in his mind, distracting him, forcing him to invent scenarios about Lucie Proctorr rather than Jim Gregory, the hero of his novel.

By Wednesday, he was pacing the apartment more than he was seated at his computer, and Thursday was worse, made even more so by the fact that Susan wasn't coming home from work. She was going directly to Jill's place, up on Riverside Drive, and they'd go to dinner from there.

The invitation to *Low Fidelity* had come in Tuesday's mail, and it had said there would be a cocktail buffet following the performance. The opening night would begin an hour earlier than usual, at seven, so Wayne fed himself left-overs out of the refrigerator at six. 'There's good and bad in everybody,' he told himself, as he paced the kitchen. 'What's *my* grudge against her? *That's* the problem.' He felt more and more tense, and had one glass of white wine to calm himself, but was afraid to drink more.

It was a cool night in early November, not cold enough to need a topcoat. He wore his blazer, a blue shirt, and a red tie, and walked down to Grove Street, arriving at ten to seven, to see the usual cluster of people on the sidewalk out front. He didn't know any of them, and was the only singleton there. He recognized Lucie at once, from her picture in *People*. She stood talking and laughing with two other women, all three of them fortyish and very good-looking, in a Don't Touch The Merchandise way. The other two women were smoking, Lucie was not.

The only reasons to stand outside were to smoke or chat or wait for friends. Wayne had none of those reasons, so he went on inside and showed his invitation to a girl at a folding table set up just to the right of the door. She checked him off on a list, and gave him his ticket and the program.

He went on into the auditorium, which was small, under a very high black ceiling, with steeply raked seating up to the right from the entrance, the stage to the left. There was no curtain fronting the stage, and the set was a busy one, a living room and a kitchen and a staircase, lots of furniture and lots of doors. The stage lights were off, so that the set was faintly mysterious and faintly threatening.

The theater was less than a quarter full, and he saw that in here there were a few other loners like himself. His seat was the last one on the far side, two-thirds of the way up. He crossed between the seats and the stage, aware of people who glanced at him and then away when they didn't know him. Would it matter, later on, if people remembered he'd been here tonight? No, it couldn't.

The program was the off-Broadway version of *Playbill*, full of chatty news about a world very different from his own. The writers he knew were novelists or short-story writers, or they had moved to California to be screenwriters and would occasionally come back to tell their horror stories. Theater people lived in a parallel universe.

The *Playbill* contained the usual pocket biographies, so he read the one about Jack Wagner, the playwright. This was his first play, it seemed. He was a journalist by profession, came from Missouri, had graduated from Antioch, lived near Rhinebeck with his wife, Cindy, and two sons. He had been nominated three times for journalism awards Wayne had never heard of.

More people came in, the theater filling, and then a cheerful older couple claimed the seats to his left. They wore lots of coats and scarves, and she carried a big black leather clunky purse, so it took them some while to get settled, during which Wayne read the list of individuals and organizations that helped support this theater, and then read the biography of the director, Janet Higgins, a native Floridian, who had directed half a dozen off-Broadway plays Wayne had never heard of and had considerable experience as well in 'regional theater.'

'Good evening.'

It was the woman to his left. Her husband was next to Wayne, so she had leaned forward to smile past him.

'Evening,' Wayne said.

'Isn't this wonderful for Jack?'

'From journalism to playwrighting,' Wayne said, with admiration, as though describing some difficult acrobatic performance. 'Quite a leap.'

'No one deserves it more,' she said, which Wayne thought a non sequitur, but he agreed anyway. 'You're right.'

'Fred Gustav,' the man said. 'My wife, Molly.'

'Wayne Prentice.'

'Wasn't the traffic terrible tonight?' Molly asked. 'I couldn't believe it.'

'I walked,' Wayne told her. 'I live nearby.'

They both looked at him as though he were an interesting freak of nature. Molly said, 'You live in the Village?'

'Uh huh.'

'Well, that must be fun,' she said.

'It is.'

'We live in Yonkers,' Fred told him. 'Our boy Perry went to school with Jack.'

'At Antioch.'

'*That's* right!'

Some people a few rows down called to Fred and Molly, who called back, and farther down below Lucie Proctorr came in by herself and took a seat toward the right end of the first row. Her blond hair glittered like gold shavings in the direct beam of one of the ceiling spotlights. The gray unlit set beyond her looked like a grave.

Wayne felt a little sick.

He had no idea what the play was about, except doors were slammed a lot, people stood four-square to shout at one another, and there was a great deal of laughter and even some applause from the audience along the way. Wayne was mostly aware of that blonde head down there, picking up light from the stage.

The odd thing was, he mainly thought about *The Shadowed Other*. Details about Jim Gregory, the people he would meet when he got to Guatemala, how he would go about his search, all these things ran through his head which they hadn't been doing all week.

Wayne suspected there was more applause at the close tonight than there would be at subsequent performances; everybody here, after all, was connected to somebody involved in the show. The actors got sustained applause, and then 'Author!' was called several times, and a beaming bookish man in pebbly brown sports jacket and navy blue turtleneck came out to receive a standing ovation. He had dark-framed eyeglasses that bounced the stage lights at the audience and a neat Vandyke beard. He held his hands together in front of himself as though he were handcuffed, and bobbed his head a lot, and smiled and smiled.

Then, at what Wayne thought was just the right moment, the man on stage raised his hands for the people to be quiet, and they were, and he said, 'None of this could have happened if it wasn't for our wonderful director, Janet Higgins!' and she came out, and was one of the women Lucie had been talking to in front of the theater. There was another standing ovation, during which Lucie, excitedly jumping in the front row, clasped her hands over her head to let Janet Higgins know she was the champ.

Janet Higgins gave a brief laudatory speech, and introduced the founder and general manager of the theater, a rumpled man in a sweater, who gave one more laudatory speech, and then invited everybody up on stage for 'drinks and goodies.'

It was strange to be at a cocktail party on a stage set. You were in a living room, and yet you weren't. People chattered happily, Fred and Molly seated themselves comfortably on the audience-facing sofa, and a number of people sat on the staircase, which didn't actually go anywhere. The kitchen counter became the bar, complete with tuxedoed bartender, and tuxedoed waiters and waitresses circulated with platters of finger food. Wayne nursed a glass of white wine, wandered between living room and kitchen, and wondered how he was going to meet Lucie Proctorr, who was always in the middle of some conversation.

At last he saw that Jack Wagner was free, so he went over, stuck his hand out, and said, 'Congratulations.'

'Oh, thanks,' Wagner said. 'Thanks.' He was very bright-eyed, and his hand when he grasped Wayne's was vibrating. His other hand held a glass of white wine with wavelets in it.

Wayne said, 'I'm Wayne Prentice, I'm the guy Bryce foisted off on you.'

'Oh, *that's* who you are!' His expressions kept swerving, a kaleidoscope of different kinds of joy. 'I'm so glad you could make it,' he said.

'So am I. It's a terrific play.'

'Thank you.'

Looking around, Wayne said, 'Bryce's ex-wife is here someplace, isn't she?'

'Oh, Lucie! Sure, she's a buddy of Janet's. You don't know Lucie?'

'Bryce and I hadn't seen each other in years, until just recently. I guess he started looking up old friends after the marriage died. Listen, I'd love to meet Lucie Proctorr, but I don't know how to go about it.'

'Easiest thing in the world,' Wagner said. 'It's just, I tell you what, we won't mention you're a friend of Bryce's.'

'Good idea. What if I know you,' Wayne suggested, 'because I called you one time to get some background about journalism for a novel I was writing.'

'Perfect. Come on.'

Lucie was in the kitchen, in a little cluster of people by the refrigerator, next to a door that had a stub of porch outside it and beyond that the darkness of offstage. Wagner waited his moment, and then said, 'Lucie, I want you to meet somebody.'

She had a bird's alertness, Wayne noticed, in the way she turned her head, and in the brightness of her eyes. She stepped out of that conversation like stepping out of a tub. 'Yes?'

'Lucie Proctorr, Wayne Prentice.'

'How do you do?'

'Wayne's a novelist, but he's all right.'

'Oh, *some* novelists are all right,' she said, and grinned slightly at Wayne as she said, 'Are you a famous novelist, Mr Prentice?'

'Oh, no,' he said, 'I'm just a door-to-door novelist, I sell books out of the trunk of my car.'

'You must be a very persuasive salesman.'

'I try to be.'

'Sell me,' she said.

He didn't follow. 'What?'

'Sell me a book,' she said.

'Excuse me,' Wagner said, being called away, but neither paid any attention.

'Sell me your latest book,' she said.

That would have been too complicated. He said, 'No, I'll make it easy on myself. I'll sell you my first book.'

She watched him with amused keenness. 'Why is that easier?'

'I was very enthusiastic then.'

'Aren't you enthusiastic now?'

'Sometimes. My first book was called *The Pollux Perspective*, and it was about two army men whose job is to safe-guard a doomsday machine. One of them decides it's a manifestation of God, and has to be protected at all costs, and the other decides it's Armageddon, and its release should not be thwarted. They both think of themselves as the good guy.'

'Very arty,' she said.

'Actually,' he said, 'I was trying to be very commercial. Blowing everything up, you know.'

She looked thoughtful. 'What did you say that was called?'

'*The Pollux Perspective.*'

'But I've *read* that book!'

Astonished, he said, 'You have?'

'My husband had it. Ex-husband. Had it, probably still has it. Do you know him?'

'Your husband?'

'Ex-husband, or at least eventually. Bryce Proctorr.'

'Oh, *he's* famous,' Wayne said. 'I don't think he sells books out of the trunk of his car.'

'No, it might be better for him if he did,' she said. 'Would you fill my wineglass?'

'Delighted,' he assured her, and carried it away, and filled both glasses.

When he got back, she was in a different conversation, but she left it immediately, took her glass, and said, 'Thank you. *The Pollux Perspective*. Why aren't you famous, Mr Prentice? You're as good a writer as my former. Don't you push yourself?'

'Maybe not enough,' he said.

'Well, you're never going to get anywhere being a shrinking violet,' she told him. 'How many books have you published?'

'Twelve.'

'And still among the great unwashed. I think you should be

ashamed of yourself.'

'It might not be entirely my fault.'

'All the losers say that,' she commented.

He could not let her see him become annoyed. 'Have you been around a lot of losers?' he asked her.

'Not for long. What are you working on now?'

'A man whose brother disappears, and he goes looking for him. I think it'll turn out, what he's searching for is himself.'

'Arty but commercial again?'

'Lots of skulduggery,' he said. 'South American generals.'

'Oh, don't we know all that?'

'We don't know my guy and his brother.'

'I'm not sure we need to know them,' she said. 'Sell it to me.'

'Not here. Too much distraction.'

Again, that sharp bird look; a bird of prey? 'Are you asking me for a date?'

He hadn't been. She was so aggressive, so fast, that all he could do was struggle to find immediate answers. Being with her was like being in a tennis match, not having known you'd be expected to play.

'Sure,' he said, because closer to her was where he would have to be, no matter what happened next. He remembered Bryce warning him that *he* had fallen in love with this woman once, and mightn't Wayne do the same? No. He'd said no before because of Susan, but now he could say no because of Lucie; she wasn't restful enough to fall in love with. You might lust after her, to see if it was possible to pin down with your cock that quicksilver quality, but that wouldn't be love.

He said, 'Dinner next Monday?'

'I'm busy Monday. Why not call me Tuesday?'

'Because I don't know your number.'

'Oh, you're about to know my number,' she said, laughing at him, 'and I do believe I'm about to know yours.'

Susan was waiting up when he got home.

'I met her,' he said, and went to the kitchen for another glass of wine, and found Susan expectant in the living room when he got back. He sat down and said, 'Susan, I don't think I ought to talk about this from now on.'

'Just tell me,' she said, 'did you like her?'

'She's interesting but repellent,' he said.

'Good.'

He said, 'I think, Susan, it's time for us to go to bed and have a sexual encounter.'

Amused, she said, 'So Lucie turned you on, did she?'

'She reminded me how much you turn me on,' he said, which was almost the truth.

And later, after Susan fell asleep, he lay thinking how that kind of woman could be a strong draw for a confident, high-powered personality like Bryce. She'd be a challenge to him, and he would never give up believing he was up to the challenge. But she would be relentless, there would never be any cease-fires with her, there was no way to bring that war to an end.

Well, one.

Next day, in the mail, came four copies of a contract, between Bryce Proctorr and Tim Fleet, resident at this address. The wording was careful but straightforward. It described exactly the agreement Bryce had offered when they'd met. 'I notice,' he told himself, 'I get a quarter of any future earnings, subsidiary rights. Movie sales, see that? But that's okay. This is merely a passage through hell, that's all, like Jim Gregory's passage through Guatemala. If *The Domino Doublet*, or whatever Bryce changes it to, if it makes millions and millions of dollars, so what? Let him have three quarters, let him have it all. It wouldn't make a penny, if it didn't have Bryce's name on it in the first place. And after all, one way or another, it isn't about money anyway, is it?'

Along with the contract had come a note on Bryce's small stationery:

Dear Tim,

Please sign all copies, keep one, send the other three to me. Send them when you think the time is right, and

I'll carry them with me when I leave for California for a couple of weeks.

I'm sure this collaboration will be a success for both of us.

Yours,

Bryce

'California for a couple of weeks,' he echoed. 'Of course, to be a continent away when it happens.'

In his office, Wayne had a four-drawer gray metal filing cabinet, man height, beside his desk. He took from its second drawer a fresh unused manila folder and inserted the four copies of the contract and the note into it. Then he took from his wallet the torn off piece of *Playbill* on which, last night, Lucie Proctorr had written her name and phone number and address uptown on Broadway. He copied all that on to a card on his Rolodex, and then the *Playbill* scrap also went into the folder.

He considered the folder for a while, trying to decide what heading to put on the tab, then at last left it blank. He slid it into the drawer between 'LEGAL' and 'MAGAZINES.' He'd know where to find it: 'LUCIE.'

Seven

For a week and a half, Bryce worked contentedly on *Two Faces in the Mirror*. It wasn't that he forgot his troubles, merely that they felt far away.

Structurally, the book was quite good, though there was some time-frame business in the middle that could be plainer; he made it plain. Changing the tone and feel of the book from a Wayne Prentice novel to a Bryce Proctorr novel wasn't hard; instantly he knew how to phrase Wayne's thoughts in his own words.

The third chapter, a very powerful mountainside near-death scene, was now the first chapter, with the rest adapted to fit, which was partly because Bryce thought it read better with that strong opening and partly because, if one of the few people who'd seen the book in its original form were to pick it up and start to read it, the story wouldn't seem instantly familiar. If it felt familiar later on, that would be all right; most novels remind us of other novels.

On the weekend, he could be with Isabelle. A divorced woman of thirty-four, soft and round with lustrous black hair, she was the daughter of a Spanish diplomat who'd retired back to Spain not long ago from some sort of long-term post at the United Nations. Isabelle's ex-husband was Spanish, had divorced her in Spain, and had custody of their three children, all under twelve. This was Isabelle's ongoing agony and struggle, the way Lucie was Bryce's, and they could find temporary respite and forgetfulness and comfort with one another. In Madrid, Isabelle's father was doing his best to get the case reopened, but for some reason the Catholic

Church seemed to be on the ex-husband's side; Bryce thought it smarter not to delve too deeply into that situation.

They traveled separately to and from Connecticut every weekend, she driving up Friday morning and back Monday afternoon. She was a copywriter for an ad agency, working mostly on catalog copy for manufacturers of faux country-style clothing. Her arrangement with her boss was that she could work at home – at Bryce's home, actually – Fridays and Mondays, so long as she was available to have material faxed to her and to fax copy back. Otherwise, it was merely expected that her long weekends would leave her refreshed, with new copy in hand.

Bryce took the train. He used to drive, used to love it, but three winters ago he and Lucie had been a minor part of a multicar pileup during bad rain on Interstate 84, and the sight of the much greater destruction just beyond his own battered BMW – the one he'd gotten for doing the ad – had left him fearful for a long time. He was enjoying too good a life to want to throw it away. And he wasn't a commuter in the normal sense, he didn't have a job with time pressure at the New York end, so why not conveniently, comfortably, safely take the train?

Monday morning he took the train, a later one than the rush-hour people, and again he had a dual seat to himself, so he could continue to go over *Two Faces in the Mirror*. Occasionally, on the train, somebody would ask him for an autograph, but most riders on this line were more sophisticated than that. He could see them recognize him from time to time, but they left him alone.

He had done almost all he could with the manuscript. It had been a good novel to begin with, and he felt he'd made it better. Really, all that was needed now was for Wayne to return the contract.

He had. Bryce got home just before lunchtime, and Saturday's mail was waiting for him, and there was the envelope with 'Prentice' on the return address. Manila envelope, manuscript size, not too thick. Priority Mail sticker.

He saw it, on the table just inside the front door where Jorge, the doorman, always put his mail when he was away, and he felt an instant of terrible fear. He's done it! he thought. She's dead!

He didn't open the envelope then, nor look at the rest of his mail, but went beyond it, feeling weak, knees shaky, and sat in the living room, his back to the view of Central Park. He was trembling, and his throat felt constricted.

No, she isn't dead, he told himself. Calm down. He knew what I meant when I mentioned California in the note. She's still alive.

When he had himself convinced that the only reason he'd experienced that moment of dread was because he'd thought Prentice might have killed her before Bryce could establish his California alibi, he got up and went to the kitchen and found in the refrigerator an open container of plain yogurt. That would settle his stomach. Lucie hadn't liked it when he'd eat yogurt directly from the carton, then put the carton back in the refrigerator, but there was no one around to complain now.

Back in the entryway, he glanced at the rest of the mail without opening it or caring about it, then at last opened the manila envelope from Wayne Prentice, and there they were, the three copies of the contract, with an extra blank sheet of typing paper that said only, in computer printout:

Enjoy California.

There were things to do, the travel agent to be called, other people, packing to do, Isabelle. Could she come to be with him for a while in California? But instead of doing any of that, he put in a call to lawyer Bob, and was told that he was with a client. 'Would you ask him to call me as soon as he's free? It's sort of urgent.'

She said she would, and he went to the bedroom to lay out the things he'd want to take to Los Angeles with him. Too early to phone people there, and he didn't yet feel like calling the travel agent.

The thing is, what if it wasn't necessary? If this divorce thing were going to end soon, then all he and Wayne would have to do would be wait a few weeks, maybe a month at the outside, and then turn in *Two Faces in the Mirror* without the threat of having to give half the money to Lucie. Once the agreement was signed, everything could work just like before, but without that one dangerous step.

If we don't have to take that one dangerous step, he told himself reasonably, it would be better. For us. For me.

It was almost an hour before lawyer Bob returned the call. His voice was distinctive, deep but rough and raspy, as though he could almost sing bass in a barbershop quartet except he wouldn't be quite musical enough. He said, 'Helen says it's urgent.'

'Well, I don't know about urgent,' Bryce said. 'The thing is, I'm going to LA for a while, possible movie deals—'

'I'd hold them up, if you can.'

'Oh, I know, we can do that,' Bryce assured him. 'The thing is, before I leave, I was wondering, is there any chance at all we're gonna see daylight soon?'

'Daylight?' Lawyer Bob didn't seem to understand the concept.

'I mean, closure,' Bryce said. 'Is there any possibility, in the next few weeks, we'll be signing those papers, getting this thing behind us?'

'Not a chance,' lawyer Bob said. 'Next few weeks? I thought you understood, Bryce, it isn't going to happen this year. Spring, if we're lucky.'

'Oh, Jesus, Bob, it's so—'

'Bryce, we've still got unresolved issues before the court. State of residency, for instance. Your copyrights exist where you are. If you were a Connecticut resident, and Lucie remained a New York resident throughout, can a New York court distribute Connecticut property? In some cases, yes. In this case, it's not so clear-cut.'

'I thought we resolved that,' Bryce said. 'I used the Connecticut house as my residence because Connecticut didn't used to have an income tax, and Lucie kept the New York apartment as her residence because it was in her name and they couldn't go crazy with the rent on us.'

'They're appealing the decision,' lawyer Bob said. 'It's really very dry and dull, Bryce, you don't want to hear every gory detail, but believe me, at the end of the day, we'll prevail.'

'The end of the day.'

'Frankly, I think one reason they're stalling is because they're waiting for your next book to be published.'

'Bastards.'

'At some point, not yet,' lawyer Bob said, 'we can make that argument to the court, and I believe it will be persuasive. Until then, we just have to go through the process, that's all.'

'Not this year.'

'Next year. Almost guaranteed.'

'Almost?' He couldn't believe lawyer Bob was serious, but on the other hand, the man had no known sense of humor.

'These things are unpredictable, Bryce,' lawyer Bob said. 'Mostly because people are not at their most rational in a divorce. But my guess on this case, barring anything unforeseen, is sometime in the spring. Thank your lucky stars you two didn't have children, that would *really* drag it out.'

Like Isabelle's children in Spain. There's always somebody worse off than you, Bryce told himself, and an image of Lucie flashed by, immediately suppressed. 'Thanks, Bob,' he said. 'I just wanted to know where I stand.'

'Pretty much where you stood, Bryce.'

'Got it,' Bryce said.

While he was looking up the travel agent's number, he thought, call Lucie? He had the phone number at the apartment she'd taken. Call her, say to her, why don't we just get this over with, go on with our lives? You tell your lawyer to quit stalling, I'll tell my lawyer to quit stalling, we'll just end it, no more bitterness, start thinking about the future for a change.

No. He could hear her voice, he could hear her laugh, he could hear her scorn. Open himself up to her like that? She'd slice him in two.

Besides, there are phone records. There shouldn't be a record of a call from him to her just before . . .

The travel agent's number. He dialed it.

Eight

'I'll be going out tomorrow night,' Wayne said.

Susan almost asked him where he'd be, he could see it in the light of the candles as they ate dinner together, as usual, that Tuesday evening. He could see the question form, and then see her find the answer on her own, and she looked down at her plate, as though embarrassed, and said, in a low voice, 'Will you be late?'

'I don't think so.'

It was as though he were having an affair, seeing another woman, and he and Susan were keeping the marriage alive by pretending it wasn't going on, Susan waiting for it to blow over and for him to return to her, he waiting . . .

For what? For Bryce to call and say it was all a joke? You didn't take me seriously, did you, pal, it was just a bull session, of course that's what it was, a couple plotmeisters sitting around scheming.

The contract was real, drawn up by a real law firm. *The Domino Doublet* had been sent to Bryce and had not come back. He'd returned the contract, with that little note about California. If Bryce wanted to change his mind, this was the time to do it.

And if *Wayne* wanted to change his mind? But how could he? He'd given away his unpublished novel, he'd signed and returned that contract, he'd managed to meet Lucie Proctorr and now he had a dinner date with her. He was in motion, whatever this motion was, and what was the alternative? He was in the situation he was in right now because there *was* no alternative.

They finished the meal in silence, and watched something or other on PBS. When they were going to bed, her body looked strange to him, foreign, not appealing. He sensed that she felt the same way about him.

Before they turned off the lights, she said, 'Is this the end of it?'

'Oh, no,' he said, startled she'd think it would happen that fast, that easily. 'No, this is just— This isn't the end.'

He wanted to say to her, this is just the reconnaissance, really. I'm meeting her at her apartment, and we're going to dinner in her neighborhood, and this is to figure out what the possibilities are. I don't even know what, how I'm going to, what *weapon*. I think I've even been avoiding all those thoughts.

He might have to take a train south some day soon, buy a gun. He'd never owned a gun, never shot one, but maybe.

What else, what were the other possibilities? He'd have to think about it, see if tomorrow evening gave him any ideas. A number of his characters, in his books, had killed other of his characters, in various ways, but at this point he couldn't remember how any of them had done it, or how it had seemed easy.

He wanted to say, no, Susan, this is just the reconnaissance, don't worry about tomorrow. But to say that would begin the conversation they'd agreed not to hold. No conversation, not till later. Some time later.

With the lights off, he suddenly thought of the stack of resumés he'd made at the copy shop. They were still atop the filing cabinet in his office, with the partial list of college addresses that he'd stopped, incomplete, when Bryce had spoken to him. What if he were to send them out, just to see?

Not tomorrow, that would hex everything. Thursday, after his first date (!) with Lucie Proctorr. Not even mention it to Susan, just send them out, see what the responses were. Maybe there was a wonderful job out there he didn't even know about, and some way that Susan could go on with her own career.

I'll send them, he thought. First the reconnaissance with Lucie, then I'll send out the resumés.

He couldn't sleep, was restless. At one time, turning from his side on to his back, his right hand brushed her left hand, and she at once closed her fingers around his. He held tight to her fingers and they lay side by side, on their backs, not talking, grasping hands.

The reservation was for eight, and they'd agreed on the phone he'd pick her up at her place at seven-thirty. 'If the weather's decent, we can walk, it's just a few blocks from you.'

'Oh? Where are we going?'

'Salt,' he said, naming a restaurant near her on Columbus Avenue.

'Well, good,' she said, sounding surprised he'd chosen well. 'I haven't eaten there, I've wanted to.'

'See you tomorrow,' he said, and at seven-thirty Wednesday evening he paid off his cab outside her building and stood a minute on the sidewalk.

It was a cool evening, late November, but dry. Her building was a modern high-rise, taking up half a block of Broadway in the low eighties, on the west side of the street, a part of the spurt of apartment building construction in this neighborhood a dozen years ago. The façade was some kind of mottled maroon stone, highly polished, and the broad entrance was high-tech, glass doors and wall and chrome verticals, as though it were the entrance to an airport building rather than somewhere that people lived. Inside, to the right, a uniformed doorman sat at a wide high desk of the same stone, reading.

A doorman. That wasn't a problem tonight, but what about the future? Whatever he did, however he did it, whenever he did it, it would have to be away from here. And even so, would the doorman, sometime later on, be able to identify him as someone who occasionally visited Lucie Proctorr?

Wayne turned away, and walked slowly up the block, looking through the glass wall at the doorman, who remained deeply involved in his reading. It was a *fotonovela*, a kind of comic book in Spanish that used photographs of actors and actresses instead of drawings.

Wayne walked on to the corner, then turned back, trying to decide what to do. Phone her? Suggest they meet at the restaurant? Too late for that. And what excuse would he give?

It was also too late to leave. His only choice was to keep moving forward, adapt to circumstances.

This time, as he reached the building entrance he turned his coat collar up and pulled his hat a little lower on his forehead; not too much, not to look like an escaped convict. Then he walked through the entrance and immediately held both cupped hands to his mouth, blowing into them. 'Getting cold out there,' he said.

The doorman put a finger on his place in the novela, glancing at Wayne with impatience. 'Who you wanno see?'

'Ms Proctorr.'

The doorman kept that finger on the novela, holding it open, as he reached with his left hand for the house phone, laid it on the counter in front of himself, and punched out the number, saying, 'An you are?'

'Tell her it's Wayland,' he said, and turned away to look out at the street, watching the traffic, giving the doorman less than a profile of his face.

The doorman spoke into the phone, then hung it up and was already looking at his novela when he said, 'Sixteen-C. The secon elevators, back there.'

'Thanks.'

Wayne walked to the elevator feeling pleased with himself. The doorman's accent would have conflated 'Wayland' and 'Wayne' for Lucie, but if he ever had to give a name to the police it would not be Wayne.

He was alone in the elevator. When he stepped out at 16, it was into a smallish well-decorated rectangular space that was shared by four apartments. Lucie stood in the doorway to the left. 'Right on time,' she said. 'Very good.'

'We aim to please.'

'Come on in.'

She stepped back, and he went through the doorway directly into a large but low-ceilinged living room. The place was furnished tastefully but anonymously by the management, like the living room of a good hotel suite. The primary colors were beige and rust, in the sofas, the end tables, the carpet that covered most of the blond wood floor, even the several paintings on the walls, which were of southern European village scenes, steep streets and old stone walls.

'Sit for a minute,' she said, with an airily dismissive wave at the low sofas. 'I'm almost ready. Are we walking?'

'Oh, I think so,' he said. 'It's nice out.'

She said, 'Do you want a drink?'

'Only if you are.'

'One for the road. If I'm going to walk, I want wine. Red wine because it's winter. What about you?'

'Same,' he said.

'I'll be back.'

She went away down an interior hall, and he looked around, deciding not to sink into one of those low sofas. Instead, he crossed the long room to the wide window and looked out over the roofs of shorter buildings to the black river and New Jersey beyond.

Sixteen stories; quite a drop. Except the window was plate glass, and couldn't be opened. Would there be an openable window anywhere in the apartment? Maybe in the bedroom.

Not a good idea. A screaming woman dropping through the night, Wayne waiting for the elevator, and the doorman in the lobby.

She came back with red wine in a surprisingly fancy etched glass. 'Very nice,' he said, taking it.

She said, 'Don't try to figure me out from the surroundings, I rented this place furnished, absolutely everything in here came with it.'

'Everything?'

'Well, almost everything,' she acknowledged, and gave him a narrow-eyed look. 'Why?'

There was a terra-cotta statue of a chunky horse and his bundled-up rider, less than a foot tall, on an end table, too large for the space. Wayne had noticed it on the way in and thought it was probably a copy of one of the thousands of terra-cotta cavalrymen and their mounts that had been discovered buried in China a few years before. He'd read about them in the course of something he was researching. He gestured with the wineglass at the statue and said, 'That's yours, isn't it?'

The narrow-eyed look became narrower. She turned to gaze at horse and rider as though rethinking her ownership of the piece, then nodded briskly at him and said, 'Try, Wayne, not to be too brilliant.'

'That'll be easy,' he said, trying for a friendly smile, wanting to keep it as light as possible. After all, he'd want to come back here, wouldn't he? Another time?

'Good,' she said. Moving away once more toward the hall, she said, 'I won't be long. A man wouldn't notice this sort of thing, but this hair is not ready for public inspection. I'll just be a sec.'

She was fifteen minutes. He spent part of that time, wineglass in hand, wandering the beige room, thinking these apartments would mostly be rented to corporate people, businessmen assigned for a few weeks or a few months to New York. Lucie Proctorr being here showed that she, too, had put her life on hold, waiting for the divorce, the same as Bryce.

He also hefted various objects in the room, looking for something lethal. Everything seemed too lightweight. Besides, could he do that? Hit someone on the back of the head with a ... with that ashtray? All that golden hair; wouldn't it cushion her?

When at last she came out, she looked to his eyes the same as before, but she seemed satisfied with whatever changes she'd made. 'All set. Is it windy?'

'No, not really.'

'I'll bring a scarf,' she decided, and he thought about strangulations with a scarf. Isadora Duncan. He didn't see how that would work.

He helped her with her coat, and they left the apartment to wait for the elevator. Trying to find conversation, he said, 'I was thinking, those furnished apartments like that, they're mostly rented to corporate types.'

'And divorcing women who live alone,' she said, as the elevator arrived. They boarded, she pushed L, and as they descended she said, 'Women who really want to live where there's a doorman.'

'I guess so.'

'Believe me,' she said, 'a doorman is just as good as a husband any day. More reliable, usually.'

'You can feel safe,' he said.

'I always feel safe,' she said.

When they crossed the lobby, he kept Lucie between himself and the doorman, who looked up, recognized the tenant, and said, 'You wan a taxi?'

'No, we're hiking,' she said.

Looking back at his novela, the doorman pushed a button that opened the glass door as they reached it. They went outside and she said, 'Which way?'

'Over to Columbus, I guess, and up.'

They crossed Broadway at the corner and headed down the side street. 'Oh, it's a great night,' she said. 'I can smell winter, can't you?'

'Yes, I can.'

'Oh, God, then Christmas,' she said, and made a disgusted sound. 'Family.'

'You don't like your family?'

'I like them where they are. And I like me where I am.'

'Where are they?'

'A place called Carmody, outside St Louis.' She sounded affectedly weary when she said, 'You fly to St Louis, and some relative has to drive and drive to pick you up and take you home, and then four days later they have to drive you all the way back, and you fly in another airplane, and you say, "Please, God, never again," but there's no escape.'

'What's wrong with your family?'

'Oh, nothing, really, nothing,' she said.

They turned north on Columbus, the herds of headlights descending the avenue toward them, one with every cycle of green, and she said, 'If I'd stayed in Carmody, married somebody I went to high school with, they'd all be just great, and I suppose I'd be a nicer person, too. But I went away, I'm more than fifteen years away, and we don't think like each other any more. I can't *stand* the television they watch. Their jokes are so stale and old, and they *insist* on telling them. And they never understand a word I say, of course. I've been in New York all this time. I was married to the rat for seven years, and when you're married to *him* you go first class, my dear, you meet the elegant and the swellegant. It's not just that I'm a big girl now, I'm a big city girl now. But enough about me, tell me, what do *you* think of me?'

'I think you're funny,' he said, a bit surprised to find that was true. I'm not going to like her, I hope, he thought. I don't have to make Bryce's mistake and fall in love with her, all I have to do is like her, and everything's messed up.

'Funny,' she echoed. 'That's been my goal all these years, to have somebody too cheap to take a taxi think I'm funny.'

Oh, good, he thought, let's have more of that, and they reached the restaurant. 'Here we are,' he said.

They sat at one of the tables in the raised section at the rear, where they could look out and down at the bar, already half full, the pretty brunette bartender in constant motion. Later on, there'd be live jazz, and the bar would fill entirely, and there'd be a second bartender.

After they'd ordered, Lucie turned to him and said, 'So how long have you been divorced?'

Startled, he said, 'What?'

'Oh, come on,' she said, 'everybody our age has been married, and you're not a faggot, and if you're taking me out you're not married any more, so you're divorced. I mean, this is not as brilliant reasoning as you and my dynasty horse.'

'I'm not divorced,' he said. 'Like you, you aren't divorced.'

'Oh, I get it,' she said. '*En train*, the separation in place, the lawyers at the trough. You know, a friend of the rat's once said he'd never heard of a trial separation that didn't work, but I say the trial comes before the separation. So who left who? What's she like?'

What to say? How to handle this? He had to tell some lies, but not too many. He could describe Susan as she was, but give her a bit more of that hard edge she could sometimes have, not with him, but that tough flat voice he'd heard her use on the phone a few times, talking with people about things related to her job. 'Her name is Susan,' he said. 'Susan Costello.'

'She kept her maiden name?'

'On the job.'

'What job?'

'She works for an outfit called UniCare,' he told her. 'They allocate money to charities.'

'What does she do there?'

'She's the assistant director.'

'Of the whole thing?'

'Yeah, the whole thing.'

'It sounds like a big deal,' she said. 'Is it?'

'Yeah, it is. She's testified before congressional committees a couple times. Mostly, though, it's just keeping everything running.'

The waitress brought a small dish, then an *amuse gueules* 'compliments of the chef': avocado puree on sesame-crusted salmon with a dab of Japanese barbeque sauce. When they'd admired it and eaten it, Lucie said, 'So your Susan makes good money.'

'Pretty good,' he agreed. 'Charity work isn't that great, but pretty good.'

'That explains it,' she said.

The waitress took away the small plates and brought their first courses. Lucie started to eat, and Wayne said, 'Explains what?'

She held her fork up to say, *wait, my mouth is full*, then put it down to sip some wine. 'Very good wine.'

'Thank you.'

'And a really good restaurant. You chose well.'

'Thank you again.'

He waited, but she didn't say anything else. When she reached for her fork, he said, 'Explains what?'

'Oh,' she said, as though it hardly mattered. 'I looked you up in Amazon.'

'Oh, did you?' She was that interested, at least.

'You haven't published anything for years and years.'

'Eight years.' No point getting into the tribulations of Tim Fleet.

'And everything's out of print,' she said. 'I clicked for used copies, and there were just a few, for not much money.'

'I've never looked myself up in Amazon,' he said. 'I suppose I ought to.'

'Don't,' she advised, 'you'll find it depressing. But I wondered, what were you living on? I mean, you don't have a job, you go around saying you're a writer. But now, I guess, the only question is, what will you live on after Susan divorces you? She's the one leaving, isn't she?'

'Yes,' he said. 'But I'm not living on Susan, if that's what you mean.'

'Oh?'

'I've had editorial work,' he said, 'other writing work. I support myself.'

'Well, you don't have to be defensive about it,' she said, but there was a gleam in her eye.

Between the appetizer and the main course, she said, 'Will you get alimony?'

'What, *me*? From Susan? No, of course not.'

'Men can, you know. And, God knows, she won't get any from you.'

'You'll be getting alimony,' he said.

'You're damn right I will,' she agreed. 'Once the lawyers get finished with their little dance, and I don't care how long it takes, the longer the better for me, I'm going to be rich, and glad of it. And don't think I haven't earned it. Seven years of *his* ego. And let's not even *talk* about sex.'

'I didn't intend to,' he said.

She looked at him with laughing surprise. 'Wit!' she cried. 'I had no idea you could be witty! Wit *and* brilliance. What a catch you'll be for some solvent girl.'

He paid cash, to avoid any record in this neighborhood. Walking homeward, Columbus Avenue traffic behind them now, giving the sidewalk ahead of them a shifting dull gray gleam, the sky above them featureless, not black but like a thick black cloth over a faint source of light, she said, 'I had fun.'

I'm sure you did, he thought, but said, 'So did I. That's a good place.'

'Do you miss writing?' she asked.

'I write,' he said, but he himself could hear that he was being defensive again.

'I mean novel writing,' she said. 'Come on, you knew what I

meant. The rat had to do it, I told him it was like an addiction, take him away from it a few days, it was like withdrawal, he turned into an absolute bear.'

'I guess that's pretty normal,' he said, thinking how much Bryce must have enjoyed having Lucie describe him to himself, time after time. While he was probably trying to get back to work.

'*Nothing's* normal with a writer,' she said. 'If you swore off, and I guess you must have, left it or it left you, you are no doubt a better person for it.'

'No doubt,' he said.

They were mostly quiet as they walked the side street over to Broadway, crossed, and turned south. Then she said, 'You're very calm, aren't you?'

What now? 'Am I?'

'Oh, I see a little edginess in you sometimes,' she said, 'but not a lot. I think you're basically a calm person.'

'You do?'

'Oh, dear. That sounds dull, doesn't it?' She pretend-smacked herself on the side of the head. 'I didn't mean dull,' she said, 'you're not dull. I just mean you're not antsy all the time.'

He had to smile. 'Like the rat?'

'Exactly. Why did Susan leave you?'

'Maybe because I was dull,' he said.

'Ouch,' she said, and briefly touched his arm, as though to ask forgiveness. 'I really didn't mean dull,' she said. 'Really.'

'Okay.'

'So what was it? Were you playing around?'

'No, of course not,' he said.

'Of course not?' When he glanced her way, he could see her give him a measuring look. He faced front again, as they approached her building, and she said, 'I can see you as a very unfaithful guy. Saying, "Oh, it doesn't count because I only really *love* Susan, but boy, I would like to get next to *that* one, and *that* one." Do you still ove her?'

'I don't know,' he said, wishing she'd ride him on some other topic. 'I suppose we go on loving the person we used to love, one way or another.'

'Are you kidding?' They'd reached her building, and both stood on the sidewalk while she said, 'Do you think, do you honestly think, I have any love in me for the rat? My dear, he wore that off me a long time ago.'

'Was *he* playing around?'

'No,' she said, sounding disgusted. 'I don't think so, anyway. The great love of Bryce Proctorr's life, you know, is Bryce Proctorr. Why would he need to play around?'

'Well, he should be happy now, I guess,' Wayne said.

'I certainly hope not,' she said. 'I suppose you want to come up.'

This was the problem he'd been worrying over since part-way through dinner. She was so aggressive, and so fast, that he had come to realize she would expect more from him on a first date than he'd expected, or was prepared for.

I'd kill her, he thought, but I won't sleep with her, I didn't come here to be unfaithful to Susan. But what was he going to do? He didn't want to alienate Lucie, because he needed to be able to come back, to see her again, take her somewhere safe, when he was ready, when he knew exactly how to go about it, when he was *armed*.

Go with it. For a while, at least, go with it. 'I suppose so,' he said, to echo what she had said: I suppose you want to come up.

'Well, there's enthusiasm,' she said.

'I don't want to push myself on you.'

She tapped his chest with her fingertips. 'Don't worry, my dear, you'll never do that. But you can come up for a few minutes, if you really want. Just so you understand, I will not go to bed with you.'

He hid his relief by pretending to hide his disappointment with a deadpan, 'Okay.'

'We'll have one more glass of wine,' she told him, 'and we'll have a nice chat, and then I'll throw you out.'

'It's a deal,' he said, and would have shaken her hand to confirm it, but she'd already turned away toward the entrance, and the doorman had already seen her and pushed the button to open the door.

Once again, he hid behind that head of golden hair as they went past the doorman's desk.

*

'I'll just be a minute.'

'Fine.'

On one side wall of the living room stood a glass-doored, glass-shelved cabinet that contained a sparse display of trophies and commemorative plates from the fifties and earlier; some decorator's idea of what the nomadic businessman would like. Wayne looked at them, the honors and memorials bleached of meaning in this beige room, while Lucie went off down the interior hall again, and soon he heard a toilet flush.

The end table with the Chinese horse and rider was near the cabinet. Wayne studied it without touching it. This artifact *did* have meaning for her. What?

She came in with two glasses of the red wine, not as good as what they'd been drinking in the restaurant, but in better glasses. 'You don't mind the same glass,' she said.

'Not at all.' He accepted the glass she reached toward him, and she held hers up for a toast, saying, 'To divorce.'

'Sure,' he said, grinning, tapping glasses with her. 'Why?'

'Because you get to meet all new people,' she said, and laughed, and sipped her wine.

'Like Alzheimer's,' he said, and drank.

She made a disgusted face. 'Oh, don't be *morbid*, for God's sake. What did you think of the play the other night?'

Apparently they were to stand here, a two-person cocktail party. He said, 'It was fun.'

Another wrong answer. She made a scrinched-up face, and said, 'Did you really like it?'

'I take it you didn't.'

'What trash,' she said. 'Poor Janet, that's all she gets are these lighter-than-air yuppie comedies; supposed to be all about sex, they're just about some loser's idea of witty repartee. She wants to do better work, she wants to direct at the Public, but she has to build a body of work and all it is is this trash. I told her once, "Janet, you'll have to tie weights to the actors or they'll float up into the flies," that's how lightweight they all are.'

'I bet you did,' he said.

'Of course I did. I always tell the truth, it's easier that way. You like the truth, don't you?'

'Love it,' he said.

'I knew you did. Is Susan any good in bed?'

'Very,' he said, and put his wineglass down on the table next to the dynasty horse, and punched Lucie as hard as he could in the stomach.

They were both astonished. He thought, not now! This is wrong, this isn't what I meant, this is too messy, this isn't right!

Her eyes were widening, her arms were moving in slow motion to fold across her belly, her mouth was opening, she was folding forward. He punched her again, hard, this time in the face, and she jolted back into the cabinet, knocking plates and trophies awry, and he moved in after her.

It's started, it's too late now, I can't go back, what am I going to do?

She leaped at him! He hadn't expected that, either, and his deflection was clumsy, both arms swinging around, thrusting her lunge to his left. He'd thought she would keep falling, back and back, as he would go on hitting her, but her instincts were so aggressive, it was as though they were both acting without thought, even though his brain was full of thoughts, a vast confusion of thoughts, while outside his brain everything was happening too fast.

She came at him with nails, fingers into talons, and he ducked back and away, knowing he couldn't permit her to scar him, mark him, he couldn't leave traces of his flesh under her nails. He kicked wildly, hitting the front of her right thigh, half-turning her as he backpedalled.

She came at him again, blood on her face, mouth distorted, not screaming yet, but soon she'd scream, and he couldn't have that, either. He jumped back a pace, this time aimed, and kicked her solidly, the outside of his right shoe squarely against her right knee. She jerked toward him, and looked astonished as she fell, and he kicked her in the mouth as she was going down.

Loud thump. Let the people downstairs be at the movies. She landed face down, and he dropped heavily to his knees on to her back, reached down, grabbed her jaw in his right hand, the golden hair clutched in his left, and tried to jerk her head around to the right.

He couldn't do it, whatever he was trying to do he wasn't doing it, break her neck or twist off her head or whatever it was, it wasn't working, and he abandoned that and reached out to his left and found the table with the dynasty horse and his wineglass on it, and pulled it to him, horse and glass both flying somewhere.

Rectangular, thin-legged table, but thick solid wooden top. He raised it over his head with both hands and brought the edge of it down hard on the back of her head. And then again on to her neck. And then again on her head.

She wasn't moving. Her arms were half bent, up beside her head, fingers curled. He reached out to move her right arm, and it waggled. He put the table on the floor, leaned down close to her, to the bloody mess of the right side of her face, and very faintly he could hear the ragged breathing.

Until this instant, there had been nothing sexual in it. The whole thing had been so unexpected, so unplanned, so much the result of the tension he was feeling, the fear, the doubt. She had not been a woman, she had merely been something that moved and made sound and it was his job to stop the movement and stop the sounds.

Now, the smell of her, the warmth of the body under his, that faint sound of her breath in and out of her broken nose, and he became aware of her as a sexual being. Oh, don't, he told himself, straightening, still kneeling on her back. Don't be aroused by *this*, for God's sake.

He climbed off her, shaky, tottering. He went down that interior hall and found the antiseptic bare kitchen. Her plastic-bag collection was in a plastic bag inside the doored space under the sink. He chose two large bags from the supermarket and brought them back to the living room.

Her bowels had released. No fear any more of being turned on. He knelt beside her, fitted first one bag and then the other over her head, twisted them at the back of her neck to improve the seal. Then he closed his eyes and knelt there, holding the twisted bags.

He stayed there like that for a long time. He didn't want to think about what he'd just done, he wanted to think about what he had yet to do. Fingerprints. The wineglass, on the floor unbroken. The end table. The doorknob. The door handle under the sink in the kitchen.

Somewhere, she would have a datebook, probably by the phone in her bedroom. His name would be in it, for tonight. Take the entire datebook. Look around for anything else that might have his name on it, or anything about him.

Robbery. This should be a robbery, not a boyfriend, not a crime of passion. Find jewelry, something obvious, anything, something of value, take it away, get rid of it. Rings, necklaces, cascading into the sewer. Not in this neighborhood, he'd walk close to Times Square, Ninth Avenue, where it's darker, drop the stuff into the sewer, take the subway home from the Port Authority Bus Terminal.

Planning. Planning, eyes squeezed shut. Slowly, the thoughts calmed down, and when at last he opened his eyes, he felt so drained he could barely move. All his limbs were stiff. The fingers holding the twisted plastic bags were stiff. He moved himself, this way and that, freed his fingers from the bag, then looked down at her, touched her, inspected her.

She was dead.

As he slid into bed, Susan rolled over in the darkness and said, 'Wayne? What's wrong?'

'It's over,' he said.

'You aren't going to do it?'

'It's done.'

He turned toward her, and she put her arms around him, and he nestled his face in against the warm side of her throat, felt the beating of the pulse there. Her breath was regular in his ear, strong and regular, not weak and ragged.

After a while, she said, 'Was it bad?'

'Worse than you can know,' he said.

Nine

Friday afternoon, Bryce got back to the Bel Air a little after three. He'd had lunch with an actor, a star of tough-cop roles, who wanted to make a series of films based on the characters in Bryce's *Twice Tolled*. Bryce had thought he'd used up those characters by the end of that book, that there was nothing more to say about them, but the actor had a vision.

He kept using the word 'franchise,' which out here apparently didn't mean Burger King but meant a continuing role in a series of films that the actor could be identified with, so that the audience would want to see him play the part again and again. The actor said the general belief out here was that audiences liked that sense of the familiar, given how much a movie ticket costs these days, but Bryce suspected it was the moviemakers themselves who needed that sense of the familiar – remakes, sequels, series, franchises – given how much a *movie* costs these days.

He didn't know if the actor had any kind of studio support behind him for this idea, but saw no reason to throw cold water on it. He wished the actor well, honestly enjoyed the anecdotes, had a very nice lunch, and when he reached the hotel he didn't go at first to the bungalow but inside to the desk, to say, 'Has Ms de Fuentes arrived yet?' Isabelle was supposed to have been on the morning flight out of Kennedy, which should have arrived at eleven-thirty.

'Yes, I believe she's in the bungalow,' the clerk told him, and gestured away to Bryce's left, saying, 'And these two gentlemen are waiting for you.'

Gentlemen? He turned, and saw two men rising from lobby sofas, moving toward him, and his first thought was that they were both the actor he'd just had lunch with. A second later, he realized, no, these were the real thing. And a second after that, he knew what it meant.

Poker face, he told himself, though inside he was flabbergasted. Wayne had done it! He'd actually done it! Somehow, even though he'd come all the way out here to get out of the way, Bryce had never truly believed it, that Wayne would actually go through with it, that this story they were making up together would burst into real life.

Wayne's done it, he thought, and something icy touched his spine.

'Mr Proctorr?'

'Yes?'

'Detective Grasso,' showing a gold badge in a soft black leather case, 'and Detective Maurice, LAPD. We'd like to speak with you for a few minutes.'

'Yes, of course.'

He stood waiting, with a half smile, but Detective Grasso said, 'It should be in private, sir.'

'I don't understand.'

Detective Maurice said, 'We'd like to go to your room, sir, if we could.'

'Oh.' Bryce frowned, reacting to the complications. 'The problem is,' he said, 'my fiancée just arrived from New York, I haven't even seen her yet, I don't know if she's showering or what she might be doing.' Gesturing at the sofas where the two men had been seated, he said, 'Couldn't we talk here?'

'We'd prefer not to be in public, sir,' Detective Grasso said. Both men were polite, but cold, and insistent.

Bryce said, 'Let me call the room, okay?'

'Good idea,' Detective Grasso told him.

They waited near the desk, both watching him, not talking together, as he went over to the house phones. Isabelle answered on the second ring, and he said, 'Sweetheart, hi, it's me, I'm in the lobby.'

'Why?'

'There are two detectives here, police detectives, I don't know what it's about, but they want to talk to me in the bungalow.'

'Detectives?'

'Could you – I don't know, could you go to the coffee shop for a few minutes? I'm sorry to do this to you, sweet—'

'Of course, Bryce, not a problem. I'll leave now.'

'Thank you.'

'I'll be in the coffee shop, burning with curiosity, when you're finished.'

He went back to the detectives: 'She's leaving there now.'

'Sorry to disrupt things, sir,' Detective Grasso said, but he didn't sound sorry and he didn't look sorry.

Bryce led the way along the outside path through the lush green plantings to the bungalow and unlocked them in, then said, 'Can I get you anything? Seltzer? Juice?'

'No, thank you,' Detective Grasso said. 'Could we sit here, sir?'

'Yes, of course.'

The living room area had two short sofas placed in an L shape with a large square glass coffee table. Bryce sat on the sofa to the right, Detective Grasso on the sofa to the left while Detective Maurice brought a chair over from the dining table.

Detective Grasso had a small notebook and pen out now, and he said, 'You say that was your fiancée, sir?'

'Yes, that's right, she just came out from New York.'

'And what's her name, sir?'

'Isabelle de Fuentes.'

'Is she an Angeleno, sir?'

'No, from New York. Spanish, really, her father was at the United Nations, but she's an American citizen. Excuse me, but, could you tell me what this is about?'

'I'm afraid it's bad news, sir,' Detective Maurice told him.

'Bad news?'

Detective Grasso said, 'About your wife, sir.'

'My – Oh, *Lucie*! We're getting a di— What do you mean? What about her?'

'She's dead,' Detective Grasso said.

Those four cold eyes looking at him, weighing him. An *innocent* man would feel guilty! *I'm* innocent, *I* didn't do it! 'Dead? But why would she— How?'

'She was beaten to death in her apartment,' Detective Maurice told him.

That *was* surprising, and horrible, too. He hadn't known, or wanted to know, how Wayne would do it, but he would have guessed a gun, or maybe poison, something like that. '*Beaten? Lucie?*'

'Wednesday night, sir,' Detective Grasso said. 'That would be the day after you checked in here.'

'Tuesday, yes, but— Wait, please, I'm trying to understand this. *Beaten?*'

And now he was thinking, it wasn't Wayne, that couldn't have been Wayne, it's an absolutely insane coincidence, never get away with that in a novel, there wasn't time for Wayne to have done it already, somebody broke in, some drug addict, rapist . . .

'Somebody,' he said, and found his throat dry, and swallowed noisily. 'Somebody,' he said, 'broke in?'

'There was no indication of forced entry,' Detective Grasso said.

'She knew her attacker,' Detective Maurice said.

'But – why? Was it – was it, you know, rape?'

'No, sir,' Detective Grasso said, and Bryce astounded and horrified himself by laughing. They didn't react, just both kept watching him.

'She's dead,' he told them, in explanation, still helplessly grinning, 'beaten to death, and I'm worried about rape.'

Detective Maurice said, 'Sir, I think you could use a glass of water.'

'I want to hear this,' Bryce told him. 'Wednesday. Why didn't anybody tell me?'

Detective Maurice got up and went over to the kitchen area, as Detective Grasso said, 'She was found this morning. She was supposed to see friends last night, go to a movie, I believe, and never showed up. They tried phoning her, and this morning when she still wasn't around one of them phoned the local precinct there.'

Detective Maurice came back with a tall glass of clear water and extended it to Bryce, saying, 'You ought to drink this, sir. A bit at a time.'

'Thank you,' Bryce said, but when he took the glass he almost dropped it, and then had to hold it with both hands. He drank some, and the edge of the glass chattered painfully against his teeth. He put it on the coffee table with a clatter, then held his hands out, palms down, and stared at them. 'I'm shaking,' he said.

'Take it easy, Mr Proctorr,' Detective Grasso said.

Bryce stared at Detective Grasso. He felt he was laughing again, or smiling maniacally, but he didn't seem to have any control. 'We're getting divorced,' he explained, 'we don't love each other any more, we don't care about each other, why would I— Why am I shaking?'

'It's a shock,' Detective Grasso told him.

'If you feel faint, Mr Proctorr,' Detective Maurice said, 'put your head down, or lie down on the sofa there. You don't want to hit your head on the coffee table.'

'No, I'll be all right,' Bryce said. 'I'll be all right.'

'I'm sorry, sir,' Detective Grasso said, 'but there are a few questions.'

'Of course, sure.'

Detective Maurice said, 'Would it help you if your fiancée was here, sir?'

'Maybe so,' Bryce said. 'Yes. Maybe so. She's in the coffee shop.'

'I'll call,' Detective Maurice offered, and Detective Grasso gave him his notebook, in which he'd apparently written down Isabelle's name.

'I'm just bewildered,' Bryce told Detective Grasso, while Detective Maurice was on the phone over by the kitchen area. 'Why would anybody do that?'

'That's what the NYPD is working on,' Detective Grasso said. 'And they asked us to help.'

'Anything,' Bryce said. 'Anything I can do.'

Detective Maurice came back and sat on his chair again, saying, 'She'll be right along. She sounds very pleasant, Mr Proctorr. No accent at all.'

'No, she's really American,' Bryce said. 'She works for an ad agency in New York, she writes copy for clothing catalogues, her ex-husband was Spanish, the divorce was in Spain and he got the children, three children, it's been very tough on Isabelle, her father's doing what he can, he's retired now, back in Spain, he lives in Madrid.'

I'm babbling, he thought, they don't care about all this, but he couldn't control the babbling either, any more than the expressions on his face. He picked up the water glass, again with both hands, and this time he managed to drink without hitting the glass against his teeth.

'I'm sorry,' he said, as he put the glass down. 'Usually, I'm better than this.'

'It's been a shock,' Detective Grasso said. Hadn't he said that before?

They heard Isabelle at the door, and all looked that way as she came in. She had changed into a summer blouse and skirt, from whatever she'd worn on the plane, and looked very beautiful.

The detectives stood, but when Bryce started to stand he lost his balance and almost fell sideways on to the coffee table. Both detectives reached quick hands in his direction, but he found his balance, stood upright, and smiled shakily at Isabelle as she hurried to him, frowning with concern.

'Bryce, what is it?'

'Isabelle de Fuentes,' he said, feeling formal introductions were absurd but necessary, 'these are Detectives Grasso and Maurice from the Los Angeles police. They're here because somebody killed Lucie.'

'Lucie!' Isabelle stared from him to the detectives, and back to him. 'They don't think you did it!'

'No no, I was here already, it was when, Wednesday.' To the detectives: 'Wednesday?'

They both nodded, watchful. Isabelle said, 'What happened?'

'She was beaten to death—'

'Oh, my God!'

'—in her apartment.'

'Mr Proctorr,' Detective Maurice said, 'I think you should sit.'

'Yes, thank you, yes.'

They all sat, Isabelle now at Bryce's right, holding his upper arm with both hands. Bryce said to Detective Grasso, 'Her apartment. I've never seen that apartment. I can't, I can't picture it.'

'Just as well,' Detective Grasso said.

Detective Maurice said, 'She didn't live there during the marriage?'

'No, we have an apartment on Central Park West, and a house in Connecticut. She moved out, it was her idea to get her own place, temporary, a furnished apartment, and at the end of the divorce we'd see who'd get what place, what, what we wanted.' Frowning, he said, 'It's a furnished apartment, who knows how many keys there are.'

'The detectives in New York have established,' Detective Grasso told him, 'that the management changes the lock code with each new tenant.'

'There'll be a funeral,' Bryce said, and looked helplessly at Isabelle. 'I have to go to the funeral, don't I? I suppose I have to go to the funeral.'

'Mr Proctorr,' Detective Grasso said.

Bryce faced him. 'Yes?'

'Could you tell me the reason for this trip, sir? Vacation, is it?'

'Well, a working vacation, I guess,' Bryce told him, thinking, they want to know if I did what I did, got out of the way so someone else could do it for me. He said, 'I'm a novelist, and—'

'Yes, sir,' Detective Grasso said, 'we know who you are.'

'Oh, okay. Well, three of my books have been made into movies, and there's interest in more, so I'm here to talk to people about them. For instance, I had lunch today with George Jenkins, he has an idea to do a series of cop movies – sorry.'

Detective Grasso seemed amused. 'That's okay, Mr Proctorr, we're cops.'

'Okay, fine. Well, anyway, he thinks he'd like to do this series from a book of mine called *Twice Tolled*. What I do, I come out every once in a while, remind everybody I exist, meet with people, and usually something comes of it.'

'And had this trip been planned for some time?'

'Well, talking about it for some time,' Bryce said, 'but didn't finalize it until the last minute. I ran into a snag in the book I'm working on – Isabelle, you remember, I was working on it last weekend.'

'Yes, sure,' she said. 'You seemed very happy with it.'

'I was, until Monday. Then I saw I'd really written myself into a corner, I'm going to have to think about it for a while, so I called Jeff – he's my agent out here – and he said he could set up meetings this week, so I came out Tuesday.'

Detective Grasso said, 'And when do you go back?'

'Well, I planned to be here for another week or so, I've got appointments most of next week, but now, I suppose I really do have to go to the funeral.'

Isabelle said, 'Oh, Bryce.'

'It's very hard to believe Lucie's dead,' Bryce told the detectives. 'We didn't get along at all, the last couple of years, it hasn't been an easy divorce, but to have her suddenly gone, I can't fathom it. She's one of the liveliest people I know. Right now, I can hear her voice.' And he could.

Detective Grasso said. 'Do you expect to be back in New York by Monday?'

'Probably sooner, depending on the funeral.'

'A Detective Johnson in New York will want to talk to you.'

'Sure, of course. Does he know how to get in touch with me? I'll be in the New York apartment.'

'Why don't I take the address and phone number,' Detective Grasso suggested. 'Just in case.'

'Sure.' Bryce gave it to him, and they all stood, and Detective Grasso said, 'Sorry to be the bearers of bad news.'

'Thank you. You did it about as well as it could be done, I guess.'

At the bungalow door, Detective Grasso gave Bryce his card, saying, 'If anything occurs to you.'

'All right.'

Detective Maurice said, 'At least enjoy our weather a day or two more.'

'I will. Thank you.'

They left, at long last they left, and Isabelle folded herself against him. 'Oh, Bryce, I feel so badly for you. What a terrible thing.'

'Yes. Yes.'

Arms around her, feeling the trembling in her body, his eyes squeezed shut, Bryce thought: Wayne. He has me now, he has me in his power now.

Ten

The strange thing was, he had no problem sleeping. When he was awake, Wayne was troubled by quick images of what had happened in Lucie's apartment, sharp shocking instants kept exploding suddenly like flashbulbs in his mind, and he'd physically recoil, or make a sudden muffled shout: '*Huh!*'

But at night, in his sleep, apparently there were no bad dreams, or at least nothing he remembered the next day, and Susan assured him he was sleeping heavily, almost too heavily. If she awoke during the night, no movement or sound by her would disturb his deep sleep. And then he would feel rested in the morning, physically fine. It was as though he were drugging himself, creating some secretion in the brain that kept him tranquil at night, that kept the bad things at bay.

They hadn't talked about it at all, it, since he'd come home Wednesday night. Every morning, they got up as usual, behaved as though everything were normal, and Susan went off to work in the regular way. Wayne usually bought just the *Times*, but this week he was buying the *News* as well, in case for some reason the *Times* didn't carry it, and he was reading both papers much more extensively than usual.

In the evenings, now, they'd go out for dinner and a movie in the neighborhood. By unspoken mutual consent, they didn't watch any television news, morning or night; maybe they didn't want to face anything more graphic than newsprint.

What amazed him was the work. Thursday and Friday, immediately after the murder, he'd done phenomenal amounts of work on *The Shadowed Other*, and kept thinking about those characters and their story in the times when he was away from his desk. It was as though the land inside *The Shadowed Other* were his real life, and this out here was make-believe.

But when would it *start*?

Finally, it was in Saturday's paper.

Both papers. Of course the *Times* would carry the story, it was on their own best-seller list that Lucie's husband had become famous.

The *News* devoted more space to the story, with two pictures, one of the building on Broadway on the Upper West Side where Lucie had died, the other a shot of Lucie and Bryce arm-in-arm, smiling at the camera in front of their Connecticut house; probably from the same photo session as the picture in *People*.

Both papers had the same meager details of the murder: beaten, no evidence of a break-in, no neighbors saw or heard anything, police were working on it. The building itself was meant for transients, none of whom had known Lucie, who had moved there after filing for divorce.

Both papers reminded their readers who Bryce Proctorr was, the *News* mentioning the actors who'd starred in the movies made from his books, the *Times* mentioning their own best-seller list. The *News* said that Lucie was beautiful; the *Times* did not.

Both papers mentioned the divorce proceedings, and both reported that Bryce had been in Los Angeles at the time of the murder, there in connection with potential movie projects. The *News* had found a scene in one of Bryce's novels, *Twice Tolled*, that was vaguely similar to Lucie's death: 'In the novel, the husband is a suspect at first, but is proved to be innocent.' That was enterprising of them.

Susan was home today, it being Saturday, so when Wayne brought the papers back to the apartment they sat together in the living room, she on the sofa, he in his regular chair, and read both pieces, trading back and forth. Then Susan said, 'No one heard anything.'

'I saw that,' Wayne said. 'That's good.'

And it was good they could let the story into their lives now because it wasn't exclusively *their* lives any more; Lucie Proctorr was dead in everybody's life now.

Susan at last put the *News* aside and said, 'We should go out today, somewhere outside.'

'It's cold.'

'We shouldn't just stay in here all day,' she said. 'Cooped up in here.'

They didn't own a car; what did they need a car for in New York? Just another expense, and the constant fuss of moving it from place to place. Those rare times when they went out of town, they'd rent a car. So Wayne said, 'You want to get a car? You want to go away for the weekend?'

'We could do that.' The *News* was open on the sofa beside her, to that page. Looking at it, she said, 'I'd like to see that house.'

'What, Bryce's house? What for?'

'I don't know, I'd just like to. It's a sunny day, even if it is cold, it might be nice to drive around Connecticut, maybe even up to Massachusetts, spend tonight in a bed-and-breakfast up there, drive back tomorrow.'

'I've been working—'

'Too much,' she said.

He smiled at her, comfortable with her. 'Too well, I was going to say. The book is moving along.'

'You can take a day off from it.'

Suddenly his mood changed, he felt lousy, and he flopped back in his chair. 'I could take forever off from it,' he said. 'It isn't going anywhere.'

'Wayne, no,' she said, 'you'll find a publisher.'

'Sure.'

'No, you will,' she insisted. 'You can make Bryce help you.'

'*Make* him?'

'Of course. He owes you now.'

'I'm getting money from him,' Wayne said. '*If* he doesn't stiff me.'

'What do you mean, stiff you?'

'Just take my book and thumb his nose at me. What am I going to do, take him to court? "I killed this man's wife for him, and now he won't pay me." Sure. And he could switch the book around so I wouldn't even be able to prove it was mine.'

Susan sat forward on the sofa, leaning toward him. 'Wayne,' she said, 'Bryce doesn't dare cross you. He *owes* you now, and he knows it, and he'll do whatever you want. Don't you know why?'

'No,' he said. 'I don't see what you're getting at.'

'You don't see it because you know who you really are,' she told him. 'And I know who you really are. But *he* thinks you're the person who did . . . *that*, on Wednesday night. He talked to you in the library in the first place because he thought you were a desperate man, and now he's sure you're a desperate man, and he'll do anything to keep you happy.'

He looked at her, not liking what she was saying. 'Or I'll beat *him* to death, too? Maybe all his children?'

'*No*, Wayne. If you're desperate, he can't predict you, and he can't control you. I know who you—'

'Listen, wait a minute,' he said. 'Wait a minute. I don't want to talk about, you know . . .'

'Of course you don't, and you don't have to.'

'But just one thing,' he said. 'I didn't plan it that way, I *wouldn't* plan a thing like that, it wasn't supposed to happen Wednesday at all, not for who knows how long, and certainly not *brutal*, not, I was as, as, as surprised and scared as she was when it started. I didn't know it was going to start—'

'Wayne, stop.'

'—and then it started, and there was no way—'

'Wayne, please stop, you're crying, Wayne, *stop!*'

'—to stop it, I had to keep on – Oh, Jesus Christ, Susan!'

She came over and knelt and held him for a long while, until the shaking and the crying stopped, until he took a long deep breath and said, 'Okay, now.'

'All right?'

'It's over now,' he said, and he could feel that it really was, that some balled fist inside his chest had finally unclenched itself. 'I'll be all right now,' he said.

She continued to kneel beside his chair, and now she leaned back, still holding his arms, to study his face. 'You're sure?'

'I'm sure.' he said and smiled at her. 'Let's go for a drive.'

They couldn't find the house. There weren't enough clues in the stories in the newspapers nor in the photo in the *News*. They knew the house was somewhere near Bethel, but all the country roads looked the same, meandering through patches of woodland, charming in the sunlight even with their leaves down. The old low stone walls undulated with the land along the roadside, and Wayne made random turns at the intersections in the little red rental Saturn. There wasn't much other traffic, and the mere fact of driving around was pleasant.

But they couldn't find the house. The large houses and estates around here were mostly set well back from the road, in among trees, hard to see, sometimes impossible, and most of these people didn't put their names on their mailboxes. After a while, they were just looking at attractive houses for their own sake.

He only raised the taboo subject once, when they were on a rare straight stretch, black and white dairy cows in a large open field on their left, tangled brushy woods on their right. 'I'm just glad,' he said, 'I'm not dreaming about it.'

'That's kind of a surprise, really,' she said.

'And a relief. What if I had nightmares?'

'You don't think you will?'

'No. If it hasn't started by now, it won't.'

'Good.'

A little later, Susan said, 'I don't really need to see his house. I just needed to get out of the apartment for a while.'

'I'm glad you talked me into it.'

'So what do you want to do now?'

He said, 'We'll go on up to Massachusetts, like we said.'

'We can go antiquing.'

'Why not?' he said. 'We'll be rich soon.'

Eleven

The funeral was Sunday, so they flew back on the late afternoon plane Saturday, getting into Kennedy at midnight. They traveled together, because there was no reason to hide any more, no more private detectives lurking around. Everything had changed now. The burden was gone.

There was a message with a phone number from Detective Johnson on the machine when they arrived. It was a black man's voice, calm and gentle, not tough-sounding at all, which was a surprise. In the morning, before leaving for the funeral, Bryce phoned that number, spoke briefly with Johnson, and agreed to meet with him at the apartment that afternoon.

Isabelle had stayed with him Saturday night, but she wouldn't come to the funeral. While he was there, she'd go to her apartment way east on Thirty-first Street and pack some things, enough so she could be comfortable in his place.

Bryce hadn't thought ahead of time about how terrible the funeral would be. Everybody there knew he and Lucie had been going through that endless miserable divorce, so nobody could quite treat him like a grieving husband. On the other hand, nobody could offer him a big smile and a hearty 'Congratulations!' either. Generally, people behaved toward him as though they had a toothache that they vaguely blamed him for.

Not that there were so many people present, maybe twenty in all. Lucie's parents had flown in from St Louis, and did their best to avoid Bryce entirely, since of course his legal battle with their daughter had made him their enemy, and they couldn't figure out any other way to react to him now.

His own family was no better. All three of his children were present, but none sat near him. There was twenty-three-year-old Betsy, a postgraduate architecture student at Brown; twenty-one-year-old Tom, studying engineering at MIT; and nineteen-year-old Barry, an English lit major at Rutgers. With them all away, in Rhode Island and Massachusetts and New Jersey, he rarely saw them or spoke with them. His accountant paid their bills, and that was the extent of the relationship. They'd sided with their mother, Ellen, in his first divorce, and had never liked Lucie, who had coldly disliked them in return. The estrangement was not deliberate on anybody's part, but by now it was habitual.

Their mother, Ellen, was there, too, which surprised Bryce, accompanied by Jimmy Branley, the architect she lived with in Connecticut. She solemnly shook Bryce's hand, saying, 'I hope you find happiness, Bryce, after all this.'

'Well, thank you,' he said, and thought again that he really should have stayed with Ellen, not only because Lucie had been so much worse. There was an honesty in Ellen that could have anchored him, if he'd let it.

Also at the funeral were ten or so women friends of Lucie's, all her age, all looking more or less like her, women who found it easy to wear black to a funeral because they wore black all the time anyway. Lucie'd always been more comfortable with women than men, and had always had a lot of girlfriends; they'd chat endlessly on the phone and buy little gifts for one another.

The setting was an upscale funeral parlor on Park Avenue, with quiet efficient dark-suited men moving it all along. The service was muted and nondenominational, vaguely religious without committing anybody to anything. Three people spoke, the first being Lucie's father, who'd written out what he wanted to say on two sheets of lined yellow paper, which trembled like leaves in his hands. He could barely get through it, gulping and weeping and choking up.

Then one of Lucie's girlfriends, a woman named Janet Higgins, spoke about the last time she'd seen Lucie, which happened to be at the première of a play she'd directed, and how supportive Lucie had been then, and had always been, and how hard it was to believe that wonderful friend wouldn't be around any more. Bryce realized with sudden shock and unease that the play must have been *Low Fidelity*, where Wayne and Lucie had met. He found himself trembling, thinking of what he'd started, what he'd destroyed. *Why couldn't the two of them have just gotten it over with?*

His mind drifted, and he thought, why not just leave New York for a while? Leave New York and Connecticut and everything.

Spain. He could move to Spain for two or three years, take Isabelle with him, maybe he could help her get her children back. At that thought, he couldn't help but look over at his own three, clustered with their mother, isolated from him. No, he was isolated from them, wasn't he?

He'd never met Isabelle's children. He'd met her father a few times, thought he was stuffy but all right, wouldn't mind being around him for a while.

But they wouldn't live in Madrid, where her father lived. No, they'd go east, over to Barcelona, find a nice villa outside the city, toward the Med. There were a dozen beaches you could go to there, a different one every day. He could find a story set in Spain, set up an office there in a sunny corner room, do his research in Barcelona. He could see the office, dark wood gleaming in the sunlight, a tiled terrace outside the large office windows. He wished he were there now, instead of here. Seated at his computer writing his Spanish novel, seeing Isabelle on the sunny terrace outside, with her three children.

The business with Wayne had to be gotten out of the way first, that's all. Wayne and *Two Faces in the Mirror*. Next Monday he could send Joe Katz, his editor, the manuscript, maybe call him this Thursday or Friday to say, 'I'm almost done, at long last!' He smiled at the thought, then stopped himself from smiling.

In the funeral, the worst was saved for last: another Lucie girl-friend, who wanted to tell them all the funny things she remembered Lucie saying, most of which had probably not been that funny in their original context and were just ghastly here. The woman had no sense of her audience, but just prattled on, and

Bryce found himself thinking, I should have Wayne kill *her*, too.

At last she finished, and the funeral parlor men wheeled the closed casket away for cremation, and it was over. People stood in small hushed murmuring groups, none of which included Bryce. Nobody in this place, he realized, is on my side. Feeling very alone, he left there and hailed a cab.

The interview with Detective Johnson was brief and easy. He was a tall rangy man, not burly like the cops in Los Angeles, and he seemed to have no suspicion of Bryce at all. He began by going over much the same territory as the two detectives in Los Angeles, Bryce's reason for being out there, but in shorter form, since clearly he'd already talked with Detectives Grasso and Maurice.

Then he wanted to know what Bryce knew about any men Lucie had been dating since their separation, and he said, 'I'm sorry, I'm probably the last person who could help you on that.'

'I suppose that's true,' Johnson agreed. 'But we have an Identikit picture that might be the guy. I'd like to show it to you.'

'Okay,' Bryce said. He was thinking, How can I claim I don't recognize Wayne? But I can't possibly say the killer looks like Wayne Prentice, not even remotely. And how did Wayne manage to get himself seen?

Taking a tan manila envelope from his coat pocket, Johnson said, 'We potentially have two witnesses, but the truth is, we're not sure they're both identifying the same man.'

'I don't follow,' Bryce admitted.

Johnson seemed reluctant to show the picture, but went on holding the envelope in both hands. 'One witness,' he said, 'is the doorman in Ms Proctorr's building. He saw a man come for her, go up to the apartment, come down with her, go out, come back with her later, and then go out again alone.'

'Saw him four times,' Bryce said. 'That's a lot.'

'You'd think so,' Johnson said. 'But not everybody's as observant as we'd like.'

'I suppose that's true.'

'The man told the doorman his name was Wayland,' Johnson said. 'Does that ring a bell?'

Oh, clever Wayne, Bryce thought, realizing at once what he must have done. Shaking his head, he said, 'I don't know anybody named Wayland. No first name?'

'No, unless that is a first name.'

'I suppose.'

'Ms Proctorr definitely knew him,' Johnson said. 'She told the doorman to send him up.'

'Wayland,' Bryce said. He shook his head.

'It seemed as though they might have gone to dinner,' Johnson said, 'in the neighborhood, given the time they went out and how long they were gone. So we canvassed local restaurants with Ms Proctorr's photo, and we've got a waitress at a place called Salt on Columbus Avenue who thinks she might have seen Ms Proctorr that night. She's not absolutely certain, and she didn't notice the man that much.'

'But maybe,' Bryce said.

'The man paid cash, so we don't get a name from a credit card,' Johnson said. 'The witnesses disagree on several points, so this is limited to what they could agree on.' And at last he brought out the artist's drawing.

Which didn't look at all like Wayne! Astonished, Bryce held the picture and stared at this stranger, trying to see, if not *Wayne*, someone he knew in there. This was some sort of tough guy, with thinner lips and flatter ears and a higher brow and darker, bushier hair than Wayne. The high forehead could have come from the waitress. seeing him from above.

Staring, Bryce could finally see Wayne's eyes, they'd got that part right. Wayne's eyes, in a stranger's face. Wayne in a mask. 'No,' he said. 'I'd know if I'd seen this man before.'

'Well, it was worth a try,' Johnson said.

Handing back the picture, Bryce said, 'So this is the guy, anyway, you're sure of that much.'

'Well, no,' Johnson said. 'It looks like a date rape that got out of hand, but it could be something else entirely.'

Bryce shook his head, showing bewilderment. He was feeling hollow, more and more hollow, as though a cavern were in his chest. A high cavern, with cold sharp stalactites. He said, 'What else? What else could it be?'

'Well, it *could* be robbery,' Johnson said. 'Those buildings over there are pretty secure, all in all, but it's possible someone got in, saw this man leave Ms Proctorr's apartment, waited till he got into the elevator, then went and knocked on the door, pretended to be the man coming back.'

Save Wayne, Bryce thought. He said, 'You think that's possible?'

'Possible, yes,' Johnson said. 'Some jewelry was taken, drawers left open, that sort of thing. But it had a kind of stage-set look. And apparently she had a week-at-a-glance type datebook, and that's gone missing, too.'

'Ah,' Bryce said.

Johnson smiled at him. 'No burglar's gonna be in the datebook, is he?'

'No, I guess not,' Bryce said.

Johnson shook his head. 'But then,' he said, 'you turn it around, let's say the burglar took the datebook so we'd blame the fella she had the date with.'

'Tricky,' Bryce said.

Johnson nodded. 'A lot of them look tricky at first,' he said. 'Sooner or later, most of them turn out to be simple.'

An hour later, Bryce and Isabelle were seated quietly in the living room, both reading magazines, when the phone rang. He answered, and the voice said, 'Hi, it's Wayne.'

Coldness ran through Bryce's body. How dare you call me? he raged, inside his head. How dare you speak to me, how dare you show your face? He said, 'Oh, hi, Wayne, hold on a second.'

'Sure.'

Putting the phone down, standing, he said to Isabelle, 'Business. I'll take it in the office. Hang up this one when I pick up, okay?'

'Of course.'

He went to his office, sat at the desk, and picked up the phone there. 'Okay, Isabelle.'

There was a click, and Wayne said, 'Isabelle. That was fast.'

'You probably want to talk about the book,' Bryce said. He didn't need Wayne to tell him that it was fast to have Isabelle here.

'I sure do,' Wayne said.

'I thought I should wait a week,' Bryce told him. 'The funeral was this morning.'

Wayne said nothing. Bryce waited, then said, 'Next Monday, or maybe this Friday, I'll call Joe Katz, he's my editor, I'll say the book's finally done, then send it over.'

'That's terrific. Thank you, Bryce.'

Bryce couldn't help himself, he had to say, 'How are you?' Meaning, how are you now that you've beaten a human being to death?

'Oh, fine,' Wayne said, but then gave a little laugh and said, 'Shaky for a while there.'

'I suppose so.'

'Things don't happen the way you think they're going to happen, you know what I mean?'

'I guess I do,' Bryce said.

'Well, I'll be here, Bryce,' Wayne told him. 'I'll wait for your call.'

'Okay.'

Bryce hung up, and looked grimly at his computer, silent, unforthcoming. Wayne's there, he thought. He'll be there, right there, from now on. Forever.

Twelve

Wayne wished they'd all just leave it alone. The story was as dead as Lucie; why wouldn't they let it die?

What they had was skimpy enough. Somehow, they'd traced Wayne to Salt, and they had an artist's drawing of the suspect that was ridiculously off. Laughing at it in the paper, Susan said, 'Is *that* the man I married?'

But after that, nothing. No new leads, no clues, no suspects, no changes or additions of any kind. But the newspapers and the local television news programs had to rehash the same damn empty details day after day. Even the networks touched on the story in their news broadcasts.

It was the usual, and Wayne knew it was merely the usual, and that it shouldn't bother him, but it bothered him. The usual was the mix of sex and celebrity, but to Wayne's eye this was a pretty watered-down version of both. It's true Bryce was a best-selling author, a commodity, a name brand, but he wasn't O.J. Simpson, for God's sake. And the police kept saying there was no sign of sexual attack, but the media didn't care, they went with it anyway. If a beautiful blonde has been bludgeoned to death, there's got to be sex involved in it *somewhere*.

'Beautiful blonde bludgeoned' was the nicely alliterative phrase most of the media had settled on, though Wayne could have told them they'd got that all wrong. It hadn't been like that at all. Bludgeoning a beautiful blonde hadn't in any way been what it was about; more like beheading a snapping turtle.

He and Susan had started watching the TV news again, once the story went public, but Wayne was regretting that now. Still, he could see Susan was as caught up in the story as if she didn't know what was actually going on. She'd become another spectator among all the spectators of the bludgeoning of the beautiful blonde.

There was something else also building in Susan, he could tell, but he didn't know what it was. They were having sex more frequently, and during it she was clinging to him more, as though he were a floating timber from the shipwreck and she in a raging sea. But she seemed to like it, whatever was coursing through her mind in those moments, so he knew better than to question it.

Then, Wednesday night, as they were about, Wayne thought, to go to sleep, she asked him, in a very low, almost little-girl voice, 'Can I ask you a question?'

Of course, she didn't have to mention the topic. I'm not going to like this, he thought, but there was no way out of it: 'Sure. What do you want to know?'

'Was it a turn-on?'

'No!' He was appalled she could ask such a thing. 'How could it?' he cried. But then he realized that the bald denial wasn't enough, it wouldn't quiet her doubts or change her mind or alter whatever picture she'd formed in her head, so, with the disgust he still strongly recalled, he said, 'She shit her pants.'

'Oh!' A shocked silence from her side of the bed; and then, 'I'm sorry you told me that.'

'I'm sorry you asked.'

Another longish silence. Then, in the little-girl voice once more, 'I won't do it again.'

'It's all right, Susan,' he said, sorry he'd been harsh. 'I know it's natural, you want to know and at the same time you don't want to know.'

'I don't want to know. Not now. Maybe some day.'

'Yes, I'd like that,' he said. 'I've been thinking that, hoping when it's, when it's all calmed down and long over, we could sit down someplace and I could tell you the whole thing.'

'But not yet,' she said.

'No, not yet.'

He knew part of the problem, for both of them, was this empty period of waiting. There was always suspense when a novel manuscript was submitted to its editor. Even after years of writing, and however much success, there was always that blank tense period between handing in the manuscript and getting the editor's reaction.

And this time, it was so much more complicated. It wasn't even his manuscript, not any more, and it wasn't his editor, and he had no control over the submission. He just had to wait, and wait, and that's why the continuing crime-of-the-moment attention from the media was getting to him so much.

It was affecting his work, too. He'd done damn little this week on *The Shadowed Other*. Last week, before they'd gone away for their driving weekend in New England, he'd been racing through the book, but this week it was coming hard. The characters resisted him, refused to let him know how they would act and react, and more important, *why* they would act this way and not that way. He didn't necessarily have to explain all the motivation to the reader, but *he* had to know. He had to know them well enough to be absolutely certain how they would react to any possible stimulus, and he was just having trouble, this week, seeing his people clear.

And then, Thursday afternoon, as he sat glooming at the computer, wondering how this one important character in the book – not the lead, but still important – would behave in response to a piece of bad news he'd just received, the phone rang, and it was Bryce. 'I just wanted you to know,' he said, 'the book's gone in.'

'Oh, Bryce, that's great!'

'I phoned Joe Katz this morning and told him it was done, and he sent a messenger up this afternoon, and he'll read it over the weekend.'

No one had ever sent a messenger to pick up a book of Wayne's before. That detail pinged off him like ironic revelation, and made him smile. 'Oh, I hope he loves it,' he said.

'Why shouldn't he?' Bryce said. 'We both gave it our best.'

Wayne beamed from ear to ear. 'Yes, we did, didn't we? Bryce, on Monday, I'll be waiting right here by the phone.'

'We both will,' Bryce said.

Thirteen

Joe Katz called just after eleven Monday morning. 'Well, Bryce, it's terrific,' he said.

Until that instant, Bryce hadn't realized just how worried he'd been. Scenarios had run through his head, and he'd squelched them, in which Joe would call this morning and say, 'What is this crap, Bryce? You didn't write this,' or, worse, 'Bryce, I hate to tell you, buddy, but you're slipping.' It's a cuckoo's egg you've got there, Joe, but which the cuckoo and which the foster parent?

He'd been hiding all these doubts from himself, but now that Joe had said those wonderful words – 'Well, Bryce, it's terrific' – he could let all those goblins out of their cupboard, let them all fly away out of his head and into the air as he beamed into the phone and said, 'I'm glad to hear it, Joe.'

'And this has some of the best writing in it you've ever done.'

Bryce's beam faded slightly. 'Thanks, Joe,' he said.

'As always, you know, I've got to pick a few nits.'

'Oh, sure, I'm ready,' Bryce said. 'I trust your nits, Joe, you know that.'

'Thanks. You've got the manuscript there? We could go over a few points, I don't need answers now, we could do lunch later in the week, or whenever you're ready.'

'Sure, wait a second, just pulling it out of the drawer here, okay.'

For ten minutes, they discussed the story and the characters and the pacing, with smallish problems that Bryce could usually fix

98

right away, over the phone. But then Joe said, 'Here on page three twelve, Henry lashes out at Eleanor and storms out of the diner. Later on, here, page three forty-seven, they seem to be back together again, no problem. I suppose we could figure out what happened in between, but I just felt as though you might have left a scene out there that we could use.'

In fact, Bryce had added a scene, Henry's departure from the diner. In Wayne's version of the book, Henry's rebellion against Eleanor had been all internal, not turning into action at all, and Bryce had found that just too undramatic, particularly in a section of the book where not much else was moving forward. He'd thought the reader would understand that a gesture of independence from Henry at that point would be no more than a gesture, and wouldn't need to be told why Henry was still under Eleanor's thumb the next time they appeared. Leaving out Wayne's original version, he tried to explain his approach to Joe, but Joe just didn't see it.

'Henry was building toward something all along through there,' Joe said. 'I could sense it. So when he finally spoke up, I really expected some sort of follow-through. I mean, he can wind up at the status quo ante, that's fine, in fact he has to for what happens later in the book, but I just need to see the step that turned him around again. You know, if on three twelve he *didn't* explode, if he kept it all internalized, then I could see that that's where the fuse is getting wet, the spark is going out, and Henry's stuck forever.'

Wayne's version, in other words. 'I felt,' Bryce said, 'we needed something dramatic at that point in the book.'

'Oh, I agree with you on that,' Joe told him. 'I'd hate to lose that little moment of rebellion. But then you've got to bring him back down again, I think, show us how it fizzled out. If it doesn't fizzle out before he makes his move, then it has to happen afterward.'

Joe was right, and Bryce knew it, but he couldn't help resisting, because he also knew that only one reader in a thousand would ever even notice the problem. Henry wasn't the hero of the book, he and Eleanor didn't constitute the main story. 'I felt,' he said, 'that we would know why he was back with Eleanor, that even when he was leaving, the reader would say to himself, "He'll be back." '

'Yes, but that just makes Henry a joke then,' Joe said, 'if we don't see the process of the turnaround, and he's too important later on to turn him into a joke at this point.'

'Joe, I'm gonna have to think about that one.'

'Fine, fine. Let's move along.'

They had another five minutes or so, Bryce taking notes, continuing to do the smaller changes immediately, and then he hung up and spent the rest of the day trying his damnedest not to think about Henry and Eleanor.

The fact is, he didn't *know* how Henry had managed to succeed with his rebellion, even briefly. The way the man was written, he'd do what Wayne had suggested in his version of the book, he'd plan to escape and then he'd fail. When Bryce had changed that, his own motives had been plot-driven, not character-driven, and damn Joe Katz was good enough to have picked up the glitch.

How had Wayne worked it? Bryce had thrown away the original manuscript, not wanting anything around here that would suggest the true origin of this novel, but now he wished he'd held on to it a while longer. But it was gone, and all he had was his own version, and it was a connect-the-dots spot where the dots simply refused to connect.

Well, he was supposed to call Wayne anyway, so at four that afternoon he did, saying, 'I just heard from Joe Katz.'

'I just about gave up for today,' Wayne said. 'I figured you'd hear from him tomorrow.'

'I think Joe had editorial conferences most of the day,' Bryce said, feeling vaguely guilty for not having phoned Wayne immediately, this morning. 'Anyway, he thinks the book is terrific. That's the word he used.' He didn't see any reason to mention the 'some of your best writing' remark.

'That's nice,' Wayne said. 'That's a real relief. You don't know what a help this is.'

'Well, I think we helped each other,' Bryce said, because it seemed to him that somehow Wayne was leaving out the other part of their collaboration.

'I know we did,' Wayne agreed, 'and I'm glad we could, you know?'

'I do know,' Bryce said. He wanted to say, How *could* you have done it, Wayne? But that was the one question that would never be asked. 'Well,' he said, instead, 'we've got this book to think about now, and I need to ask you something about it.'

Sounding surprised, Wayne said, 'Sure. Go ahead.'

'Joe had some little problems,' Bryce said, suddenly awkward, because he was going to have to admit this one lumpish revision he'd made in the book, 'and we dealt with all but one of them, but on that one I'm kind of snagged.'

'Something I got wrong?'

'No, as it turns out,' Bryce said, 'something you got right, and *I* got wrong.'

'Oh. Some change you made.'

'You know where Billy almost leaves Janice?' Using the names from Wayne's version of the book.

'In the diner? Yeah, sure.'

'Well, I felt we needed a dramatic scene there, more—'

'Oh, no, you didn't. You had him walk out?'

'Yeah.'

'He wouldn't do that!'

'I thought he could have this one little moment—'

'No, no, Bryce, that's the whole point with Billy, that's how I use him later on, with him it's all internal, he never translates it into real-world action, that's not who he is.'

'Well, I made the change,' Bryce said, 'and Joe caught it that it was a glitch—'

'Of *course* he did.' Wayne sounded very upset over this.

'But now, the problem is,' Bryce said, 'he agrees with both of us. He agrees with me that we need more drama at that point, an *event*, but then he feels we have to have a scene to show Billy go back to what he was before.'

'You mean, he violates character, then notices it, then rushes back.'

'I guess so. Anyway, that turnaround scene is what Joe feels it needs. The book needs.'

'You can't just put it back the way it was?'

'You can't take a dramatic scene out of a book after the editor's seen it.'

'Shit. Goddam it, Bryce, I wish you'd talked to me about that move. Are there other things like that?'

'I made little changes, you know I did, but that's the only one Joe had problems with.'

'So you've got this internal guy suddenly makes an external act, and then what? I mean, the way you have it.'

'Then the next time we see them, they're back together. Like you had it.'

'No explanation.'

'No.'

'Jesus, Bryce, what are you gonna do?'

'I don't know, I was hoping you'd have an idea.'

'I had an idea. You replaced it.'

'I just can't think of a scene,' Bryce admitted, 'where Billy undoes it.'

'Neither can I,' Wayne told him. 'I can't imagine Billy outside that diner, alone.'

'Let's,' Bryce said, 'both sleep on it, and I'll call you again tomorrow.'

'Okay,' Wayne said, but he sounded doubtful.

That evening, eating dinner at Gaylord's with Isabelle, Bryce said, 'I was thinking, once the editing of *Two Faces in the Mirror* is done, I'd like to leave town for a while, leave my whole life for a while.'

She looked at him with some amusement. 'Leave your whole life?'

'All except you,' he assured her. 'In fact, what I was thinking about, what if you and I moved to Spain for a couple of years?'

She reacted with astonishment, but not, he thought, with pleasure. 'Spain! For God's sake, why?'

'It's a beautiful country,' he said. 'I could set my next novel there. I don't like the city right now, the reminders, or Connecticut either. Just to take a break from all this. And maybe I could help you to get your children back, it might make a difference if you were there.'

She turned very cold at that. 'I think we leave that to my father,' she said. 'I don't believe I should mess in it, and I don't think you should get into things you don't understand.'

'Okay, okay,' he said. 'So you don't want to go to Spain.'

'I *left* Spain,' she said. 'I like New York.'

'Fine,' he said.

'And you know, Bryce,' she went on, 'this would not be a good time for you to leave the country, don't you realize that?'

He had no idea what she was driving at. 'No. Realize what?'

'You're a suspect!'

'What? You mean in—'

'I mean,' she said, 'the husband is *always* the main suspect, and you were in the middle of a very bitter divorce, and wasn't it a nice coincidence you just happened to be in Los Angeles when Lucie was murdered?'

'But I *was* there.'

'You're a rich man,' she told him. 'You could have hired some-body. Don't you think the police are investigating that? To see if you spent any extra money recently, if you had any meetings with strange people.'

'Well, I didn't,' he said. 'Neither of those.'

'If you try to leave the country,' she said, 'they will be sure you paid to have Lucie murdered, and they will harass you unmerci-fully.'

'The point is,' Bryce said, not at all wanting to think about what she was telling him, 'you don't want to go back to Spain.'

'Not for one minute.'

'Fine. We'll stay here.'

And, irrelevantly, he thought, this is where Henry got up and left Eleanor. Wayne was right, and I was wrong.

In the morning, he called Wayne, but Wayne had no suggestion for him on how to smooth over the glitch in the story. Bryce said, 'Normally, if I have a problem like this, I go in and do a head-bang-ing session with Joe, and we'd come up with something, but this time, I just don't think that's gonna work. I'm realizing, those people are yours more than they're mine. You can tap into them, keep them consistent.'

'Not once Billy is off the rails, Bryce, I'm sorry.'

'I had a brainstorm this morning,' Bryce said. '*You* could meet with Joe, the three of us meet, I know for sure we'd work it out.'

'Me? How could I meet with *your* editor?'

'I have a story I can tell him,' Bryce said. 'You and I knew each other years ago, you were a successful novelist, he's probably heard of your name, but then it all kind of dried up for you. I was having a hell of a time with the book, couldn't concentrate on it, because of the divorce, and then we ran into each other again, and I hired you to be my editorial consultant.'

'Editorial consultant. That's what it says in that contract.'

'Exactly. I'll tell Joe, I want to keep it quiet, because it could be publicly humiliating if there was any suggestion I couldn't do my own books all by myself.'

'Jerzy Kosinski,' Wayne said.

'That's just precisely it,' Bryce said. 'Kosinski never got his reputation back, not completely, after all those rumors that other people wrote his books.'

'So I'm your undercover editorial consultant,' Wayne said. He sounded a little insulted. 'How does that get me into a meeting with your editor?'

'You understand these characters,' Bryce told him. 'Better than I do myself sometimes. And in fact, and I'll explain this to Joe, when I was working on that part of the book, you argued against Billy walking out of the diner. You can tell Joe all that internalizing stuff you told me, I couldn't tell that to Joe and get it right.'

Wayne said, 'But haven't you switched the book around since I saw it? Changed the character names, moved some chapters, all that? How could I talk about the book?'

'I'll messenger a copy of the manuscript down to you this morning.'

'Messenger. That's nice. Who are Billy and Janice now?'

'Henry and Eleanor.'

'Henry and Eleanor,' Wayne echoed, as though tasting the names on his tongue. 'Sure. Why not?'

'You'll see when you get the manuscript, I tried to keep your ideas, not do a Frankenstein's monster here, I think this is the only real glitch.'

'Fine. So I'll read it, and you'll set up this appointment, and I'll go in with you as your sort of pre-editor editor—'

'The guy who helped me through the bad patch caused by the divorce.'

'I certainly did. But then the three of us all sit around and solve the . . . Henry problem, and then I go back into the shadows, like the Phantom of the Opera.'

Bryce was reluctant to say this, but he thought he had to: 'If you and Joe get along,' he said, 'and I don't see any reason why you shouldn't, you might pitch him a story idea of your own.'

'Oh.' A short word, but quick with interest.

'Not right away,' Bryce said. 'When we get this book put to bed, then take your shot.'

'I will,' Wayne said. 'Thank you, Bryce.'

Fourteen

It was very strange to read your own book after it had been taken over by somebody else. It wasn't even a matter of whether Wayne thought the changes made the book better or worse, it was simply the otherness of it. Like a dream in which you're in your own house, but the details are all wrong, the furniture's different or in the wrong place and the doors lead to rooms you don't know. Disorienting, disturbing, almost frightening; and yet, fascinating. A parallel universe.

He had to read it through twice before he could see it clearly; the first time had been just too through-the-looking-glass. With the second run-through, though, he saw that this was a valuable learning experience, a wake-up call for some sloppy habits he'd developed over the years. Also, some of Bryce's changes struck him as brilliant. Moving the third chapter up to begin the book was just exactly the right thing to do, for instance. Other changes Bryce had made, though, struck him as pointless. What was wrong with 'winced'?

Susan read *Two Faces in the Mirror* as well, and insisted she liked the original better, which he knew was more loyalty than critical comment. She did agree with Wayne that the Henry-Eleanor scene was a mistake, but had no more idea than he did how to solve the problem.

Susan had always been his first reader, and had been valuable to him just because she was *not* a literary or artistic type, but was a solid realist. She didn't admire good writing or clever plotting for themselves, but enjoyed his books for their approximation to the truth. Whenever she did find fault with his work, it was because some striving for effect had left plausibility behind. A more artistic type, say another writer or a painter, would have forgiven such flaws or not even seen them, but Susan needed to feel solid ground beneath her feet, and he'd come to rely on her judgment to give his work ballast.

They joked sometimes about opposites attracting and absolute opposites attracting absolutely, but they knew it was true. They were devoted to one another and dependent on one another because they were so foreign to one another, so close together because they were so far apart. It was the very depth of their differences that made her his perfect reader; she admired his ability to create entire worlds out of the merest air, and he admired her ability to find the real world not boring.

The appointment with Bryce's editor, Joe Katz, had been set for ten-thirty Thursday morning. Bryce's publisher, Pegasus-Regent, was one of those who'd moved their offices down to the Madison Square Park area in the early eighties, when midtown office rents went through the roof. The firm had most of an old building now, on Twenty-sixth Street off Park, with a ground-floor luncheonette as the only other tenant. It was an easy walk from Wayne's apartment, though the early December day was cold and windy and overcast. But Wayne liked the weather, it gave him the impression of having a little struggle on the way to victory.

That other struggle, last month, he seldom thought about any more, though during the half-hour walk across and uptown the scene did keep coming into his mind; probably because this meeting was one more result of it. But these days, when he remembered that night in Lucie's apartment, it wasn't as though it had been anything he himself had done, but more like a scene from a particularly grisly movie. He remembered the experience the way you remember something you've seen, not something you participated in. It was as though, in his memory, he were three or four feet behind the attacker, observing from up close, but not a participant. However, like a scene from a particularly powerful movie, the memory did stay with him.

The entrance to Pegasus-Regent was unprepossessing; the loss of elaborate office-building lobbies was one of the trade-offs when the publishers moved south. A glassed door with the firm's name on it stood to the right of the luncheonette. Inside were a narrow hall with an old mosaic-tile floor, a steep metal staircase leading back and up, and two elevators.

Editorial was on six, the top floor, the closest hope to a view in this neighborhood. Wayne rode up, and when the elevator door opened he might as well have been in midtown after all. Editorial had a very modern, very elaborate large reception area with two separate clusters of sofas and magazine-laden coffee tables to left and right, and a receptionist at a broad multimedia desk straight out of *Star Trek*.

Wayne was two or three minutes early, but Bryce was already there, reading a recent *Economist* on a sofa to the right. He jumped up when Wayne walked in, waved to him, and called to the recep-tionist, 'Okay! Tell Joe we're ready.' Then, as she turned to her control panels, he came over toward Wayne, hand out, smiling, saying, 'Good to see you, Wayne.'

He looks feverish, was Wayne's first thought. Then Bryce was shaking his hand, and Wayne felt electric tension in Bryce's hand, and saw that the feverishness was deep in Bryce's eyes. And he's lost weight, Wayne thought.

This was the first they'd actually seen each other since that day in the library, the day Bryce had suggested this substitution plot. It was strange to think about that, to realize how much had happened since then. They'd talked a number of times on the phone, Bryce had arranged for him to go see that play, he'd signed the contract, he'd done ... what was required of him, now he'd read Bryce's version of *The Domino Doublet* – he didn't care for the title change, but let it go – but in all that time they hadn't actually been in the same room together. A month, a little more than a month.

'Mr Proctorr,' the receptionist called, 'Mr Katz says to please give him ten minutes.'

'Okay, fine, fine,' Bryce said, and to Wayne, 'Come on, sit over here.'

They sat catty-corner on the sofas, and Wayne said, 'Good, I wanted to talk to you about something else today anyway, this gives us time to do it.'

Why did Bryce look so worried? Though all he said was, 'Sure. What?'

'Well, money,' Wayne said.

Relief from Bryce; what had he expected? 'Oh, sure,' he said. 'It'll be coming to my accountant as soon as Joe puts through the okay, and that'll be after I do the changes based on the meeting today.'

'So in a week or two.'

'At the longest,' Bryce said. 'You know, it isn't even a check any more, it's an electronic transfer straight to my accountant. Then he pays my agent's commission, pays my bills, puts money in my checking account every month, and takes care of everything else. He can transfer your part to your accountant or however you want to do it.' With a shaky grin, he said, 'It's going to be a little too much to just deposit in your checking account.'

'Oh, I know that,' Wayne assured him. 'What I was thinking, Bryce, I'm not all that tied to my accountant, I've changed accountants three times the last eight or nine years, I'm never a big enough deal for them. If you wouldn't mind, why don't I switch over to your guy? You could introduce me, and then they just keep the whole thing in the one firm. Fewer people to know about it.'

'That would be perfect,' Bryce said. 'My guy there is Mark Steiner, I'll give him a call this afternoon, explain the situation, tell him you'll call.' He pulled out a pen, ripped off part of a page of *The Economist*, and wrote 'Mark Steiner' and the phone number on it. 'Wait till tomorrow,' he advised, 'so I'll be sure to have talked to him.'

'Thanks, Bryce,' Wayne said, and pocketed the scrap of paper.

Bryce gave him piercing sidelong glances, faintly disturbing. 'Well?' he said. 'What did you think of it?'

'Oh, the book?' Wayne felt awkward all at once. How do you react to the man who ate your book and regurgitated it as his own? 'I liked a lot of the stuff you did,' he said. 'The new opening is absolutely right.'

'Oh, thanks,' Bryce said. 'I really think the Henry-Eleanor thing is the only time I thoroughly messed it up.'

'Absolutely,' Wayne assured him. 'It's fine.'

'Mr Proctorr, could you go in now?'

'I sure could,' Bryce said, and jumped to his feet, then waited for Wayne.

They went down what would have been a wide corridor, except that secretaries' desks stood out perpendicular from the left wall, next to office entrances, and crammed book-cases covered the right wall; there was not quite room left for two people to walk abreast. Wayne followed Bryce to the end, where a half-open door showed part of a window showing sky.

This end room was Joe Katz's office, he being the senior editor. It was a large corner space, with big windows facing north and east; buildings and a bit of Madison Square Park to the east, building roofs and a bit of sky to the north. In addition to a massive dark-wood desk and four large soft armchairs – no sofas – the room was as cluttered as an attic. An Exercycle, a pinball machine, a doctor's office balance scale, an English-pattern dartboard, a spinet, a TV plus VCR, all elbowed one another for space along the walls.

Joe Katz came smiling around the desk to greet them. A short man, he was slender except for a surprising potbelly, as though he'd swallowed a lightbulb. Above a hawknosed face he'd mostly borrowed from Leon Trotsky was a tangle of black-and-white Brillo hair. His glasses were rectangular, black-framed, and halfway down his nose, so that usually he looked over them rather than through them. His hand was already out in greeting.

'Joe Katz,' Bryce said, 'may I introduce the skeleton in my closet, Wayne Prentice.'

'I knew you had one,' Katz said, grinning, grasping Wayne's hand. His handshake was strong, affirmative. 'Everybody does.' Peering over his glasses at Wayne, he said, 'Don't tell me yours.'

'I won't,' Wayne promised.

Katz released his hand and patted Bryce on the shoulder, having to reach up to do so, and the gesture reminded Wayne of somebody patting a favorite horse. 'Come on and sit down,' Katz said. 'What have you and your alter ego figured out? No, first – Sit, sit.'

They all sat in the armchairs, turning them to make a group, Katz ignoring his desk. Leaning forward, hands clasped together, elbows on knees, small feet just touching the gray carpet, he said to Wayne, 'I don't think I ever read anything of yours, remiss of me.'

'You're not alone,' Wayne assured him.

'Well, I looked you up, found *The Bracket Polarity.*'

The fourth of Wayne's novels under his own name, and the beginning of the downhill slide. The first downhill slide. 'Oh?'

'Well, it was terrific,' Katz said.

Wayne was delighted. 'You think so?'

'I had no idea Louie was a mole! Usually I see those things coming. I mean, my God, I'm an editor, I'm supposed to see those things coming, but I absolutely did not! And it was fair, too, you didn't cheat. How'd the book do?'

'Moderate,' Wayne said. What else was there to say?

Katz shook his head, disliking that. 'Shitty marketing, it must have been,' he said. 'Don't blame yourself.'

'I don't,' Wayne told him.

Katz sat back and his feet came off the floor. 'Now,' he said, 'turning to today's disaster. Bryce tells me you never did want Harry to leave that diner.'

'Not without Ja – Eleanor.'

'And there are ways in which you are right,' Katz told him. 'If he'd never left, it wouldn't have bothered me. But now I see we can goose that part of the book, make it better, give it a little jolt from the thruster, *if* we can get Henry and Eleanor back together without bending ourselves out of shape.'

Doubtfully, Bryce said, 'Maybe he could phone her the next day, apologize, grovel.'

'Too late,' Wayne said. 'By the next day, she's cement, she's hardened, she won't even answer the phone.'

Katz nodded. 'I'm afraid you're right about that,' he said, and scratched his chin. 'I used to have a beard,' he explained, 'and I shaved it off last year, and I still feel the damn thing. What was the point shaving it off?'

Bryce said, 'Grow it back.'

'Then I'd have to look at it, too,' Katz told him. 'It's bad enough to have to feel it.'

'Anyway, you don't have to trim it,' Wayne said, feeling they'd wandered into some conversation from *Alice in Wonderland*.

'That's it,' Katz told him. 'Always look on the positive side. For instance, what can we do about our suddenly impulsive Henry?'

'I was thinking about that on the walk up,' Wayne started, because that was the other thing he'd been thinking about.

Katz said, 'Walk? From where?'

'West Village.'

'Where?'

'We're on Perry, between Bleecker and Fourth.'

'My God,' Katz said, 'I'm around the corner from you on Fourth. I do my best thinking on that walk, back and forth, every day.' To Bryce he said, 'Two people live in the same neighborhood a hundred years, walk all over the place, never meet once. *That's* New York.' Back to Wayne, he said, 'So what did you think, on our walk?'

'I think he gets as far as the car,' Wayne said. 'Bryce has it that he leaves the car for her to use and takes a taxi, and she stays in the diner and broods about the relationship, and then drives off. We can keep all of her thoughts, that's the good part, but I think he only got as far as the car, and then got into the car on the passenger side.'

'Oh, nice,' Katz said.

'That's the apology right there,' Wayne said. 'She pays the check, she's mad, she steps outside, he's submissive. In the car on the passenger side, ready for her to take over.'

Katz said, 'She gets *into* the car. Eleanor doesn't make flamboyant gestures like hailing a cab.'

'No no,' Wayne agreed, 'she gets into the car.'

'And what does he say?'

'Nothing,' Wayne said.

Bryce said, 'Wouldn't he apologize?'

'He won't do anything at all until she gives him permission,' Wayne said.

'That feels right,' Katz said. 'So what happens?'

'She puts the key in the ignition,' Wayne said, 'but she doesn't start the engine. She looks at Henry, he's in profile, he just keeps looking out the windshield, waiting. She says, "Feel better now?"'

He says, "No." She says, "Good," and starts the engine, and drives them home.'

Bryce said, 'We don't have to go home with them.'

'Bryce, you're right,' Katz said. 'They drive off, and then, when we meet them again, we know everything, we understand everything. Wayne, you're a very productive walker.'

'Thank you,' Wayne said.

'Now,' Katz said, bouncing forward to get his feet on the floor so he could stand, 'we still have a few more little pleats in the fabric. Bryce? Did you share these with Wayne?'

'I didn't feel he needed to sweat them,' Bryce said. 'I figured, let him think about Henry and Eleanor.' He grinned at Wayne and said, 'I know you didn't like what I did there, but you made it come out just perfect.'

'Thanks,' Wayne said. 'So we were both right, it needed the action, but it also needed to be undone.'

Katz had gone over to his desk, and now he came back with a clipboard with several manuscript sheets on it. Bouncing into his chair again, feet off the floor, he said, 'Let's begin.'

The next half hour contained little for Wayne to do. It was his novel they were discussing, and yet it wasn't, and he was expected to have either no input or at best the occasional kibitzer's remark. It was a strange position to be in, so after a while he got to his feet and spent his time instead studying the various artifacts with which Katz had filled his room.

At one point, Katz called to him, 'Shoot a little darts, if you feel like it.'

'I'm very bad at darts,' Wayne told him.

Katz said, 'Take a look at the holes in the wall. You won't be the first duffer we've had. I'm not that great myself.'

So Wayne pulled the darts out of the board, and had added a few more holes to the wall by the time Bryce and Katz were finished. Then they both rose, Katz bouncing out of his chair again, and Katz said, 'Twelve-twenty. How about lunch?'

'I can't, Joe,' Bryce said. 'I'm supposed to meet Isabelle, we're moving more of her stuff over to my place.'

'By God,' Katz said, 'it's nice to see things finally begin to turn around for you, Bryce. A good woman, a good friend' – with a gesture at Wayne – 'and at last a good book. How about you, Wayne? You on for lunch?'

'Sure,' Wayne said.

Although you couldn't see anything on Bryce's bland surface, Wayne knew he wasn't happy to leave these two alone together. Wayne was ecstatic.

Over lunch, Wayne found himself telling Joe Katz his secret. They were in Union Square Café, one of the trendy lunch places that had sprung up once the publishers moved into the neighborhood, and their conversation was interrupted from time to time when Katz had to return a hello from some other passing diner, but still, in this crowded noisy public place, Wayne found himself telling another person his secret for only the second time. Bryce had been the first.

Katz had trouble getting it. 'Wait a minute, you're Tim Fleet?'

'Yes.'

'But I've read you, you're very good. But what's the big secret? It's a pen name.'

'The publisher doesn't know,' Wayne said. 'My editor didn't know.'

'Didn't know it was you.'

'Didn't know it was a pen name.'

Katz shook his head. 'I'm not following this,' he said. 'Pitch it to me like an outline.'

'Writer has successful novels,' Wayne told him, 'sales begin to slide. The big chains' computers turn against him, cut orders, sales get worse, finally he can't get a decent advance, nobody wants him. He rigs up a phony identity that only his agent knows, claims to be living in Italy or wherever, submits the next book as a first novel by Tim Fleet. The computer doesn't know Tim Fleet, so it can't put the hex sign on him. But after a while it does know Tim Fleet. End of story.'

'And you're telling me your publisher has no idea it's you.'

'They've never met me,' Wayne said. 'For all I know, they've never heard of me.'

'That's fantastic,' Katz said.

'Joe,' Wayne said (they were on a first-name basis by now), 'it's happening all over town. It's like the blacklist, writers hiding behind fronts, except, instead of Commie hunters, it's the computer they've got to hide from. What was tragedy the first time comes back as farce.'

'It can't be happening all over town,' Katz said. 'How many people could pull a thing like that?'

'Joe, do you have any writers you've never met? They live in some remote place, you communicate by E-mail, everything comes strictly through the agent, you don't really have a useful address for them?'

'Well, two or three,' Katz said, 'but, you know, not everybody can live in New York.'

'More than you know can live in New York.'

'You're creating terrible doubts in me,' Katz said. 'But why go through all that? Why lie to the publisher? Why not just do a pen name?'

'Because of the sales staff,' Wayne told him, 'and publicity and advertising, all those people you need behind you. If they know Tim Fleet is Wayne Prentice, even though it's supposed to be a secret outside the publishing house, it has that stink of failure on it already. But if they think Tim Fleet is Tim Fleet, really think that, and he's brand-new, and he's never failed because he's never been tested before, they can be excited. They can do wonders, when they're excited.'

Katz nodded. 'You're right about that,' he said. 'I'll tell you truthfully, Wayne, if I have a reconstituted virgin somewhere on my list, I'd rather not know about it. I'm sorry you told me as much as you did.'

'It's probably not as prevalent as I think,' Wayne reassured him. 'I'm aware of it, you know, because I did it.'

'And what of Tim Fleet now?'

'Dead,' Wayne said.

Katz was startled. 'Really? But he's very – you, I mean – you, he, whoever you are, you're very good.'

'Sales aren't.'

'You have a new book?'

Wayne almost said, I did have, but you have it now. Instead, he said, 'Part of one. But my publisher doesn't want it.'

'Let me not promise you anything, Wayne,' Katz said, 'but this afternoon, when I get back to the office, let me crunch some numbers, talk to some people in sales, see if there's anything we can do.'

'That'd be great.'

'No promises,' Katz said. 'You know, I can't argue with the computer, either.'

'Why did we give up autonomy, do you suppose?' Wayne asked.

'I hate to say it,' Katz told him, 'but it's too late to ask that question.'

When he walked home, Wayne felt as though he were floating above the sidewalk. What a great guy Joe Katz was! And how many good things he'd said about Wayne's own work! If there was any way at all to get around the computer, Wayne knew, Joe Katz would be his next editor. He could hardly wait for Susan to come home, tell her about his fantastic day.

The answering machine light was blinking. He pressed the button, and heard, 'This is homicide Detective Arthur Johnson, trying to reach Wayne Prentice.' He left a phone number, and said he would try again.

Fifteen

Isabelle had changed her mind. When Bryce got to her place, a one-bedroom, elevator building, third floor, no view, furnished minimally and decorated with travel posters, she was seated on the sofa, drinking coffee, and had done no packing. 'We have to talk, Bryce,' she said.

He said, 'Don't you have to get back to work?'

'Eventually. But first we have to talk.'

He looked around the room. 'You haven't packed anything.'

'It isn't working out,' she said.

'What isn't working out?'

'You and me. When I thought about actually moving over there, out of here, I realized it. It isn't working.'

He sat beside her on the sofa. She looked at her coffee rather than at him, and he tried to think of what he should say.

It was true, they'd been growing farther apart, but he had no idea why. She seemed to be holding herself aloof from him, in a way that hadn't used to be true. He said, 'Is it because I talked about moving to Spain?'

She smiled, sadly, and shook her head, still not looking at him. 'It's nothing at all,' she said. 'It's you and me, it's everything.' Now she did look at him, and he saw that she was sad but also remote. She said, 'It stopped being good when Lucie died. I know it should have worked the other way, but it didn't. The . . . whatever it was we had, it seemed to need Lucie to keep it going.'

He knew at once that she was right, though he hadn't realized it before, had very successfully managed not to notice, and couldn't begin to understand why it should be true. He said, 'Isabella, we can't let Lucie come between us *now*.'

'But she is between us. You dream about her, lying in bed with me.'

'I do? No, I don't.'

'In your sleep,' she told him, 'you moan and you make muttering sounds, never words, and you thrash around as though you were hitting somebody.'

'Me?' He hadn't been aware of that. He'd known he was feeling more tired lately, less alert when he woke in the mornings, but he didn't remember bad dreams. He'd known they were there, really, the dreams, but he never remembered them. He said, 'Why do you say it's about Lucie? If I don't say words.'

'Who else would you be beating?'

'Beating?' He sat back, as far from her on the sofa as he could get. 'Isabella,' he said, 'you *know* where I was when Lucie died.'

'Detective Johnson thinks we were there on purpose.'

'Johnson? He talked to you? When?'

'Tuesday. Day before yesterday.'

'I thought he was done, I thought that was all over.'

'I think it's just starting, Bryce.'

'But why? You *know* I didn't have anything to do with Lucie's death!'

'But I don't know it,' she said. 'Nobody knows it, because nobody knows what really happened. They'll find out, the police will find out, and then maybe it'll be all right again. But now ... Bryce, you're frightening, with those dreams, your shoulders moving, punching under the covers, muttering, frowning. And when you're awake you're depressed, there's no joy in you. Not since we came back from California.'

'That's why I want to go away for a while,' he said. 'Somewhere warm. It doesn't have to be Spain.'

'I can't go away with you,' she said. 'I can't live with you. I'm sorry, Bryce, I've been thinking about this all week, and I think about moving into that apartment with you, and it's like I'm moving into a grave.'

'Oh, God, Isabelle, don't say something like that.'

'It's what I feel.' She put down her coffee cup at last and held his left hand in both of hers. 'We have to stay away from each other for a while,' she told him. 'There's something you have to work through, I don't even know if you know what it is yourself but you have to work through it, and I can't be there. Later, when you feel better, when Detective Johnson knows what really happened, then maybe we can get back together. I'd like to. We had fun a lot of times. The weekends . . .' She trailed off, looking away from him, but still holding his hand.

He'd never told her he loved her, because he wasn't sure he did, and he was afraid of what the word might entail. He almost said the word now, but stopped himself, knowing it wouldn't be real, it would only be a tactic to try to hold on to her. And knowing, too, that she would see it for what it was, and turn away from him even more.

He said, 'Isabella, the idea of not seeing you—'

'For a while.' She looked at him again, squeezed his hand. 'I hope, for just a while.'

He looked around the small characterless room. This is where she preferred to be. He said, 'We were going to have lunch.'

'I'm not really hungry, Bryce, I'm sorry.'

He smiled a little and shook his head. 'I don't think I am, either. First time in my life, I bet, I'm not hungry for lunch.' He looked at her again. 'I'm going to miss you.'

'I already miss you,' she told him. 'The you from before.'

Suddenly restless, realizing he was becoming angry, not wanting to be angry, not wanting Isabelle to know he was angry, he pulled his hand from hers and abruptly stood. 'I miss the me from before, too,' he told her. 'God knows I don't want Lucie back, but I want something back. Is it okay if I phone you sometimes?'

'I hope you will,' she said.

He nodded. 'Maybe we could date, after a while. Dinner and a movie.'

'And a kiss goodnight,' she said.

He laughed. 'Oh, I think just a handshake at first.'

She stood. 'I wish you'd kiss me now,' she said.

He kissed her, holding her too tight, aware of her struggle to breathe, and finally forced himself to let go. Her eyes looked frightened, but she still smiled as she said, 'I'll see you.'

'See you,' he said, and left, knowing, at the end there, he'd wanted to hit her. The way Lucie was hit.

Three-thirty. He sat at his computer, in the apartment, trying to think of a story. *Two Faces in the Mirror* was virtually finished now, once he did the little Henry-Eleanor insert and a few other things. Half a day's work, he'd probably do it in Connecticut this weekend. Alone in Connecticut this weekend, but to be alone here would be even worse. He had weekend friends, sometimes dinner invitations on the Saturday. Nothing this weekend, but somebody could still call. And in the city, on the weekend, nobody would call.

What he had to do now was think of the next book. It had been over a year and a half since he'd written anything - the rewriting of Wayne's book didn't count - and he felt all those muscles were stiff now. He had to get limber again.

Most books began for him with a character abruptly being put into motion. Sometimes the setting was important, too, but the main thing was to find a character, somebody he could stay with for six hundred pages, and give that character a reason to get moving. So what he was doing at the computer now was trying to find that character, the entry, the starting point.

A doctor? He'd have to do an awful lot of research, but that was all right. He'd never written about a doctor before.

A doctor who finds a disease where it shouldn't be, something that's only found above the Arctic Circle, say, and his patient has never been north of Tarrytown, and . . .

Not a doctor.

He hadn't known he was dreaming about Lucie, but Isabelle must be right about that. Beating Lucie in his sleep. And then the dreams were always gone in the morning, leaving nothing but a sense of heaviness, weariness, sorrow.

Life was supposed to be better without Lucie, that's what it had all been about. And it was better, the financial crunch was over, the aggravation was over, the book deadline had been solved. He was the only fly in the ointment, he was the only reason things weren't better. He was doing it to himself.

A real estate salesman finds drug money hidden in the basement of a house he's offering, and the drug dealers want it back. No; older money. Prohibition money from the thirties, a third-generation private eye has been looking for it, like his father and his grandfather. Yesterday and today, linked. Neither of them has any right to the money, so both of them have the same right. But the private eye is tough and ruthless, and the real estate agent is just an ordinary guy, trying to keep from being swallowed up.

Is the real estate agent a woman? No. Bryce didn't think he'd ever successfully written from a woman's point of view, not for more than a few pages at a time. He'd get too many things wrong. He didn't even want to think about the sex scenes.

He and Isabelle hadn't had sex for almost two weeks. He hadn't even noticed, not till this second. Nothing in Connecticut last weekend, nothing here since, nothing here last week. Connecticut, two weeks ago. Her idea. And he hadn't noticed.

These characters weren't characters, they were wallpaper. He breathed on them, and they failed to stir into life.

Maybe he should just take the train to Connecticut today, not wait till tomorrow, see if the change of scene—

The phone rang. Isabelle, he thought, though he knew it wouldn't be. He picked up, and it was Wayne. 'Oh, hello,' Bryce said.

He'd felt strange today in Joe's office, with Wayne, almost as though he were jealous, as though he didn't want them to get along. It was irritating they lived in the same neighborhood, he wasn't sure why.

Wayne said, 'I just got home, and—'

'You and Joe got along great, I see.'

'—your Detective Johnson was on my answering machine!'

Oh. Isabelle was right, Johnson wasn't finished. Bryce could hear panic in Wayne's voice, and panic was the last thing Wayne should do right now. Making himself sound calm, unconcerned, Bryce said, 'Yeah, he's making the rounds, Isabelle told me, he talked to her on Tuesday.'

'But what does he want with me? Why does he even know about me?'

'Well,' Bryce said, 'my guess is, he talked to Janet whatever her name is, who directed that play—'

'Higgins.'

'—and from there to Jack Wagner, and Jack would have said he'd introduced you to Lucie at the play, so now he wants to know what you and Lucie talked about, and did you ever see her again, and you never did.'

'I never did.'

'Have you called him back?'

'Not yet, I wanted to talk to you.'

'It's not a big deal, Wayne,' Bryce said. 'He's following every lead, that's all, that's what his job is. You won't give him any reason to look twice at you, and he won't look twice at you.'

'I guess so.'

'Call him now, Wayne. If you don't call him back, he will look twice at you.'

'All right. I'll call him now.'

They hung up, and Bryce continued to sit at the computer, but he'd stopped trying to think of a character. He was thinking about Wayne instead.

Wayne had done what Bryce had sent him out to do, and it was supposed to stop there, but it wasn't stopping there. Wayne kept moving, acting, and Bryce didn't like the ways he was going. Cozying up to Joe Katz. And now, going into a panic, just because a cop wanted to talk to him. Cops had talked to Bryce, cops in Los Angeles and cops here, and he'd handled them all with no problem, no problem. Why can't Wayne do the same? Johnson's just following his leads.

But Johnson was a good detective, Bryce was sure of that. Would he smell something on Wayne, see something, sense something? Don't the good detectives begin with that sixth sense, the feeling that something's wrong, not yet knowing what?

Wayne had a power over Bryce that Bryce hadn't truly appreciated until now. When they'd made their agreement, that day they'd met at the library, they'd put themselves in each other's hands, they were absolutely dependent on each other's solidity and reliability. Bryce was solid, Bryce was reliable, God knows he'd proved that.

Is Wayne going to be a problem for me? Bryce wondered. If he's going to be a problem for me, what do I do about it?

Sixteen

The appointment with Detective Johnson was for eleven the next morning. Normally, Wayne didn't like to dose himself indiscriminately with drugs, but this morning, after Susan left for work, he took half a Valium. It was her prescription, rarely used, for those times when her job became too stressful. Wayne had almost never taken one, and didn't want to be zoned out when Johnson got here, but that would be better than being hopped-up, manic.

He hadn't mentioned Johnson to Susan yet, because what was the point? She'd have all day to worry about it, for no reason. When it was all over, he'd tell her what had happened. With, he hoped, a relieved laugh.

Johnson was exactly on time, and when he came in he didn't seem threatening at all. A moderately dark black man, tall and not too heavy, mild in his manner, he seemed more like somebody who worked in a bank or for some bureaucracy than a homicide detective. 'Thank you for seeing me, Mr Prentice,' he said, as though Wayne had had a choice in the matter.

'Anything I can do,' Wayne assured him. 'Would you like a cup of coffee?'

Johnson smiled. 'Oh, I better not,' he said. 'I drink coffee all day long sometimes, I think I'm putting the people at ease, the end of the day, *I* got the heebie-jeebies.'

Wayne grinned, liking the man. 'Then I guess we just sit down,' he said.

They sat in the living room, and Johnson said, 'You know what this is about.'

'Lucie Proctorr.'

'You met her fairly recently, I believe,' Johnson said. He wasn't taking notes, seemed just to be having a casual conversation.

'I guess it must have been the weekend before she died,' Wayne said. 'Or the Thursday, really.'

'It was at a play?'

'Yes. The playwright introduced me. I asked him to.'

Johnson was interested in that. 'You asked him to?'

'I'm an old friend of her husband's,' Wayne said. 'Bryce. We knew each other twenty years ago, more than twenty years ago, here in the city, we were both trying to make it as writers.'

'You did some novels yourself,' Johnson suggested.

'Yes, sure,' Wayne said. 'When the first one was published, I went to Italy for a year, research for the second book. When I got back, I'd lost touch with some of the people I knew, including Bryce. Then he became famous, and I didn't' – Wayne shrugged – 'it seemed awkward to get in touch with him, after a while.'

'But you did it, finally.'

'No, he called me. What I think it was,' Wayne said, 'when his marriage broke up, I think maybe he was lonely, or the friends they'd had were mostly her friends. I think he looked up people he hadn't seen for a while, including me. We met a couple of times, we had coffee—' Wayne broke off, and laughed, and said, 'Not too much coffee.'

'No, that's good,' Johnson said, and smiled. 'But how did you get from there to this play?'

'Well, Bryce really talked against Lucie,' Wayne said. He'd been working out this story in his mind since yesterday afternoon, and thought it was solid now. 'Any time her name came up,' he explained, 'there was more from Bryce about how rotten she was. You begin to wonder, can anybody really be that bad? I finally said it to him, I'd like to meet her, see for myself, he said be my guest.'

'So he's the one who knows Jack Wagner, the playwright.'

'I don't know any of those people,' Wayne said. 'I went there, I didn't know a soul. Usually there's at least somebody you know vaguely, but not there, no. Bryce couldn't go because Lucie was going, because the director was a friend of hers, so Bryce called Jack Wagner and asked if I could go instead, and Wagner said yes. I don't think Bryce said I wanted to meet Lucie, but I told Wagner that myself, at the party.'

'And that it was curiosity.'

'Sure. An old friend's horrible marriage, what does it look like?'

'Like rubbernecking at an auto crash,' Johnson suggested.

Wayne laughed. 'Guilty,' he said. 'That's just what it was. You know, like when Tom Sawyer charged his friends to look at his wounded toe. Everybody wants to see the really icky things.'

'Yes, that's true,' Johnson said.

'Which in this case,' Wayne said, 'was Lucie Proctorr.' And without warning there came into his memory, as clear and vivid as a movie poster, that final moment when Lucie Proctorr *had* been the icky thing. It stopped his breath, it stopped time, it almost destroyed the flow of the story he was telling, but then, desperate, afraid Johnson would see something, guess something, he *used* it, sitting back, letting the shock show on his face, crying, 'My God, what am I saying? That's horrible!'

Soothing, Johnson said, 'That's okay, Mr Prentice, I know what you mean. The question is, what did you think of Lucie? As bad as you thought?'

'No,' Wayne said. 'She couldn't have been as bad as Bryce was saying, nobody could, but she wasn't very good, either.'

'You didn't like her.'

'Not at all. I'm sorry to talk about her like that when she's dead and all, but I thought she was just negative, and a put-down artist. I mean, it was her friend who directed the play, and she's there as a guest, drinking their wine, and all she wanted to do was talk about what trash the play was, and how her friend Jane deserved better than that, she should be directing at the Public Theater.'

Johnson smiled. 'I take it you didn't talk with her for long.'

'Maybe five minutes. Then I thanked Jack Wagner for inviting me, told him what a great play it was – it wasn't really very good, but you don't say that—'

'No, you don't.'

'And I came home and told Susan about it. My wife.'

Johnson looked interested. 'She didn't go along?'

'No, she didn't want to,' Wayne said. 'She wasn't interested in Bryce's ex-wife, in fact she's never met Bryce. And she didn't care about the play, and she has a full-time job, so she didn't feel like coming out with me. She had dinner that night with a woman friend of hers, and was home before I was.'

'When Lucie left the theater that night,' Johnson said, 'do you have any idea who she was with?'

'Not at all,' Wayne said. 'I was gone by then. I was probably the first one to leave the party.'

'You didn't know anybody,' Johnson suggested, 'and the mission was accomplished.'

'That's right.'

'Did you discuss Lucie with Bryce Proctorr, later on?'

'Not really. I mean, just a little bit. I told him what I thought, what I just told you, that I more or less agreed with him that she wasn't a very nice person.'

Johnson nodded. 'I guess Bryce must have felt Lucie mistreated him quite a bit,' he said.

'I guess so.'

'Did he ever tell you he wanted revenge against Lucie?'

Startled, because everything had been so easygoing, Wayne said, 'Revenge? No, all he ever said was he wanted it over with, the lawyers were dragging it out.'

'But he wanted it to end.'

'He sure did.'

'Did he ever suggest there might be any kind of shortcut to end it that he might take?'

'You mean, like killing her?'

Johnson grinned. 'Well, that's one way, sure,' he said. 'But I was thinking, some of these rich fellas, they just pack up everything and leave the country, and tell the wife, "Catch me if you can." '

'I don't think that idea ever even occurred to Bryce,' Wayne said. 'He's got his life here. Besides, whatever money he gets paid, that's here, too, in New York. I don't think it would do him any good to go to Europe or anywhere.'

'That's probably true.' Johnson seemed to consider for a minute, and then he said, 'Do you think of Bryce Proctorr as a good friend?'

'In a funny way, yes,' Wayne told him. 'We hadn't seen each other for years, whenever I thought about him or saw his name in the paper, what I mostly felt was jealousy, because he was so much more successful than I am, but now that I've seen him again for a while I like the guy. He isn't stuck-up or anything like that. I don't say we're close, but we get along. Yeah, I like him.'

'You didn't mind his success.'

'It's his. He isn't stealing anything from me.'

'Well, that's true,' Johnson said. 'And what are you doing these days, Mr Prentice, if I may ask?'

Acting surprised, Wayne said, 'Still writing.'

'Really? Novels, like before?'

'Sure. I've been using a pen name, the last few years,' Wayne told him, 'but I'm thinking of going back to my own name with the new one.'

'You're working on a book now?'

'I'm always working on a book.'

'To tell the truth, Mr Prentice,' Johnson said, 'I'm something of a wannabe writer myself. I won't inflict anything of my own on you, don't worry about that, but I wonder. Could I take a look at what you're working on?'

'Sure,' Wayne said. 'Come along.'

As they left the living room, it occurred to Wayne that he might actually be a suspect in the case, even if just in the way that everybody is a suspect at first. Or had Johnson recognized some element from that drawing of the suspect in Wayne's face? Susan had finally seen some similarity in the eyes, but not enough, she thought, to lead anyone else to the likeness.

But asking to see his novel in progress. Wasn't it likely that Johnson wanted to know if Wayne could support himself with his writing, or if he was somebody who needed money, maybe needed it enough to kill a pesky ex-wife for an old friend? You won't get me that way, Detective Johnson, Wayne thought.

They went into Wayne's little office, which Johnson admired, calling it 'compact' as though that were a synonym for 'efficient,' and then Wayne had him sit in front of the computer while he booted in the disc of *The Shadowed Other*. It didn't have a title page, because he wasn't sure of the byline yet, but began with Chapter One.

'Well, look at that,' Johnson said. He read the first paragraph, then scrolled a dozen pages or so, read another paragraph, then sat back and shook his head in amused wonder.

'You professionals make it look so easy,' he said. 'That's why I know I'll never get anywhere.'

'Everybody started,' Wayne told him. 'No one was born a pro.'

'That's very nice of you to say,' Johnson told him, and got up from the computer. 'Thank you for your time, Mr Prentice,' he said.

And that was that.

Seventeen

Bryce couldn't seem to get out of his temporal confusion. He usually took the train up to Connecticut sometime on Friday, spent the weekend, left Monday. This week, the New York apartment had just become too oppressive by Thursday, so he'd taken the train up shortly after Wayne had told him about the message from Detective Johnson, and now it was Friday morning, and he was already here, and he just couldn't keep the day straight in his mind.

He phoned several weekend friends, wondering what if anything might be doing, this early in December, not yet massively Christmas, but of course none of them were here. Today is Friday, he had to keep reminding himself, and they are in New York. They work in New York. They live in New York. This is their weekend place.

And me? Where do I work? Do I work? Where do I live? Where do I call to find *me*?

He still didn't have his new story, and he needed it, he needed it *now*. Story ideas had never been a problem for him, there'd always been more ideas than time to write them, he'd reject one perfectly good notion because he felt more simpatico toward a different one. But of course he could never go back to any of those ancient story stubs, they wouldn't still have juice in them.

For him, creating a novel was like gardening: you choose your seed, you treat it exactly the way the package says, and gradually a thing of beauty – or of sturdiness, or of nutrition – grows up and becomes yours. The seed you don't nurture doesn't wait to be doted over later; it shrivels and dies.

One seed, that was all he needed. Of course, also this weekend he had to do the tiny remaining revisions on *Two Faces in the Mirror*, but that was no problem. No matter when he turned the work in, Joe Katz surely wouldn't read the pages until after the holidays. *Two Faces in the Mirror* was scheduled now for June, which was tight, in publishing terms, but Bryce Proctorr was a known quantity – and a known quality, too – so there was no doubt in anyone's mind the manuscript would be ready in time. And it had been too long since a Bryce Proctorr novel had been published, so the sooner the better.

Meaning the sooner the better, as well, for whatever was to come next. He should already know what it was by now, so he could do some preliminary plotting out, so he could spend the winter months in whatever travel and research might be necessary, spend the spring writing the book, turn it in in June just as *Two Faces* was being published. That was the kind of scheduling a publisher liked; the new one comes into the shop as the old one goes out the door.

Bryce thought on the train Thursday afternoon, he thought in front of the television set Thursday evening and in his waking hours in bed Thursday night and at the computer Friday morning, between useless phone calls to absent weekend friends, and he never got anywhere. A character in motion. Every character he thought of, whatever profession, age, nationality, residence, sex, economic status or relationship with the law, every single character, arrived already carrying its body bag.

That's when he thought maybe the thing to do was go away for part of the winter, somewhere different, somewhere warm. The Caribbean, maybe, or Hawaii, or southern Europe. Not Spain; Capri, maybe.

He was entering into the computer:

James Bond arrived on Capri with his right arm in a sling. I recognized him from the surveillance photos, and approached with my left hand out. 'Chris Dockery,' I said. What happened to the wing?'

'It got winged,' he said.

Breep breep, went the phone. Bryce frowned at what he'd just typed. A novel from the point of view of a James Bond sidekick? An ambiguous fellow, without Bond's Queen and Country stuff. An ironic contrast, a way to contemplate the issue of patriotism in a world where history has ended.

Breep breep.

Artificial, juvenile, unsustainable; and a mare's nest to clear the rights.

Breep breep.

'Yes.'

'Oh, there you are. I left a message on your New York machine.'

It was Wayne. James Bond's sidekick, the more ruthless one. License to kill. 'Hello, Wayne.'

'Detective Johnson just left.'

Bryce heard the tone of self-satisfaction in Wayne's voice and was reassured by it. 'It went okay, I guess.'

'No problem at all,' Wayne said. 'Only, I should tell you what I told him, so we both have the same story. In case he checks back with you.'

'Very good,' Bryce said. He imagined he was on the phone with Chris Dockery, receiving some plot point information.

'I told him we knew each other more than twenty years ago, drifted apart when I went to Italy. I figured you were calling old friends after your marriage ended, you called me.'

'How did I know where you were?'

'I'm in the phone book, Bryce,' Wayne said. 'No reason for *me* to have an unlisted number.'

'Oh, sure, sorry.' He felt embarrassed, as though he'd made some sort of faux pas with a member of the lower classes. And of course he'd *found* Wayne in the phone book once, to leave that message: You'll meet her. Yes.

'Anyway,' Wayne said, 'you called me, and we met and had coffee a few times, and—'

'Coffee?'

'I don't know, it just came out that way.'

'We sound like an AA meeting.'

'You could give us a few drinks, if you want, it isn't important.'

'Good.'

'Anyway,' Wayne went on, 'you said so many negative things about Lucie that I got interested to meet her just once, see if she could possibly be that bad. There was a play opening that you couldn't go to, because she would be there, and I asked if I could go, and you—'

'*You* asked?'

'I was curious.'

'All right.'

'You called the playwright,' Wayne said, 'Jack Wagner, and I went, and I asked Wagner to introduce me to Lucie. I talked with her maybe five minutes, didn't like her, left the party early. First one to leave. Which I was, by the way.'

'He have any problems with any of that?'

'None,' Wayne said. 'He told me he was a wannabe writer, and—'

'Oh, God.'

'No, it's okay, I think he was lying. I think he wanted to know if I had any way to support myself, or if I'd become a contract killer. So I showed him the book I'm working on—'

'A new one?' Bryce felt a twinge.

'Didn't I tell you? Yeah, it's coming along pretty good.'

'That's nice,' Bryce said. 'I figure I'll get started on my next after the holidays. You know, it's tough to get stuff done in December.'

'Try impossible,' Wayne said. 'Anyway, the point is, Johnson came and left and I think he's satisfied. I think that's the end of it.'

'Let's hope so,' Bryce said. 'And thanks for letting me know.'

'Well, sure, of course.'

Bryce sensed that Wayne would have liked to prolong the conversation, but he did not. 'Talk to you soon,' he said.

'Sure,' Wayne said.

Off the phone, Bryce deleted Chris Dockery and his friend Bond, and entered:

When my marriage ended, I was feeling kind of lonely and adrift, so I tried looking up old friends from my first days in the city, and there was Wayne Prentice in the phone book. I called him, and we met a few times, had coffee or drinks, and I guess I unloaded my dissatisfaction on him because he got curious about my ex-wife and wanted to meet her. There was a play premiere I was invited to but I couldn't go because she would be there, so Wayne asked if he could go in my place. I arranged it, and he went and met her and I guess he didn't much like her. We haven't talked about it since, obviously.

Bryce read what he had written, and he didn't like it. In the first place, there was the fact that Wayne had no trouble saying Lucie's name, talking about her, while Bryce found it increasingly difficult to refer to her as a real person. Shouldn't *Wayne* be feeling this? But clearly he was not.

But that wasn't the main point. There are moments in almost any novel when it's necessary to move a character from one position to another, so that you can go on with the story, and this was like that. Once the character is moved into the new position, everything is fine, but in order to make the transition the writer has to bend something out of shape. Some behavior is wrong, some reaction is wrong. It's a rip in the fabric of the novel, but it's necessary to get the story where it has to go, so the novelist merely sighs and shakes his head and *does* it. Other writers, reading the book, might notice the lump in the batter, but most readers won't.

This was one of those junctions. Once we get Wayne to the premiere of *Low Fidelity*, everything's fine, everything moves along as though on rails. But the flaw is before that.

Under no circumstances, never, would Bryce Proctorr, after the breakup of his marriage, be feeling lonely enough and nostalgic enough and sentimental enough to start looking up people he'd known twenty *years* ago, for God's sake. Utter strangers to each other, by now. And who else did this Bryce Proctorr look up and phone? *Just* Wayne Prentice?

A novelist would see through this, he thought. Would Detective Johnson? Probably not. Even if he felt something was just a little off in the story he'd been told, there wouldn't be anything there to get hold of, nothing concrete. And in any case, he probably wouldn't even notice the false note.

So long as the New York Police Department doesn't hire a lot of novelists to track me down, Bryce thought, I should be okay.

Eighteen

Christmas, which at least in theory should be the best season for a charitable organization like Susan's, was in many ways the worst. All of the needs were increased, all of the problems were magnified, all of the requirements became more urgent, and people who could keep their egos in check very nicely the rest of the year suddenly became vastly important in their own eyes.

Every evening, now that Detective Johnson had come and gone, now that the whole Lucie episode seemed to be finished with and fading from their minds (as well as from the media, thank God), now that Wayne's rejected novel had found a good home (however anonymously) so that soon a great deal of money would be coming their way, Susan was spending the dinner hour each evening telling Wayne the latest horror stories and comedies and comedic horrors from her days at UniCare.

There was rich material here. If Wayne weren't already at work on a novel, and if in fact it weren't the case that he had no market for any novel at all, he'd certainly try to find a story in the varied stories Susan was telling him. The setting was both Dickensian and very modern, sentimental but still ironic; perfect.

Finally, for the hell of it, he sat down one morning after breakfast, the week after the visit from Detective Johnson, and banged out a six-thousand-word non-fiction piece on the subject of the economics of organized charity. He welcomed the irony, and wallowed in the sentiment. He had no idea what to do with such a thing, but wrote it anyway, because it was fun, because he preferred to be

136

writing than not to be writing, and because he seemed to have bogged down in *The Shadowed Other*.

He knew what that was all about, and he wasn't made anxious by it. There'd been a moment, very briefly, when he'd realized *The Shadowed Other* was grinding gradually to a halt, that he'd wondered if this were a delayed reaction to the Lucie thing. (He called it that in his mind now, the Lucie thing, knowing what he meant, all the details and the surroundings and the circumstances, and he didn't need any further definition for himself.) But the Lucie thing wasn't bothering him, wasn't incapacitating him. He regretted it, of course he did, he regretted the necessity of it, and God knows he regretted the *messiness* of it, but it was over now, and whatever his regrets, whatever the horror of the incident itself, it was finished and they were now in the post-Lucie world, which was a much better world for Wayne.

Also, he had begun to suspect that the only way he could have done the Lucie thing was the way it had happened, by surprising himself, forcing the issue, creating a situation where there was no way to turn back. His vague plans about traveling to some southern state to buy a gun, then track Lucie anonymously through the canyons of New York, had all been a fantasy, a daydream. He couldn't have done it that way. Shock himself into action; that was the only possible route he could have taken.

So it wasn't the Lucie thing that was blocking *The Shadowed Other*, it was Joe Katz. After the holidays, Joe Katz would have a conversation with Wayne about his potential future at Pegasus-Regent. If it were thumbs-up, *The Shadowed Other* would spring immediately back to life. If not, not.

That evening, Wayne showed 'Charity Begins in the Out Basket' to Susan, who had a couple of small corrections to suggest but otherwise thought the piece terrific. So he made the changes, and the next day he called Willard Hartman, his agent, with whom he had not spoken since the dooming of *The Domino Doublet*.

'Wayne! Good to hear your voice, my friend. Happy holidays.'

'And you, Willard. I thought I should warn you . . .'

'Yes?' Said in jolly fashion, but with wariness underneath.

'I seem to have descended into the sinks of fact,' Wayne said.

'I've done some sort of article about the charity biz, based on stuff Susan told me.'

'Aimed where?' Willard asked, sensibly.

'I haven't the vaguest idea,' Wayne admitted. 'I don't know that world. I just want to mail it to you, Willard, and if there's no market for it, you'll know better than me.'

'Well, I'll certainly enjoy reading it, Wayne, I know that much,' Willard told him. 'You know I'm a fan of your stuff. I just wish there were more of us out here.'

'Me, too, Willard,' Wayne said, and the next day sent him a copy of the piece, with a note reading, 'Think of this as a Christmas card.'

Nineteen

Early in December, Christmas settles over New York City, and refuses to permit anything else to be talked about or thought about. Bryce took the train in to the city three times in search of Christmas presents for his kids, and for Joe Katz, and for Jerry Mossman, his New York agent, and for Gregg, the groundsman who mowed the lawns in Connecticut in the summer and kept an eye on the place the rest of the year, when Bryce – and before that Bryce and Lucie – were less often there.

But this year he was more often there. He found the apartment uncomfortable, didn't like to spend the night there, but twice he had to, once after Pegasus-Regent's Christmas party, an annual event he had no choice but to attend. The probable reason that he drank too much at the party this year, a thing he didn't normally do, was because Wayne was present.

He hadn't expected Joe to invite Wayne, who wasn't after all a Pegasus-Regent author. (In a way, of course, he was, but not in a way Joe Katz could know about.)

'Well, hello,' Bryce said, walking over to where Wayne stood, a plastic glass of pink punch in his hand. 'Fancy meeting you here.'

Wayne was very happy, maybe a little high. 'To tell you the absolute truth, Bryce,' he said, 'I feel like Cinderella. This isn't my real gown, and that isn't my real coach outside, and I wasn't really invited to the ball.'

'Don't tell the prince that,' Bryce advised him, 'and things could work out for you.'

Wayne was tipsy enough to be sincere, in a way Bryce found crude, almost ghoulish. 'I want to thank you, Bryce,' he said. 'You made all this possible.'

'You made a lot possible, too,' Bryce reminded him.

But Wayne was off on a voyage of his own, looking past Bryce, gazing at all the people at the party, book people chatting about books. 'God, I love this,' he said.

Bryce knew what he was thinking. This is his world, he belongs in this world because he doesn't belong in any other, doesn't fit anywhere else. The teaching-in-college fantasy had been just that, a fantasy, and one way or another it would have ended badly. This is the only pond in which this fish can swim.

And so, he has to be telling himself, whatever I had to do to be here is all right. To stay here where I belong, not to strangle in some alien world, simply to get what I deserve, the bare minimum I deserve; to be in my own world. Nothing is too much to do, to get that.

I did this to him, Bryce thought. I made him an offer he couldn't refuse. If no price is too high to pay, then the price I charged him wasn't very high at all, was it?

Bryce too looked around the room, trying to see it through Wayne's eyes, but knowing his own eyes saw differently. He *did* belong in this world, his bona fides were proved, and he *had not done anything*. Yet he felt he was the outcast. Why should that be? Why should the loser be lapping this up like cream, while the acknowledged winner feels like the interloper, the nobody, Caliban, the bumpkin rubbing elbows with his betters?

'Maybe this is a masked ball,' he said, but was immediately glad that Wayne was inattentive and didn't pick up on that. Because he knew at once what would be beneath Wayne's mask: openness, eagerness, sincerity. But what would be beneath Bryce's mask?

'Oh, I want you to meet Susan. Susan? Come here, meet Bryce Proctorr.'

Bryce turned, and she offered him a cool hand and a cool smile. 'How do you do? Wayne has told me so much about you.'

Has ever a stock bit of dialogue contained such gross subtext? *Jesus Christ*, Bryce thought, what a horrible secret we three share, in the middle of this party, we three and nobody else.

He and Susan Prentice took an instant dislike to one another, and Bryce could see her recognizing it as much as he did. She was a good-looking woman, he supposed, but too controlled, her light brown hair too much of a helmet to her head, her body too neatly trim, as though it had been pruned like a Christmas tree, her movements all too small and careful.

'Merry Christmas,' he said, and showed his party smile, and toasted her with his glass of punch.

'This is really a lovely party,' she said. 'Much better than Romney.'

Romney had been Wayne's first publisher, years ago. Tim Fleet, Bryce knew, had been published by Antelope, but of course if Antelope hosted any parties – not all publishers did – Tim Fleet could not have attended. What a strange thing it must have been to be Tim Fleet.

Bryce said, 'Pegasus is the only publisher I've ever had, so I have no basis for comparison.'

Surprised, Wayne said, 'Is that true? Most writers switch sooner or later.'

'Jerry, my agent, did some saber rattling a couple times,' Bryce told him, 'but Pegasus always came through. And I've been happy here. My first editor was great, and when he retired Joe took over, and that's twelve years, and I'd never leave Joe. If he ever went, I'd go with him.' If I had a book to give him, he thought.

Turning away from that thought, he said to Susan Prentice, 'What was wrong with Romney? Their Christmas parties, I mean.'

'They were very cheap,' she said, 'and it was always in their offices, and it didn't really work, and they'd just order deli stuff and the cheapest possible white wine, and all their A-list writers stayed away in droves.'

Wayne laughed, though shrilly, and said, 'That was it, right there, if only I'd noticed. If you found yourself at Romney's Christmas party, you knew you weren't A-list. You knew you were mid-list.' Grinning at Bryce, he said, 'You know my definition of mid-list? No pulse.'

Lucie! Crumbling backwards to the ground, punching, punching: no pulse. Bryce closed his eyes, and opened them. 'I've been lucky,' he said, 'and I know it. And I'd better circulate, if I want to go on being lucky. Nice to meet you, Susan.'

'And you.'

Bryce wandered the party, but found no one else to have a good conversation with, and soon left. Looking back from the door, he saw Wayne deep in happy conversation with, among others, Joe Katz.

There were as many parties up in the country in December as in the city, and he felt more comfortable at the country parties. The people he knew there were much more diverse, not all writers and editors and agents. The weekenders in the hills around him, who'd become casual friends and party hosts over the years, included lawyers, advertising workers, doctors, the owner of a chain of garden nurseries, a newspaper columnist, even a couple of actors. He felt at ease with these people because they cared more about pool services and deer repellents than about publishing mergers and the vagaries of the New York Times Book Review.

The actual holidays he expected to spend home alone in the country, but a week before Christmas he got an unexpected phone call from his ex-wife, Ellen. 'The kids are all coming up the afternoon of Christmas Day,' she said, 'and we'll have early dinner, because everybody has to get back. We were wondering if you'd like to join us.'

This offer had never been made before, and was clearly being made now because of the death of Lucie. Bryce's immediate reaction was to say no, was to continue with the idea that he'd stay alone for the holidays, but as he said, 'Well, Ellen, I—' she said, 'Are you seeing anyone? You could certainly bring—'

'No no,' he said. 'There was a, I don't know if you knew about Isabelle—'

'I don't know your life now, Bryce.'

'Well, there's nobody,' he said.

'So drive up. Oh, around one or two.'

'All right,' he said, and was glad he'd already bought presents, which he'd intended to mail. Since they wouldn't be entrusted to the Post Office after all, he gave them much more elaborate wrappings, with big bows, and large cardboard cutouts of angels declaring the name of the gift's recipient.

Christmas Eve he spent by himself, but that was all right. He watched television, switching around among choruses and comics and sentimental stories, dipping into three separate filmed versions of *A Christmas Carol* – now, there's a property with legs – and thinking how many other people were working or otherwise occupied tonight.

A little after ten the phone rang, and it was Isabelle, the first he'd heard from her since the day she'd decided not to move in with him after all. Several times he'd thought of phoning her, but it seemed too pushy to do, since she was the one who'd rejected him, and also too much trouble. What would be gained by talking to Isabelle?

She was calling from a party; he could hear the crowd noises in the background. 'What's going on?' he asked.

'I was wondering about you. Are you all right?'

'Sure, why wouldn't I be? I'm spending tomorrow with my kids. Where are you?'

'Some friends of my father's,' she told him, 'they have this penthouse just north of the UN, spectacular views out over the East River, it's really fantastic.' Lowering her voice, she said, 'I'm the only one here under sixty. I think I'm their little match girl.'

'They couldn't have done better,' Bryce assured her.

'Are you coming to town at all?'

'Not till after the holidays,' he said, knowing she was asking him to ask her out, but perversely refusing. He didn't *want* to rebuild the relationship, he wanted it to go on crumbling.

It went on crumbling, and soon they said goodbye to one another, and he went back to Christmas Eve in the world of TV. And early the next afternoon he put the shopping bags in the back of the BMW – they'd replaced the one that had been in the multicar collision – and drove the eighteen miles north and west through blustery wind under a bruised multilayer swirling sky – but not yet snow, which was predicted for a few days farther along – toward the house Ellen now shared with Jimmy Branley, outside Newtown.

Branley was an architect, and had designed his house, which

Bryce found ostentatious, all the rooms too large and sprawling, the white clapboard and fieldstone house diffused over the crest of a slope as though poured there, trailing down toward a generous swimming pool on one side and an elaborate black-granite ornamental pond on the other.

The interior was all white walls and massive blond beams and yellow brick fireplaces. Branley'd designed much of the furniture, too, all of it low and wide, as though it were being seen in a funhouse mirror. But the house was at its best, Bryce knew, at parties and festive occasions, when people seemed to flow from area to area, and the sound quality was such that you could always have a private conversation without ever feeling isolated from everybody else.

Since this was a weekend place, and by definition then at least to some extent a party house, and since it was also the showcase for Branley to demonstrate his style and skills for potential clients, Bryce had to admit that, whether he liked the house or not, it did the job Branley asked of it.

Bryce wasn't entirely sure what he thought of Branley himself, who was a cheerful, amiable man without a bad word for anybody. An ex-wife's new husband was one thing, but the guy she was living with was something else, even when it had been going on for several years, and when that guy was nearly fifty, with two grown kids of his own. Why Ellen and Branley didn't just go ahead and get married he didn't know; maybe Bryce had turned her permanently away from marriage.

The one thing he knew for sure about Branley that he didn't like was the way the man cheerfully announced, at every opportunity, that he wasn't a reader. Had never read any of Bryce's novels, no doubt never would. Too busy, too content with his architecture career, totally uninterested in fiction.

Bryce sometimes wished he could express such total lack of interest on his part in architecture, but that would just sound silly. Of course he was uninterested in architecture; only architects are interested in architecture. But all literate people are supposed to be interested in literature, or at least that's what Bryce had always believed.

He was the last arrival, and was welcomed cheerily if not effusively. The presents he'd brought were put under the huge tree in the living room with all the other presents already piled there, and he was re-introduced to Kathy and Jack, Branley's children, both mid-twenties, both doing something in cable TV.

Bryce soon regretted coming. The problem was, everything was normal, everything was fine, everyone accepted him, even his own kids seemed warmer than usual. The early dinner was fine, and he was seated next to Kathy Branley, who it turned out had just read *Twice Tolled* in paperback, and wanted to tell him how much she'd enjoyed it. And throughout, he kept thinking, I'm not supposed to be here, I'm not supposed to be with these people, I'm not supposed to be around simple pleasures. He didn't know why he felt that way, and didn't want to question it. He just wished he hadn't come.

Still, however much he might feel out of place here, nevertheless he stayed on, and stayed. After dinner, they opened champagne with the Christmas presents, and then the others started to leave, but Bryce stayed on, not entirely because he wanted to but because some sort of lethargy had overtaken him. And, he realized, too, he wanted to talk with Ellen. He'd been feeling the need to talk with Ellen since he'd seen her at the funeral, and now was maybe his last chance.

Tom and Barry, Bryce's younger children, having driven up together in Tom's car from New York, left together around seven, followed shortly by Branley's two kids, leaving only Ellen and Jimmy, plus Bryce and his twenty-three-year-old, Betsy, who was of course an architecture student and therefore always had a lot to discuss with Branley.

Ellen wound up in the kitchen, and Bryce followed, sitting on one of the chrome-and-canvas chairs at the butcher-block table, listening to Ellen's small talk, understanding that Ellen simply thought he was lonely and she was trying to fill in a little empty time for him.

But it was more than that. At a pause in her chitchat, he said, 'Ellen, there's something I've been wanting to talk to you about.'

'Yes? Sure. What is it?'

'Well,' he said, feeling amazingly awkward, not knowing how to sit with these arms, these legs, 'what it is, I feel this need to confess.'

She half-smiled, expecting some sort of joke. 'Confess? Confess what, Bryce?'

'Well, I hired somebody to kill Lucie.'

She stopped whatever she'd been doing – putting plastic around a pie remnant, something like that – and turned to stare at him. 'You did what?'

'It was going on for so long, you know,' he said, 'and I couldn't work. It was that, more than anything else.'

'You killed Lucie?'

'Had it done. Paid for it done. While I was out of town.'

She strode to the kitchen door, pushed it shut, came quickly to sit at the table opposite him. He'd never seen such a deep vertical streak between her eyes. She said, 'You're telling the truth.'

'Of course I'm telling the truth.' He shrugged, looking away from her. 'It was supposed to make things better.'

'How could you have— How could you even think of such a thing?'

'Thoughts like that have been thought before, Ellen,' he said. 'I didn't invent it.'

'No, of course not,' she said, shaking her own head, as though she'd been stupid. 'And that's what you do, anyway, isn't it? Think up things like that.'

'Usually not quite this . . . effectively.'

'And what now? Is he blackmailing you? The man who . . .'

'No, no, he's all right, he's fine, he's perfectly happy.' This time when he shrugged, it was spastic, like a convulsion. '*I'm* the problem.'

'In what way?'

'I still can't work,' he told her. 'I'm trying to think of a book, a new story, and nothing comes. And everything's just *drab*. I told you, that girl, Isabelle, we were together awhile—'

'I don't know her.'

'No. When she left me, she said there wasn't any joy in me any more. And it's true.'

'My God, Bryce, what a mess.'

'It was a terrible mistake,' he said. 'I realize that now, it was the worst thing I could have done. I have to make it right, Ellen. I don't know, for some reason I need you to know about it first. Be ready for it.'

She gave him a wary look. 'Be ready for what?'

'I have to go to the police, of course,' he said. I have to—'

'Don't you *dare*!'

He stared at her, astonished, and she was glaring at him as though he were her worst enemy in the world. 'What?'

'Is there no *end* to how selfish you can be?' Her face was stone, eyes burning ice into him. 'I think I'm used to it, how self-centered you—'

'Ellen, what are you saying? I don't understand.'

'Of course you don't,' she said. 'You have three children, Bryce, at the very *beginning* of their lives, all just on the verge of stepping out to become whoever they're going to be.'

'What has that got to do with—'

'You're a *celebrity*, you fool! You're a famous man! If you drag those children through a murder trial, a media circus, Bryce, I may kill you myself.'

All he could do was gape at her. 'I never—'

'Of course you never,' she said. 'That's always true with you, you *never* never. Bryce, you did a stupid and an evil and an unforgivable thing, but I will not let you make it worse.'

'I thought,' Bryce said, 'if I confessed . . .' He wiped cobwebs from his face.

'You ruin your children's lives,' she finished. 'You don't get off the hook that easily, Bryce, you don't get to be like the Catholics, just confess everything and it's all gone, the joy is back in your life. You can't *do* that. You have responsibilities.'

'Oh, Ellen,' he said.

'Responsibilities,' she insisted. 'For you, Bryce, confession is bad for the soul.'

He managed a laugh, though not a good one. 'All right,' he agreed. 'You're right, all right, I see that now, I didn't see it before, I'm glad I talked it over with you first.'

'Oh, my God, Bryce, so am I.'

'Confession is bad for my soul,' Bryce said, and nodded. His head felt very heavy. 'I'll remember that,' he said.

Twenty

Susan's grandparents, the Costellos, used to be truck farmers years ago in central New Jersey, near Hightstown, growing tomatoes for the huge Campbell Soup processing plant, as were most of their neighbors. The plant is long gone, most of the farms have been turned into bedroom communities for New Yorkers, and highways and strip malls scratch the landscape. But Susan's grandparents, both now in their nineties, were still alive and still owned the farmhouse and outbuildings and twenty-six acres, and every Christmas the whole family collected there, from as far away as Miami and Omaha, filling the house and the two barns converted into guest cottages.

This annual experience combined the wonderful and the horrible in more or less equal measure, and Wayne loved it. He himself had grown up in Hartford, Connecticut, to schoolteacher parents who couldn't have been more uptight if they'd still worn whalebone corsets. His father was dead now, his mother living in Pompano Lakes, Florida, his three siblings scattered, and they rarely if ever saw one another. Wayne supposed the main reason for that, from his family's side, was because he and Susan had no children. A lot of people, once they marry and settle down to 'normal' life with a 'normal' job and 'normal' kids, are completely uninterested in anyone who isn't exactly like themselves. Wayne did not have a 'normal' job, Greenwich Village was not a 'normal' home, and, most damning of all, they didn't have their own batch of dirty, loud, sticky, offensive kids.

All of which was fine with Wayne. Susan's family was enough for him, a large, variegated, tolerant, cheerful, boisterous clan, heavy into ribbing and joking but slow to take real offense. Wayne had a great time every year during those four days on the farm, forgetting completely his other life in New York, and the same thing happened this year. Not a thought about his perilous career, not a thought about Bryce, not a thought about Joe Katz, not a thought about that article he'd somehow written just before they'd left, and certainly not a thought about Lucie Proctorr, who was now in his mind not even a gruesome movie he'd seen once long ago but was a story, a horror story someone had told him once that his own vivid imagination had elaborated on but which was nevertheless not quite real.

They got back to the apartment on the twenty-eighth, refreshed, enjoying the accumulation of mail, seeing they now had invitations to *three* New Year's Eve parties, and of course they'd go to all three, and did, and met no one anywhere who could trouble their minds.

The Tuesday after New Year's, Wayne got two morning phone calls. The first was from Willard Hartman, his agent, who said, '*Vanity Fair* wants your charity piece.'

'Fantastic!' Wayne hadn't really expected anything from that piece, it had just been something to do, filling the time, writing something because writing something was better than not writing something.

'They have a few questions,' Willard went on, 'and a few changes to suggest. And they want to talk about photos to illustrate the piece, they always have to have photos.'

'Oh, sure, we can figure something out.'

'Laurie Simons, the editor on this one, sub-editor, she could just E-mail it to you, or fax it, whichever you prefer.'

Tim Fleet's life had existed almost entirely in E-mail, putatively sent to and from Milan. 'Give her my E-mail address,' he decided. 'What do they pay?'

'They've offered six thousand.'

'Hah,' Wayne said. 'Go figure.' Not bad, he thought, for a morning's work.

The second call, half an hour later, was from Joe Katz, who said, 'Let's do lunch.'

Wayne's heart fluttered. 'Sure. When?'

'One o'clock?'

'Oh, you mean today!'

Joe laughed. 'Wayne,' he said, 'I eat lunch every day. Walk on up, I'll see you at one.'

They ate at Campagna, on East Twenty-first Street, where Joe was known and they got a table for two with a little privacy, which wasn't the case throughout the restaurant. They talked about the holidays and Joe ordered a glass of white wine, so Wayne followed suit. Once they'd ordered their lunch, Joe said, 'Let's talk about your career.'

'I didn't know I had one,' Wayne said.

'I'm sorry, Wayne,' Joe told him, 'but you just jumped to the last chapter.'

A cold lump formed in Wayne's stomach. He was glad he'd ordered the wine. He'd known the news was almost certain to be negative, but he hadn't been able to keep himself from hoping. Joe Katz was a senior editor, he had clout, he was respected. Couldn't *he* tell the computer to go fuck itself?

Apparently not. Joe was truly apologetic, wishing it were up to him, but the numbers were the numbers. 'This is a bad time in publishing,' he explained.

Wayne didn't really feel like laughing, but he laughed. 'It's always a bad time in publishing.'

'Then this time is worse,' Joe said. 'The publishers are merging, more and more imprints under the same umbrella, and the result is, everybody's publishing fewer books.'

'I know about that part.'

'Of course you do. But on the other side, there's less room in the media for book reviews, attention to books, because now they're covering all these new technologies, CD-ROM and the Internet.'

'I knew I was getting fewer reviews as time went on,' Wayne said. 'I thought it was me.'

'It's everybody,' Joe assured him. 'Or almost everybody.'

'Not Bryce.'

'No, not Bryce.' Joe shrugged. 'Which brings up the other problem. Half a dozen years ago, the book wholesalers consolidated, and that means, even if you get your book published in hardcover, there's less chance to get a paperback reprint.'

'That happened to me, too,' Wayne agreed.

'I don't know if you'll appreciate the irony,' Joe said, 'but people like Bryce are seeing slightly better paperback sales, because the people like you aren't in the way any more.'

'I don't know if I'll ever appreciate that irony, either, Joe,' Wayne said. 'But what it comes down to is, you can't do anything with me.'

'The only offer I could possibly make you,' Joe said, 'is so insulting I don't want to do it.'

'You might as well try me,' Wayne said. At this point, what could an insult look like?

'I told Carew, the publisher, I really wanted you, and he did all that good-money-after-bad stuff, and then we came to a compromise. You tell me you have a book.'

'Part of a book.'

'If I think there's something promotable in it,' Joe said, 'maybe we can work something out. You know what I mean by promotable.'

'Princess Di should be a character in it.'

Joe laughed, but he said, 'It wouldn't hurt. Promotable is absolutely distinct from quality. I know your work, I know you'll produce good readable prose, I know you're good with plots and good with characters, so let's just call all that a given.'

'Thank you,' Wayne said.

'This isn't compliments,' Joe told him. 'I'm discounting everything we know you're good at. What I want you to do is go home and look at that part of a book you have, and say to yourself, "Never mind Joe Katz. What will the publicity department see here? What will the sales department see here? What's the *hook*?" You understand what I'm saying?'

'Yes,' Wayne said.

Joe shook a finger at him. 'I'm not asking you to bend your book out of shape,' he said. 'In the first place, I wouldn't be able to make it worth your while. So don't add Princess Di.'

'Okay,' Wayne said.

'But if you think,' Joe said, 'without destroying the integrity of the work, you can find a promotable element in it, call me and tell me. And *then* I'll look at the book. And if it's got all your normal strengths, plus you're right about it being promotable, I'm permitted to offer you ten thousand dollars.'

Wayne could think of nothing to say.

Joe finished his wine in a gulp, and signalled for a second glass. Wayne pointed at his own glass, and Joe showed the waiter two fingers. Then he said, 'The idea is, if we can get behind this book and promote it, and kick you up above the computer's expectations, then next time we can offer a little more and try even harder and make another increase in sales.'

Wayne said, 'You're talking about building a career from scratch, the way it used to be, when writers and publishers stuck with one another for the long haul.'

'Except,' Joe told him, 'the way the game is played now, we begin in sudden-death overtime.'

Wayne sipped his second glass of wine. There was nothing promotable in *The Shadowed Other*. You could only promote it as a novel, a story, something you might like to read. He said, 'I'll think about it.'

'Good,' Joe said.

'And I want to thank you, Joe,' Wayne said. He was sincere, and hoped it showed. 'I know you did your best.'

'We can only do what we can only do,' Joe said.

Twenty-One

Bryce had arranged with Linda, the once-a-week cleaning woman in New York, to pack up his mail every week, the stuff she thought he'd care about, put it in a manila envelope, and send it to him in Connecticut. The Thursday after New Year's, he got such an envelope, and one of the items it contained was a brisk letter from the management firm that handled the building containing his apartment. The letter was addressed to Bryce Proctorr, and it informed him that the management firm had become aware of the fact that the leaseholder of the apartment was deceased. If Bryce cared to negotiate a new lease, he should phone Ms Teraski at the above number as soon as possible. Unfortunately, it would not be acceptable for him to remain in the apartment without a lease.

What a strange thing to realize, that even though Lucie had been the one to move out at the breakup of the marriage, it was still her name on the lease. Mark Steiner, his accountant, had had reasons of his own why Lucie should be a New York resident and lease the apartment while he should be a Connecticut resident and own the house. It had seemed unnecessarily complex at the time, in the way that tax laws lead to unnecessary complexity, but now it seemed grotesque.

They understood the leaseholder was deceased. That was the most bloodless way yet to describe the circumstance by which the life had been pounded out of Lucie's body.

He didn't call Ms Teraski, not yet, because he wasn't sure what he wanted to do. He supposed he should call Mark at some point, find out what the tax laws and the accountant thought best for him at this juncture, but he didn't feel ready for that call, either.

Then, two hours later, Mark himself phoned Bryce. 'I just wanted you to know, the Pegasus money is in.'

'Oh, good,' Bryce said.

'I'll be calling Wayne Prentice next.'

'He'll be glad to hear from you.'

Mark laughed. 'I suppose he will,' he said. 'You know, I still think this is the most insanely generous deal I've ever heard of.'

'He was worth it, Mark.'

'I bet he would have taken less. If you're ever tempted to make another deal like this one, Bryce, please talk to me first.'

'It won't happen again. But I needed him right then. I wasn't working, it was going on too long, it was going to hurt the career, the reputation. He's worth the money, Mark, because the truth is, if it weren't for Wayne, *Two Faces in the Mirror* would not exist.'

'And you're sure of him.'

'What do you mean?'

'Well, I know he's a friend of yours,' Mark said, 'and he's a nice guy, I like him—'

'Uh huh.'

'But what about the future? I mean, he isn't going to come along some day and claim that book is *his*, is he?'

'Absolutely not,' Bryce said. 'I know I can trust him on that, Mark. I trust him absolutely on that.'

'Well, you usually know what you're doing,' Mark said. 'I'll call him now, give him the good news.'

Bryce hadn't asked this before, and it really wasn't any of his business, but he suddenly wanted to know: 'What's your arrangement with Wayne, anyway? I mean, you're handling his finances now, right?'

'It's essentially the same deal I have with you,' Mark told him. 'That's what he asked for, and that's what he'll get. I assume he'll have further income to back it up.'

'Oh, I'm sure he will,' Bryce said, and it wasn't till after he'd hung up that he realized he'd forgotten to talk to Mark about the apartment.

Well, he knew what that meant. That meant he wasn't going to keep the apartment. Not negotiate a lease, not live there, fifteen stories up, all alone. He'd move his furniture, what he wanted, up here, throw the rest away. Most of it he wouldn't want anyway; Lucie'd picked it all out. It was hers.

The phone call and the decision about the apartment, if that really was the decision, had left him restless, so that afternoon he drove to Brenford, the gourmet grocery store in this part of Connecticut, the place where you went for New York-style foods you couldn't get in a supermarket. At New York-style prices, too. There were things Bryce could only get at Brenford, the coffee he liked, a salmon dip, some other things, and it had been a while since he'd gone there.

Early Thursday afternoon in midwinter and the parking lot at Brenford's was half full, mostly of Jeep Cherokees and Toyota Land Cruisers and the like, with here and there a Volvo or a Saab or a BMW like Bryce's.

When all else failed, it was pleasant to receive this occasional reassurance, these visual signals that one is not alone, one belongs to a tribe, and one is firmly in the territory controlled by that tribe. The license plates were more than half Connecticut, the rest New York and a few Massachusetts. In summer there were New Jersey plates as well, but one knew they were not real courtiers, but merely bumpkins visiting the court.

The shopping carts came in two sizes, plus small hand-carried baskets for those who weren't really serious. Bryce compromised with a smaller-size cart, and the glass door slid out of the way as he approached, greeting him with a puff of warm air smelling vaguely like a bakery.

Usually he didn't like shopping, but preferred to hurry into a store, grab the first things he saw that approximated what he wanted, and hurry back out again. Today, though, he felt a kind of underwater stillness inside himself, as though he'd been swimming hard but now didn't have to any more. Now he could coast.

Everything was finished. Detective Johnson had phoned earlier this week, but only to get the names and addresses and phone numbers of some of Lucie's relatives in Kansas and Missouri; he was haring farther afield, he had not found the murderer's spoor. Pegasus-Regent had paid for *Two Faces*, Joe Katz had accepted it as a work by Bryce Proctorr, the distracting and harrying divorce process was eliminated, Wayne Prentice was content. His relationship with Isabelle had stalled, but maybe that merely meant it had gone as far as it could, that he and Isabelle would never be any closer to one another, that she was not at last the answer to what he would do next in that department.

'Excuse me.'

'Yes?'

An attractive face framed by soft waves of ash-blond hair, and the kind of wide innocently eager brown eyes that suggested plastic surgery. A short dark fur coat open on a dark green blouse and tan wool slacks. She seemed hesitant, but not really afraid of rejection. She said, 'Aren't you Bryce Proctorr?' Her voice was throaty, as though she smoked cigars, or liked to laugh at dirty jokes.

'Guilty,' he told her, with his meet-the-fan smile.

'I *thought* so!' She extended a slender hand in which the bones were outlined beneath pale skin. 'I was told you lived somewhere around here. I'm Marcia Rierdon, I'm a huge fan of yours.'

'How do you do,' he said, taking the hand, which was quick and strong. He'd had encounters like this before, one step beyond normal random; the follow-through depended on the circumstances. 'I always like to hear positive words,' he assured her.

Smiling, she said, 'Well, I have one negative word for you, Mr Proctorr. Where's the next book? Your readers are waiting.'

'June,' he promised her. 'I guess there'll be books in the stores in May. It's called *Two Faces in the Mirror*.'

'I will buy it at *once*. I think I have every book you've ever written.'

'Well, good.'

'In hardcover!'

'Even better,' he said.

She leaned forward, a sudden hard hand on his forearm, where he was holding his cart. 'Could you—' she said. Then she retreated, hand off his arm, shaking her head. 'No, it's too much to ask.'

'Is it?' he asked. 'How do I know if I haven't heard it?'

'I live nine miles from here,' she told him, 'toward Amenia, New York.' Looking in his cart, she said, 'I don't know how much more shopping you have to do—'

'I'm almost done.'

A sidelong smile. 'Shopping for one,' she said.

He grinned, nodding his agreement. 'That's what I'm doing.'

'I'd think a person—' Then shock changed her face, she pressed carmine fingertips to her mouth, she said, 'Oh, my God, your *wife*!'

'It's okay,' he assured her.

'Oh, what a terrible thing, I completely forgot, I am so sorry!'

'No, it's fine,' he said. 'Don't worry about it. I forget myself, sometimes.'

'Well, now I'm embarrassed,' she said, 'now I can't ask you.'

'You want to know if I'll follow you to your house,' he said, 'and sign your books.'

'Oh, *would* you?' Her hand was on his forearm again, tighter than before.

'I'd love to,' he said. 'Give me five minutes.'

'I'll be by the registers,' she told him, and permitted her bright-eyed smile to turn just a little coquettish as she lifted her hand beside her face to give him a tiny ta-ta wave, then turned away.

He didn't have that much more to find in here. Walking the aisles, finishing the selections, he thought about this as a scene in a novel, where it would always have seemed a little opportunistic and now would seem outdated as well. Twenty years ago, these hills were full of stay-at-home wives during the week, childless or their children away at school, their husbands living and working in New York, coming up only for the weekends, some of the wives on the prowl for ways to make country life more interesting while the breadwinner was away. Most of those wives were gone now, either to jobs of their own in the city – almost all of the couples Bryce knew up here had two jobs and traveled to and from New York together – or at the very least they found life in the city during the week more stimulating than life alone in the country. But there were still a few, a minority, maintaining the traditional structure, the woman tending the fire in the cave while the man was out contending with the mastodon.

And hitting on a famous person only because he's famous was an evergreen activity.

So this had happened to Bryce before, over the years, though not often; this would be the third time. The first one, he'd been happily married to Ellen, and he'd been polite and friendly, honored by the attention, but unfortunately stuck with an appointment with his wife; a lie, but it doused the fire.

The second time, he'd been sleeping with Lucie but not yet married to her and she was still resisting the idea of spending time with him in Connecticut, so then he'd been happy to follow the lady home, eventually taking her out to dinner, going back to spend the night. She'd given him her phone number, which he'd immediately thrown away, and wouldn't have been able to find that house again today on a bet. Nor did he remember her name, nor much about what she'd looked like. Oddly, the rejected first one was a little clearer in his memory.

So what was the program this third time at bat? She was attractive, she was intelligent (she did, after all, admire his books), he was completely unattached, and she was unlikely to be a problem in the future, since she already had a man who provided her this place within the tribe. If Bryce didn't want to see her again, it would be just as simple as the other time.

I'm going to follow her home, he thought, but the frisson that gave him was a strange one, almost a revulsion. Wasn't she sexy? Certainly she was sexy. Beneath the uniform of the tribe, she would be very fit indeed.

Somehow, he couldn't imagine forward to that moment. Part of sex, of course, is anticipation, imagining what is yet to be, but his mind was dull, he could only think of the here and now, we have two cars, she's waiting by the cash registers, I will follow her toward Amenia, New York.

Yes, there she was. She waved as he unloaded his goods on to the moving black belt, and then pushed her cart full of bagged groceries outside. He paid, wheeled his own stuff out, and she was across the lot, standing beside a gray-green Jeep Cherokee with Connecticut plates. Again she waved, and he waved back. She got into her car, he loaded his and got behind the wheel, and their two-car convoy left the parking lot and turned left.

All the roads around here were two-lane, winding, hilly, upscale suburban. The houses were set well back, most of the trees still in place, new plantings, fences, hedgerows, tennis courts, swimming pools, multicar garages angled beside Colonial stone. The Cherokee ahead of him glided like a dream through the landscape, and Bryce followed.

Lucie. This had been Wayne and Lucie, just two people getting to know one another, strangers in that engrossing time before sex when every sense is heightened, every gesture has meaning, every slant of shadow across cheekbone is to be analyzed, the world to be discovered approaches across the universe. And then the explosion.

Why am I thinking about Lucie? he asked himself, and clenched hard to the wheel. Am I going to spoil things? Am I going to go in there and be a pathetic grieving widower, impotent in his sorrow? *What* sorrow? I don't grieve for Lucie, I never have, I never will. I hate it that she made it all necessary, but she did make it all necessary, she did that. I did nothing.

He wanted to know. Lucie had been his enemy, his demon, his succubus, and he should have been there, he should have experienced it for himself. It was only to avoid suspicion that he hadn't been there, that someone else had done what he should have done. He knew, in the dreams he never remembered, he knew he was trying to create the scene, imagine the scene, but it wasn't working. He wanted to know.

Marcia Rierdon. The looseness of her smile, the brightness of her eyes. What would she look like—

Why can't I visualize having sex with her? He forced himself to see a white pillow in a dim room, her smiling face, bright-eyed, looking up from the pillow. But where was he?

His fist smashed down. That nose, which has also been fixed, is fixed again. The fist lifts, the wide eyes are wider, but what does it *look* like? What does it sound like? What is it like?

His eyes snapped open just before he would have driven off the road into an old stone fence. He righted the car, and saw the Cherokee slowing toward a Stop sign ahead, the right-turn signal on. Keep your eyes open, you have to drive with your eyes open.

She stopped at the Stop sign. He switched his right-turn signal on. She turned right. He stopped; he turned right.

Oh, God, is that what I'm going to do? He could feel it coming over him, knowing what it was but not wanting to know what it was. He would never have sex with this woman, this Marcia Rierdon. There was heat for her, but it wasn't in his loins, it was in his shoulders, the straining muscles of his arms, in his legs.

I wasn't there because I couldn't be there because they would suspect me, but I should have been there, it's incomplete if I'm not there. I don't know this woman, she doesn't know me, no one will ever know I was in her house, never know I was this far west in Connecticut, never know anything, at last I can be *there* because I cannot be a suspect.

Sweat ran down and out from under his hair, on to his forehead, down in front of his ears, into his collar in back. He was panting, his hands were clenching and unclenching on the wheel.

You can't do this. You don't need to know. You don't *need* to know. You can't hurt Marcia Rierdon, she isn't Lucie. She isn't Lucie.

She's married, she's self-indulgent, she's faithless, she's evil, she *is* Lucie.

Is not having the memory worse? Or is having the memory worse?

He seemed to be his own prisoner. He watched helplessly, hoping he could stop himself, hoping he wouldn't stop himself, hoping he could come out of this, whatever this was, just come out of this with his mind intact. Just not hurt *himself*.

Her brake lights lit. She turned right onto a blacktop driveway between two square brick posts, with a large dark house back there among towering trees. A black mailbox said, in red letters:

681
RIERDON

He touched the brakes. He breathed loudly through his mouth. He drove past that driveway, and on.

He stared now out the windshield as though he expected some

monster to come up out of the roadway at any second and engulf him, car and all. The way he'd stared just after the multicar collision, before he'd realized he was still alive.

He turned at random, the next intersection, the next. I can go back, he told himself, I can turn around and go back, make an excuse, she'll still let me in, she'll still *want* me to come in.

I'm going to have to resolve this, sooner or later, and I can go back right now.

He kept driving. Nearly an hour later he drove into Amenia, New York, from the south, which would not have been a straight line from her place. He turned right at the traffic light, heading back to Connecticut.

I can still go back, he told himself, though he was no longer sure exactly where she lived. If I come to her house, he told himself, I will turn in. We'll leave it to fate, or God, or chance, or dumb luck, or whatever. If I see her house, I will turn in. Absolutely, no question. I can always make some excuse.

He drove another hour, and then he drove home and unpacked his groceries.

Twenty-Two

By the middle of February, Wayne had sold three more magazine pieces, and had earned nineteen thousand dollars the first six weeks of the year. At that rate – though realistically he knew that rate couldn't possibly continue – but at that rate, if he actually could make it continue, he'd bring in just about twice as much a year from magazine articles as he'd ever made, even in the best years, from writing novels.

So far, the new career had been as much fluke as planning. Flush with his *Vanity Fair* success, he'd done another piece on the subject of charity, again with Susan as his primary source, this time with her also as lead to other sources, this piece on charity and celebrity, on the subject of which celebrities chose to support publicly which charities, and why, with an emphasis on celebrities and charities both based in New York. He'd expected that to go to *Vanity Fair* as well, but they said it was too much like other things they already had, so Willard Hartman sent it to *Playboy*, and they bought it.

All right, then, *Playboy*. He did a piece about seduction on the Internet, aimed right at the crease between *Playboy*'s one and three pin, and it proved to be a gutter ball instead. So Willard sold that one to *Vanity Fair*; go figure.

With the third piece, he decided not to even think about a market, but leave that – as, after all, he'd done with that first piece on the charities – to Willard. Using Jack Wagner and Janet Higgins of *Low Fidelity* as his entree – happily, neither of them so much as

163

mentioned Lucie – he did a piece on the current state and future prospects of off-off-Broadway.

Willard called ten days later: '*New York* is very happy with the downtown piece.'

In the meantime, *The Shadowed Other* was going nowhere. He looked at the printout from time to time, thought about it, even knew part of where the story would move next, but he just couldn't force himself to boot that disc into the computer. What was the point? No one waited for *The Shadowed Other*. He'd get to it someday, but at the moment he had a living to make. After all, he now had a major accountant, who treated him like a valued client; no point letting that slip away. With Susan's salary and his own new freelance career, he should be able to keep Mark Steiner's interest alive.

As to this sudden and unexpected success, he thought it was probably the years as a novelist that had prepared him for it, without his realizing it at the time. He'd always been a storyteller who got the details of our world right. Not just the guns and the planes and the perfumes and the whiskies, but the highway intersections and the histories of obscure clans and the reasons for the extinction of this or that species.

Much of his preparation, in his novels, had been in the library or on the phone, with experts. He had learned early on that he could phone almost anybody in the world, from the Israeli United Nations Mission to Budget Auto Rental's main headquarters, and say, 'I'm a writer working on a novel, and I wonder if you could tell me . . .' and people would stop whatever they were doing, answer the questions, look things up, spend as much time as he wanted, and wish him luck at the end of the call. It was one of the great secret resources of the fiction writer, that pleasure that the rest of the world takes in helping the fiction along.

His other strength from the novel writing was a certain liveliness of tone, a writing style that avoided the dull and the predictable, that found unexpected but good connections, that made him fun to read.

So what he was doing now, in these nonfiction pieces, was not that much different from what he'd been doing all along. Leave out the story and the characters, and sell what's left. Skim milk; sells very well.

One way this new career was different from writing a novel was how quickly it used up the ideas. Like all of his books, *The Shadowed Other* was essentially one idea, which he elaborated and ran changes and variations on, and rendered, and used, until it was completely emptied out. That meant one idea every year or two. Writing for magazines, you had to have two or three ideas a month; so far, he could keep up.

His next idea was a piece on celebrities who chose to make Manhattan their primary residence, rather than flee either to the seclusion of Connecticut or the warmth of California or the more exotic choices of London, Paris, Rome, Geneva. His entree on that one, of course, would be Bryce, who would be his first subject and then would pass him on to other celebrities he personally knew who fit Wayne's profile, who would in their turn pass him on to others, and in less than a month he'd have a piece. And let Willard decide who wanted it.

But when he called Bryce's New York number he got a recorded announcement that the phone had been disconnected, and no referral number was given. What did that mean?

All at once, Wayne thought, I'm vulnerable to him. If he goes nuts, he could make trouble for me. But why would he want to do that? Doesn't he have everything now? Didn't he get everything he asked for?

Nevertheless, Wayne found himself reluctant to phone the Connecticut number. He didn't want to just stride on into that darkened room. So he phoned Mark Steiner instead, the accountant he now shared with Bryce, left a message that he'd called, and when Mark got back to him that afternoon Wayne said, 'Mark, is there anything wrong with Bryce?'

'Wrong?' Mark sounded wary. 'What do you mean, wrong?'

'I haven't seen him for a month or so,' Wayne said, 'and I tried to call him in New York just now, and the number's disconnected. I didn't—'

'Oh,' Mark said. He sounded relieved. 'Bryce gave up the apartment.'

'Gave it up?'

'It was in Lucie's name,' Mark told him. 'Bryce is a Connecticut resident, something you and Susan might want to think about one of these days. He didn't particularly like the apartment, when it's just himself, so rather than renew the lease he's given it up. Technically, it's his till the end of the month, but he's already moved out. I think he left some furniture there that he doesn't want, that's about it.'

So much for celebrities who live in Manhattan. Or, at any rate, so much for Bryce as the entree. 'Oh, good,' Wayne said, 'I'm glad it isn't a problem. I was afraid to call him up there, I didn't know if he'd got sick or moved to Timbuctoo or what.'

'No, he's fine,' Mark said. 'Staying up there full time. Working on the next book, I think.'

'Great. That's what he needs.'

'It certainly is,' Mark said.

Over their usual candlelit dinner, Wayne told Susan about this change in Bryce's living arrangements. 'I'll tell you the truth,' he said, 'I suddenly got kind of a queasy feeling. You know, sometimes Bryce can act like he isn't wrapped real tight.'

'At that Christmas party,' she said, 'I thought he was very hostile.'

'Withdrawn,' Wayne said. 'He can be withdrawn, but it isn't hostile.'

'It looks hostile. So he's gone from there? Central Park West?'

'Mark says he's still got the lease till the end of the month, but he's out except for some furniture he doesn't want.'

She said, 'What would an apartment like that cost?'

'I don't know. Six or seven thousand a month, maybe more. Why?'

'Dealing with people every day,' Susan said, 'who pay two hundred dollars a month and can't afford it, it's just interesting to know what other people pay.'

'Whatever it is,' Wayne said, 'Bryce can afford it.'

Susan said, 'Let's go look at it.'

'What? Why?'

'Remember when we tried to find the house in Connecticut, and we couldn't? We can certainly find an apartment on Central Park West!'

Wayne said, 'But why?'

'You say there's still furniture there,' Susan said. 'I want to see the way they live, the way they used to live. I don't know why, I just do.'

Wayne said, 'If you want, sure. This Saturday. Then we could do lunch at Tavern On The Green.'

'It's a date,' she said.

'I'll call the rental agent,' Wayne said, 'tomorrow, find out if they're showing it. I bet they are.'

'Why wouldn't they?' Susan asked. 'They want a new tenant in there the day Bryce is out. And I read in the paper, just a couple weeks ago, there's a glut of those high-end apartments now.'

'You're right, it would be interesting,' Wayne said, pouring more wine for both of them, 'to see where Bryce used to live.'

There was an amazing amount of furniture still in the apartment, including the bed and two dressers and a rocking chair in the master bedroom, most of the living room furniture, most of everything. The dining room was the only absolutely bare space.

The woman from Price-Cathcart, the building management firm, was named Ms Pered, and she was birdlike under a glorious pink-gold wig. She chattered like a bird, constantly, as they made their way through the rooms, seeing where Bryce had removed most of the things from his office except a wooden revolving book rack and a black leather easy chair; Christmas gifts from Lucie, no doubt.

The terrace, even now in February, was extraordinary, with its views everywhere except to the north, and Central Park over there like a Christmas card, seen from far above.

Susan almost vibrated with pleasure as they moved through the rooms, her hands trembling slightly on his arm, and at the end she said, 'What is the rent?'

'It would depend on the lease. With the shortest lease, two years, it would be sixty-three hundred.'

'And a longer lease?'

'A seven-year lease would be fifty-nine. But that would require a larger deposit. And the cost-of-living increases would be the same.'

Susan said, 'Let me look at the kitchen again.'

They looked at the kitchen again, and Susan said, 'Will the previous tenant be removing this furniture?'

'No, he's taken what he wants. He would prefer to sell to the new tenant. Much of it is custom-built for these rooms.'

'Let me look at the master bathroom again,' Susan said.

'Of course.'

Susan looked at the master bathroom again, and then at the terrace again. Wayne by now was looking at his watch, because they had a reservation at Tavern On The Green.

Back in the living room, Susan looked around and said, 'What a pity.'

The birdlike Ms Pered cocked her bird-head. 'Yes?'

'We do have a budget, and it's really ironbound. Our accountant, you know,' she said, and smiled sadly at Ms Pered.

Who smiled sadly back, and nodded her head, and said, 'They can be hard taskmasters, many of our tenants find that.'

'We wouldn't be able to go above six, for the two years,' Susan said, while Wayne gaped at her. 'As for the furniture, we'd undertake to dispose of it, but we wouldn't want to buy used furniture.'

'I'm sure something can be worked out,' Ms Pered said.

Twenty-Three

B ryce sat at the keyboard. He typed:

The man had a wife and she disappeared in Kyrgyzstan, where she went scouting locations for a movie on the Mongol hordes that was a money-laundering operation for the Russian Mafia, with money from their operations drug-smuggling across the Black Sea, using small patrol boats from the Russian Navy that had been taken over by the Ukraine after the breakup of the Soviet Union because Russia no longer had access to the Black Sea, but these patrol boats through bribery were dropped from the official records and are now being used in acts of piracy, operated by a renegade group from the Afghan rebels, to raise money for terrorists linked to the Arab fundamentalists, to get enough money to disassemble a powerful destroyer from the Russian Navy, also no longer existing on the official records, and reassemble it in a tiny fishing village on the North African coast. When he learns, because he is an executive with an international bank, that somewhere this ship, in disguised form, is on its way to New York City to blow up the United Nations from the East River, he goes to North Africa where he meets the woman who looks so like his wife that he believes it must be her, but she claims not to speak English. He must find

the destroyer and he must solve the mystery of this
woman.

Bryce nodded. He didn't reread what he had written, he never
did these days. He merely reached to the rear of his desk, where
there was a half-full box of fifty floppy discs. He took a fresh one
from the box and inserted it in its slot in the computer, then clicked
File, ran the cursor down to click *Save As*, and went over to *File
Name*. In that box he typed *Kyrgyzstan*. All of these movements were
automatic, so that he barely even thought about them while he was
doing them, nor was he thinking about much of anything else.

After giving the file a name, he switched it to a disc drive and
pressed *Enter*, to put the story he'd just written on to the disc. Then
he went back into File, and closed down. Removing the disc from
the computer, he put a fresh white label on it and wrote *Kyrgyzstan*
on it. Then he slid the disc into the rack above his desk with the
others already there.

Every one of those discs, each with its own name on its label,
contained nothing but a brief story synopsis. They, and a hundred
more, could all fit on just one disc, of course, which would be the
normal way to do it, but he believed that sooner or later he'd return
to one or more of these ideas and add further detail. He had an
endless supply of floppy discs, so why not keep a visual record of
his accomplishments?

And now, it was time to go shopping.

Almost every day, recently, he did a new plot after breakfast, and
then went shopping. He went to different stores, and wandered in
them for a long time, and waited for some woman to speak to him.
Twice, he'd tried approaching women himself, but both times their
reaction was so negative and hostile that he realized it couldn't be
made to work that way. He had to wait for one of them to come to
him, but so far none had.

He also, from time to time, drove in the direction of Amenia,
New York, looking for that mailbox that said Rierdon, but so far he
hadn't found it. Or, if he'd passed it once or twice, he hadn't
noticed.

He did not question himself. He did not look back over his days any more than he looked back over the stories he made up and saved on the discs. He knew that it was possible that a woman, sometime, in one of these stores, would start a conversation with him, and that things would be better after that. Sharper, clearer, more defined.

Late in February, somebody from Price-Cathcart, the managers of his old building in New York, had called to say they had a new tenant for his apartment, but the tenant didn't want the furniture he'd left behind. Did he want to send for it, or would he prefer the new tenant to dispose of it all? Dispose of it, he'd said, and hadn't thought another thing about it, and now it was March, and the long New England winter slowly thawed.

In his life generally, things were fine, better than ever. Now that he lived in the country full-time, he'd become closer with other friends who spent all or most of their time up here; there were more of them than he'd known. It was nice to be among people with money and leisure and the kind of work that didn't require them to commute day after day to the city. And they were happy to welcome him among their number.

His social life, particularly on the weekends, was richer than ever. He'd come to realize that a number of the people he knew hadn't liked Lucie, not at all, and the invitations to dinners and parties as a result had been less frequent than they might have been. Now his social schedule was as full as he wanted it to be, and since he wasn't deep in the writing of a new novel, he had more loose time than usual. The only work he did these days was the plot outline almost every morning, and he never thought about any of them ever again.

Sometimes, at dinners or parties at other people's houses, he met interesting women, divorced or in any case free, and there'd be flirtation, kidding around, but nothing serious, and he never did any follow-through. He wasn't ready for a new relationship yet. And meeting these women, through friends, was not at all like the wandering in the stores. In the stores he was looking for Marcia Rierdon, or another Marcia Rierdon, and that was something else. The women he met socially might be interesting to date, if he were ready to start that again, but he wasn't, not yet, so nothing came of it.

He did try to phone Isabelle once, early in March, but her phone had been disconnected, with no referral. He called the ad agency where she worked, and they said she'd left there in January. Nobody there knew where she'd gone. Back to Spain, to fight for her children? Still in New York, in some other apartment, some other job?

There was no way to trace her. He fretted for a while over that, feeling he'd had an opportunity for some sort of calm life, good life, with Isabelle, and he'd dropped the ball there somehow, failed to get that right. But there was nothing to be done about it now.

On the second Wednesday in March, after he'd done the plot outline he called *Kyrgyzstan*, he went shopping as usual, was not approached by any women, and when he drove home there was a strange car in the driveway, tucked to the side to leave access to the garage. The car was a dark maroon brown, almost black, dusty, a small-model Chevy, some years old, with a few old dents that had been hammered out and painted over. It had a blunt efficient air, as though its driver didn't care anything about style, only about getting the job done, but there was no driver in it, nobody in sight anywhere.

Bryce thumbed the control and the garage door lifted as he drove slowly toward it. As he entered the garage, he caught movement off to his left, someone coming around the corner of the house, someone dressed in dark clothing, like the car.

Bryce stopped the BMW, switched off the engine, and climbed out. Leaving his few groceries on the passenger seat, he stepped out of the garage and saw Detective Johnson walking toward him. There was a smile on Johnson's face, but Bryce didn't trust that.

'Beautiful grounds,' Johnson began. 'A really beautiful setting.'

'Thank you,' Bryce said. 'I'm kind of surprised to see you.'

Johnson stuck his hand out. 'Just a courtesy call,' he said.

Shaking his hand, Bryce said, 'A courtesy call?'

'Well, a progress report,' Johnson told him, and shrugged, with a rueful grin at himself. 'Which is to say, none.'

'No progress. With Lucie, you mean.' Which was the first time he'd said that name aloud in a few months; he was pleased to note that it didn't affect him.

'Sure, with Mrs Proctorr,' Johnson agreed. 'I tried calling you in New York, but they said you gave up that apartment.'

'It was in Lucie's name,' Bryce told him. 'The lease. You want to come in?'

'If I'm not interrupting anything.'

'No, no, come on. We'll go in this way, if you don't mind, I've got groceries to put away.'

'Sure, no problem.'

They went in through the garage, Bryce getting his plastic sack of groceries, shutting the garage door. In the kitchen, he said, 'Would you like coffee?'

'You know, I would. It's a long drive up here. *And* back.'

'You can hang your coat in that closet,' Bryce said, tossing his own on one of the stools in here, and Johnson put his black topcoat away, showing the dark gray jacket, dark blue shirt and black slacks beneath.

Putting today's groceries away, Bryce was startled to realize just how much stuff he had accumulated in here. Buying a few items every day, living alone, not using that much, he now had four identical unopened jars of mayonnaise, seven cans of coffee, six boxes of the same kind of rice, on and on. Embarrassed, afraid Johnson would see all these extra things and somehow understand what that meant, he left the sack half-full on the counter and said, 'I'll do these later. Coffee first.'

'This is a very nice place you have here, very nice,' Johnson told him.

'Thank you.' Bryce busied himself making coffee. 'Why don't you sit on one of the stools there.'

'Thanks.' Seated at the island in the middle of the kitchen, like a man bellied up to a bar, Johnson said, 'So you don't have a place in the city at all any more.'

'No. I didn't need it.'

'I envy you.' Johnson grinned, and said, 'I suppose your accountant told you we checked up on you.'

Surprised, Bryce said. 'Checked up? No, he didn't. What do you mean, checked up?'

'We got a court order to take a look at your financial records,'

Johnson explained. 'We informed your accountant, Mr Steiner. Usually the accountant tells his client.'

'I guess he didn't want to upset me,' Bryce said.

'And I suppose,' Johnson said, 'he knew we wouldn't come across anything that would be a flag.'

'When did you do this?'

'Back in December. Just before Christmas.'

Two weeks before Pegasus paid for *Two Faces*, and the big payout to Wayne. Bryce said, 'You were looking to see if I paid somebody to kill Lucie.'

'Sure,' Johnson said. He didn't seem at all troubled by the admission. 'You know you've got to be the prime suspect.'

'The husband.'

'*And* conveniently out of town.'

'That wasn't convenient,' Bryce assured him, 'but I know what you mean.'

'So we had to check on you,' Johnson said. 'You know that.'

'Of course.'

'You made no unexpected withdrawals, no unexplained payouts, nothing out of the ordinary at all.'

Bryce said, 'So that gives me a clean bill of health.'

'Not entirely,' Johnson said. 'Nobody killed your wife for you for money. There was always the chance that somebody did it for love.'

The coffee was ready. Bryce said, 'For love? I don't follow that. How do you take your coffee?'

'Just black.'

Bryce poured the cups, added half-and-half to his own, and gave Johnson a cup, as Johnson said, 'You had a girlfriend then. Ms de Fuentes. While you were out of town, she could have arranged it for you, even done it herself.'

Astonished, Bryce said, 'Isabella? But Lucie was beaten to death!'

'With a little table. A woman could have used that table. And there was no sexual assault.'

'Isabelle wouldn't— You can't be— I can't imagine such a thing.'

'That's my job,' Johnson said, 'to imagine every possibility. Check out every possibility.'

'But Isabelle. Come on to the living room.'

'Sure.'

Johnson got up and followed Bryce from the kitchen down the wide art-hung hall past the dining room to the long living room, saying as they went, 'We looked into her, too, just to see. She was at the movies with friends that night, so she had an alibi. And there was nothing off-base about her finances, either.'

'You checked *her* finances?'

'Naturally,' Johnson said. Bryce gestured for him to take a seat, they both sat, and Johnson said, 'That would be a couple months ago, early in January.'

'You went to her accountant.'

'Well, no, she didn't have an accountant, not the way you do. Just somebody to do her taxes every year. So we went to *her*, had her show us her checkbook, savings account.'

'Oh, poor Isabelle.'

'She took it very well,' Johnson said.

'But— What did you think she could have done? Paid somebody to kill Lucie? Why?'

'Maybe it was a loan,' Johnson suggested. 'You'll pay her back when the coast is clear.'

'I couldn't even *think* of such a thing,' Bryce told him.

'Well, like I say, that's what my job is, I'm supposed to think of things like that and everything else, and then check them out.' Johnson sipped. 'Good coffee.'

'Thank you.'

'Anyway, there was nothing there, and she took it fine.'

And left, Bryce thought. Got as far away from me and Johnson and the whole thing as she could. He said, 'So what else is there? My ex-wife?'

Johnson chuckled. 'No, and not your kids, either. We did a little looking into that— No, no, don't get upset, they didn't know we were around.'

Bryce suddenly remembered Ellen's response when he'd confessed to her, the immediate instinct to protect the children, and now he saw she was absolutely right. He said, 'You really do burrow in, don't you?'

Johnson shrugged. 'That's the job. Anyway, my report right now is, we don't have a goddam lead. We aren't giving up, you know, we don't give up, but at this moment we've run out of theories to check.'

He isn't even asking me about Wayne's story, Bryce thought. He bought that, too. He said, 'You're going to open it.'

Johnson gave him a surprised look, and a laugh. 'How do you know about that?'

'Research for a novel once,' Bryce told him. 'The New York Police Department never closes a case until there's a conviction. But if there's nothing more to do, you open it, open and inactive. You go on and think about newer things, fresher cases, but you're always ready to come back if something else shows up.'

'Exactly.'

'Like me moving out of New York,' Bryce said.

Johnson laughed. 'You're getting to know me,' he said.

'Anything I might do, that's just a little off from my pattern,' Bryce said, 'you're going to notice, and you're going to say, "What's that all about?" So you came up here— That's a department car, isn't it?'

'Sure. They're hard to disguise.'

'You came up here to see what the story was,' Bryce said. 'And the story is, the lease was in Lucie's name, she decorated the apartment, it was hers, the furniture was all hers, it reminded me of her. They said I had to sign a new lease or vacate, so I vacated. I don't have a job to go to every day in the city, and I like it up here. This is *my* place.'

'I can see that.' Johnson had finished his coffee, and now he put the cup on a coaster on the end table and said, 'Do you mind if I ask you a question?'

With a surprised laugh, Bryce said, 'That's all you do!'

'I suppose. But this is a little different. I know you and your wife were in the middle of a bad divorce, and you both had bad things to say about one another the last year or so. I'm wondering how you feel now. Would you like to see her murderer brought to justice?'

'I couldn't care less,' Bryce told him. 'I was wrong to marry her, I was right to get away from her, it was hell having the whole thing take so long, and I'd be a hypocrite if I said I was sorry she was dead. If she'd gone down in a plane crash or got shot in a bank robbery or whatever, it's all the same to me. You want to find the killer because that's your job. Her parents want you to find him—'

'I hear from them a lot,' Johnson agreed.

'I'm sure you do. They want him found because they loved her. It isn't my job, and I didn't love her, not any more, so I don't care. I hope you get him because I know it's important to your professional feeling about yourself, but it doesn't mean a damn thing to me.'

'Well, that's straightforward,' Johnson said. 'Thank you for answering that, and thanks for the coffee.' Standing, he said, 'If I get in touch again, it'll be because I have real news, not just to say I'm stuck.'

'Good.'

Bryce also stood, and they went back to the kitchen to get Johnson's coat. Johnson gestured at the grocery sack on the counter. 'You're a real homebody.'

'I am.'

Bryce led him through the house to the front door, and along the way Johnson said, 'I've been catching up on your books. Very enjoyable.'

'Thank you.'

They shook hands again at the door, and then Bryce went back to the living room to watch out the window as that ugly little car backed away from the garage and went out the circular drive.

Was Johnson really finished? This time, was it really over? Bryce was glad Mark Steiner hadn't told him about the search of his financial records, but he'd have to tell Mark soon that he knew about it now and was grateful for Mark's silence, but that now everything was okay. Anyway, everything seemed okay.

Back in the kitchen, he looked again at this mass of excess groceries. He opened cabinet doors, stood looking at all this stuff, wondered that he'd never even noticed it, not till Johnson was here to see it. After a while, without putting the rest of the groceries away, he went to his office. He sat at the keyboard and wrote:

I was doing a very stupid and a very dangerous thing, and I have to stop now. What if I'd found Marcia Rierdon again? Or some other woman? I would have run away again, I know I would, I think I would, I'm almost sure I would, but I could have got myself into all kinds of trouble along the way. And with Johnson watching, too.

What did I think I was going to do? Kill Marcia Rierdon? Even if I did, that wouldn't be the same, would it? It wouldn't. It wouldn't solve anything, and it wouldn't be the same as being there, and they would trace it back to me, somehow they'd trace it back to me.

I'm glad Johnson came here. Now I realize how far from shore I'd gone, how close I was to losing myself completely. It stops now.

Twenty-Four

Wayne had taken up jogging. With Central Park right there, outside the window, it seemed a crime not to. He'd work at his computer for a while every morning – he was starting to get assignments from the magazines, now that the editors had come to know him – and then jog before lunch, usually finding a snack somewhere in or near the park.

The second Friday in March, though, he'd be going home for lunch, because Susan had taken the day off. Tomorrow night, they'd have their first dinner party in the new apartment, six people in, including Joe and Shelly Katz, which was going to be a big deal as far as Susan was concerned, so this morning she had gone off to do the shopping. This afternoon she'd do the preliminary work on dinner, then finish it all tomorrow.

Wayne didn't have a specific route in the park, he was still getting to know the place, jogging at random, still finding new mini-landscapes within the boulders and low hills and specimen trees and sweeping lawns. As he ran, he usually thought about the piece he was then working on, or other pieces to come, but this morning he thought about Joe and Shelly Katz, because he'd be seeing them tomorrow night. And how oddly that had all worked out. He'd hoped Joe would be his editor, but he'd become a friend instead, and now he and his family were living in Wayne's old apartment on Perry Street.

What had happened, the two couples had had dinner together in a restaurant in the neighborhood, back in February, and Wayne had told Joe about their taking Bryce's apartment on Central Park West, and that he felt awkward about it. 'Susan just fell in love with it,' he said, and she said, 'I certainly did.'

'But I don't know how to tell Bryce,' Wayne went on. 'In fact, if I can avoid it, I think I won't tell Bryce.'

Joe said, 'Why not? He didn't want the place any more, he got out of it, what does he care who moves in?'

'I don't know,' Wayne said, 'it just feels weird. Like the cuckoo in another bird's nest, you know?'

'Don't worry about it,' Joe told him. 'If I could afford the place, I'd take it myself. If it was in the Village. We *need* more space.'

'We certainly do,' Shelly said.

The situation was, as they explained it, that Joe and Shelly, with their two sons, Joshua and Sam, eleven and nine, were still living in the too-small apartment they'd moved into when they'd first got married and were only a couple. And now Shelly was a computer programmer, working out of her home, helping clients set up websites and do links to other sites, which meant a lot of equipment jammed into a corner of their bedroom. They needed a larger place, but they didn't want to move out of the West Village, and had searched fitfully for years without getting anywhere.

Wayne and Susan's place was perfect for them. Wayne had always gotten along well with the landlords, an older Italian couple who lived in an apartment on the first floor, so a deal was cut with no trouble, and not too terrible a raise in the rent. On the morning of March first, Wayne and Susan and a moving van had moved north, and that afternoon Joe and Shelly and a moving van had moved around the corner from West Fourth Street to Perry.

From time to time, Wayne thought about showing the half-manuscript of *The Shadowed Other* to Joe, but what was the point? Just awkwardness for Joe, who'd have to say complimentary things while nevertheless handing it back. So why bother? Let *The Shadowed Other* remain where and what it was: unsung, and undone.

Wayne had even cannibalized *The Shadowed Other* in a way, using part of the research and some of the turns of phrase from the manuscript for an article on the last thirty years of unrest in Central

America, comparing the reality of what had been happening down there with the American cultural interpretations of those events, the novels and movies that had used the revolutions and unrest as the base for their stories. Willard had sold that, just last week, and it would soon be in print. The shadow of *The Shadowed Other*.

Ahead on his left, as he jogged, was a basketball court, with a pair of guys at each end playing one-on-one. It was still March, and nippy, but these players were all in shorts and T-shirts and the usual giant spaceship sneakers, and were working up a sweat. There was a bench on the right, unoccupied at the moment, so Wayne sat there, to take a breather and watch the two games.

One-on-one is a game for two players, using all the rules of basketball, but it's no longer a team game. There's no one to pass off to, no one to feint with, no one to block for. There are no easy moments, loping along while your team-mate has the ball. It is constant motion, unrelenting, one man with the ball, dribbling, moving, feinting, driving, trying to get a clear shot at the basket, while the other man defends, blocking, holding him out, dashing in to try to steal the ball, both of them straining, giving it their all, working at the peak of their ability.

The two games Wayne watched now were uneven, the guys on the left being much more practiced and skillful than the guys on the right. Everybody struggled, everybody fought, but the guys on the left moved with swift hard grace, like dancers combined with wrestlers, while the guys on the right kept flubbing, overreaching, not quite tripping, neither of them ever quite quick enough to take advantage of the other guy's mistakes. They were like a parody of the first team, but they were just as serious, just as absorbed, just as determined. And no doubt having as much fun, which was after all the point. One-on-one isn't a team sport, and it isn't a spectator sport either; it's a game for the players.

Sitting there, watching the two games progress, Wayne sensed that fiction itch starting up in him again, as though he'd actually finished *The Shadowed Other* and were ready for a new story, a new invented world. Two guys who meet in Central Park and play one-on-one, and don't know one another in any other context. Who are they really, and how does the rest of their lives begin to impinge on their game? Competition and camaraderie; the seriousness of the determination to win, and the fun of just playing the game.

Wayne looked off down the path to his right, and saw Lucie coming. He blinked, but of course it wasn't Lucie. It never was. A tall slender woman with that kind of halo of gold-shavings hair, wearing black, walking with that the-street-is-mine stride, was not a rarity in New York. Wayne saw about one Lucie a month, but of course on second look they were always significantly different.

This one, for instance. She was with two other women, she walking on the left, on Wayne's side as they moved toward him along the path, and when he'd first seen her she'd had her head back, laughing. Now, when she wasn't laughing, and she had turned her profile to Wayne to face the other two women, she didn't look like Lucie at all. They never did.

He'd been sitting here too long; he was beginning to feel the chill. He waited for the *fausse* Lucie to go on by, then stood, and jogged home.

Shelly Katz was a tiny dynamo of a woman, compact, with tightly curled black hair almost as Brillo-like as her husband's. Her whole body seemed to be tightly curled, one muscle ready to spring, but her manner was easygoing, comic, relaxed. 'I want to see the changes you made,' she said, Saturday evening, as Wayne and Susan greeted them at the door.

'Not that many yet,' Susan told her.

Wayne was helping with their coats when Shelly pointed at the hall table where Jorge the doorman would leave their mail if they were to go away. 'Isn't that Bryce's?'

Wayne, trying to sound light and casual but feeling again that flutter, as though he were about to be found out for some crime, not knowing exactly what that crime might be, said, 'A lot of the stuff here is Bryce's. He left it all behind.'

'We'll replace as we go along,' Susan explained, 'but for now, it helps to fill the place.'

Shelly gave Joe a bewildered look. 'He left his *furniture*?'

'He thought of it as Lucie's,' Joe told her. 'She decorated this apartment.'

Wayne hadn't thought of the furniture as Lucie's, he'd thought of it as Bryce's, and he'd enjoyed living in its midst. He said, 'Bryce must have had *something* to do with it. Picking it out.'

'Writing the check, I think,' Joe said.

Susan said, 'Wayne, you put their coats in the bedroom, and I'll do drinks.'

'Right.'

Wayne carried the coats to the bedroom, seeing for the first time that the furniture around him, the colors of the walls, were all Lucie, not Bryce. It made him feel odd, uncomfortable. That ghost had faded, so much so that even when he saw it walking, as he had yesterday in the park, it had no power to bother him. But the furniture? Lucie's? It was like suddenly finding yourself in enemy territory.

Everything in the bedroom was theirs, their own, brought up from Perry Street. His office, too, was all his, except for the leather armchair and the revolving bookrack. The dining room was completely their own. It was the living room, and the kitchen, and the guest bedroom, and the outdoor furniture on the terrace, and the long room-size hallway, it was all of those that had the dead hand of Lucie Proctorr laid heavily upon them, like a fog you just can't quite see.

Where Joe and Shelly will spend the next hour before dinner, Wayne thought, in that living room, that's where they'd spent so much time with Bryce and Lucie, on those sofas, with that coffee table, those end tables, those lamps.

Even the drapes kept open to frame the view of the park. He found himself reluctant to leave the bedroom, to go to the living room, as though some jaws were waiting for him in there, some trap. Or maybe some glaring bright light to shine into his soul and show him complete to Joe Katz; like the picture of Dorian Gray. We all have that picture inside us, don't we, he thought, in the locked secret attic nobody ever sees.

It had been a long while since he had visualized Lucie clear in his memory, her mocking eyes, that slightly twisted mouth and the raised head of the matador as she'd said, 'Is Susan any good in bed?' The last words she'd ever spoken.

The doorbell snapped at his attention. His own bedroom was around him, in this strangely wonderful new place. He left it, to be host. This was *his* home now.

He was seated at dinner between Shelly and a woman named Ann, whose husband worked with Susan. Again he was surrounded by his own furniture, and the easy rituals of dinner chitchat were familiar and comforting. It wasn't until they went back to the living room for after-dinner drinks that he sat near Joe, who looked around and said, 'I have to tell you, it's weird to be here like this. Without Bryce and Lucie, but with all this familiar *stuff*. I keep expecting them to walk in. Well, him, anyway.'

'It's a bigger apartment than our old one,' Wayne said, 'too big for what we brought with us, and the stuff was here. But Susan's right, we'll have to replace it. A couple things you might be interested in.'

Joe grinned. 'Because now *we're* in a bigger place ? I don't think so, Wayne.'

'No, there's one thing in particular,' Wayne said. 'I brought everything up from my office, and he left a couple things, and it's too crowded in there. One thing he left is a very nice wooden revolving bookrack, looks expensive, but I don't need it. Would you like to see it?'

'No, I remember it,' Joe told him. 'Lucie gave Bryce that for Christmas, three or four years ago. He left that behind? That surprises me.'

'Well, I don't want it,' Wayne said. 'I thought you might.'

Joe shook his head, with a rather sad, nostalgic smile. 'I was part of the conspiracy,' he said, 'when we smuggled that thing in here without Bryce's knowing, so it could be a surprise on Christmas Day.'

'Oh.'

'Every once in a while, you know, Wayne,' Joe said, 'some unexpected emotion shows up, something you didn't remember or didn't know you cared about. That bookrack— You know, now I'm thinking about it, I think Bryce always thought it was kind of over the top. Too ostentatious, you know? I don't think he ever did like it.'

'So that's why he left it.'

'But it still represents a happy moment,' Joe said. 'A moment in this room. Me sitting on this sofa, right here. They used to have the Christmas tree over there. When Lucie was pleased by something, you know, she used to clap her hands together, like a little girl.'

Wayne almost said, 'I never saw her do that,' which would have been a brainless thing to do. Instead, he said, 'I guess they had good times before the bad. Most divorced couples can say that.'

'Oh, sure.' Joe nodded, and looked toward the empty corner where the Christmas tree would go. 'I can just see her, though, clapping her hands like that, when Bryce suddenly found this huge *kiosk* kind of a thing, all wrapped in gold paper, *hidden*, believe it or not, behind the tree.'

Gold paper; Wayne could believe that. 'It sounds like a great Christmas,' he said.

'If I were you, Wayne,' Joe told him. 'I'd take that, it's on its own wheels, I'd take it down the service elevator and just put it out by the curb. That's the great thing about New York, you know. Anywhere else, you put something out on the sidewalk, either it stays there for a month or you get a ticket for littering. In New York, you can put *anything* out on the street, on West Fourth I saw a sectional sofa put out, must've been ten feet long. In twenty minutes it's gone, no matter what it is. That's New York.'

Wayne understood now that everything Joe saw around himself in New York had to be unique to the city; crackpot but benign. 'You're right,' he said.

'Wheel it out,' Joe advised. 'In twenty minutes, it'll be on its way to Queens.'

'I think I'll do that,' Wayne said.

Twenty-Five

Wednesday again, a week since Detective Johnson's visit, and the new regime was holding. Bryce had stopped prowling in stores, and now he limited himself to quick trips for perishables and the *Times*, which was also a perishable, of course. He spent most of his daylight hours now outdoors around the house, repairing winter's damage, getting ready for spring. He felt better, almost as though he'd gotten over something physical, the way you get over a low-level fever that had hung on for so long that it had begun to seem like normality; when at last it lets go, what a relief to find the real normality once more.

He had also stopped making up new storylines every morning. He didn't know how many he'd done, but there were certainly a bunch of discs in the rack on the shelf above his computer screen. He didn't remember any of them exactly, but felt that soon he would go back into the office, run through all those ideas, choose one, and finally get started on the next book.

But not yet. At the moment, all he wanted to do was physical labor by day and then watch tapes of old movies after the dinner he heated for himself every evening. Weekends, he still had plenty of social invitations, so he certainly wasn't becoming some kind of hermit.

Before now, he'd only been full-time in this house in the summer months, and hadn't been much aware of it as an entity in itself. Now the changeable beauty of the land fascinated him, and he found himself much more aware of the details of the weather than when he'd lived mostly in New York. He loved being out here, working, in the middle of his land.

He always carried the cellular phone from the BMW with him when he worked outside, and on Wednesday afternoon it rang as he was using the posthole digger to make a hole for a new support at one corner of the fence around the swimming pool. This was the kind of job he always used to have Gregg, the lawn guy, or one of the other local handymen take care of, but he was finding these days he liked to do the work himself.

He left the digger propped in the half-dug hole, peeled off his work gloves, and answered the phone just after the second ring: 'Hello?'

'Bryce. Joe. How we doing?'

'Oh, fine.' Bryce was back to telling Joe the vague non-truths about his progress on the alleged new book. 'Slow, you know, but getting there.'

'Terrific. But what I'm calling about is not to nag you, at least *primarily* not to nag you—'

'You don't nag,' Bryce lied. 'And anyway, I need it.'

Joe laughed. 'Very Talmudic,' he said. 'No, what I want to talk to you about is *Two Faces*, promotion thereof.'

'Oh, sure.' Because *Two Faces in the Mirror* would be coming out in June, three months from now.

'The first question is,' Joe said, 'a tour.'

'If I have to,' Bryce told him. 'I'd rather do phoners, you know that.'

'You can talk that over with Ricki Sussman,' Joe said, she being head of the Pegasus publicity department. 'She'll give you a call.'

'Ricki's only happy when she knows I'm on an airplane,' Bryce said.

'Talk it over with her,' Joe advised, 'and leave me out. And the other thing is, the *New York Review of Books* would like to do an interview with you.'

'*Review of Books*? Aren't they a little . . . academic for me?'

'It's been a while since you've had a book out,' Joe explained, 'you're part of the culture, part of the zeitgeist, and they won't put you down, or why should you do it?'

'Gore Vidal won't be the interviewer, in other words.'

Joe laughed. 'No, we'll have approval.'

'Sometimes,' Bryce said, 'I think the worst part of writing is getting published.'

'Other people,' Joe said, 'have suggested that's the second worst.'

'Okay,' Bryce said. 'Okay.'

'Time is short,' Joe told him, 'so the interview will have to be this month. Up at your place, okay?'

'Sure, I'd prefer that.'

'I thought you would. Let me get off now, I don't want to keep you from the new book.'

'That wasn't nagging either,' Bryce assured him, and hung up, and turned back to the hole he was digging.

Lucie had gone on tour with him, just once. Six cities in eight days. Chicago was one of them that time, and Houston, and Seattle. Was that San Francisco?

In any event, it had been her idea to come along, for what she'd thought was the glamour of it, staying in the hotels, being squired around, being the lion, being the big fish in a succession of small ponds. But then she was there for the reality, and she hated it. She hated it, and she made life on tour even more complicated for Bryce as a result. She fought with the staff at most of the hotels where they stayed, was difficult to bookstore clerks – a thing you don't do – and generally made her disaffection felt at every turn.

The problem was, she was used to attention, usually a lot of attention, but always at least *some* of the attention in the room, but in this context there was no attention left over for her at all. She was used to Bryce being famous, and very used to him being rich, but she wasn't at all used to him being a star, being the one who used up all the oxygen in the room, and she didn't like it. All the press interviews, all the television talk shows, all the fans, all the bookstore clerks, everybody everywhere had eyes and attention only for that person standing to Lucie's left. She was bad-tempered for weeks afterward, more bad-tempered than usual, and never again suggested she join him on tour.

Maybe he wouldn't have to tour this time. He'd rather not, he'd rather stay here. Looking down into the hole he was digging, thinking about the rigors of book tours, he lifted the posthole digger by its two long wooden poles as high as his arms would reach, so that the two curved metal shovel heads facing one another at the bottom were completely up out of the hole. Then he *drove* it down, the shovels punching into the packed soil at the bottom, breaking some dirt and small stones loose. When he spread the poles, it made the shovel faces scoop in toward one another, gathering the loosened soil. He lifted it out, moved it to the side, brought the poles closer together, and the dirt fell on to the mound he was building on a piece of burlap. Then he repeated the operation, *driving* the digger down into the hole.

It hit a rock. The *clang* came with a tremor that ran up the poles to vibrate inside his arms, and all at once he saw that figure again, that dark figure, crouched, seen from behind, punching, punching. That was all he could see, the crouched and punching figure, from the back. Why could he never see Lucie?

He shifted position, to flank the rock rather than hit it, and *drove* downward again. Was *this* what it was like? He lifted the digger and *drove* it down. Was *this* what it was like? He *drove* it down. Was *this what it was like?* Was *this* what it was like? Was *this* what it was like?

Twenty-Six

It had probably been a mistake to take the apartment, but Susan had been so determined that Wayne hadn't seen any way to argue about it. In fact, at that time, he hadn't even wanted to argue. The idea of living in Bryce's apartment, taking over Bryce's apartment, might have occurred to him as well, but he would have brushed it away as embarrassing and improper. But when the idea came from *Susan*, and so forcefully, as though she knew without a question it was the right thing to do, he could only go along with her, feeling a little sneaky private pleasure in what they were up to.

But now here they were, with a rent that was almost quadruple what they used to pay, and an income that had drastically shrunk. Susan still had her job, and Wayne seemed to have created this new career for himself in magazines, but it wasn't enough to keep them on Central Park West. He'd have to sell three articles to the slick magazines a month in order to net enough after taxes just to pay the rent, and there was no way he could turn out that much salable work month after month. It's true Mark Steiner was holding half a million dollars for them, investing much of it, doling out a four-thousand-dollar-a-month deposit into their checking account for their daily expenses, but eventually even that well would run dry, and then what? And why permit it to run dry at all?

If it weren't for the money question, he'd be enjoying this new career. The other difference he'd discovered between writing novels and writing magazine nonfiction was the fact that when you wrote for magazines you *knew* you were turning out forgettable words,

190

disposable, gone forever in a month, but when you were working on a novel you were always aware, in the back of your mind, that this just might be deathless prose; think of that. To be absolutely certain that what you were writing had a shorter shelf life than yogurt was a great relief.

But there was the money question, and so he'd decided to try something else. He'd decided to take a little time off to write a screenplay. He was well aware that the world was awash in screenplays written on spec, hopeless, doomed, never to be anything more than Xeroxed pages gathering dust on a shelf, orphans, almost every shelf in Hollywood a complete orphanage in itself, but *somebody* hit. *Some* movies were made. Yes, and the losers also told themselves the same thing, and Wayne was aware of that, too.

But he had to try, and he thought he did have a leg up on the orphans out there, in that he was a published novelist. He was a man with a body of work, a packet of good reviews, a bunch of actual hardcover books you could hold in your hand. Hollywood might be sharp about a lot of things, but they wouldn't be sharp about the chain-store computers. *They* wouldn't know he was roadkill. All they'd know is that he was a novelist, and not only that, a New York novelist. They would at least give him a respectful hearing, which is more than they would do for the screenwriters in their midst.

When his first novel, *The Pollux Perspective,* had been published, there'd been some movie interest, and in fact a small one-year option that had not been renewed. That novel was now over twenty years old, but he'd read it through again and it seemed to him the story still worked, the updating would not be at all difficult.

There were, it seemed to him, nine strong cinematic scenes in the novel, and the connecting matter could be condensed without a problem. He could convert this book into a screenplay in a month, less than a month. Willard Hartman had a corresponding agent on the West Coast who handled film deals for him, and to whom Willard would surely send the screenplay if it came out as well as Wayne expected it to. If it sold, wonderful. If it didn't, it would still be his calling card, it would still show Willard's associate out there what he could do, and that he was ready to do more.

He knew, of course, that *The Pollux Perspective* was not a movie title, and the speed with which he thought of a movie title to put on it – instantaneous – struck him as a good omen. '*Double Impact*,' he typed, and got to work.

His fourth day on *Double Impact*, the work going even more smoothly than he'd expected, the phone rang at eleven in the morning, and it was Willard. Wayne hadn't told him about the screenplay yet, had decided to wait until it was finished and Susan had approved of it before letting anybody else know it was in the works.

'The first thing,' Willard said, 'the *Review* has scheduled your Guatemala piece for the Sunday after next.'

'Oh, great.' The shadow of *The Shadowed Other* would see print, while its parent sank into the cold dark water of the past.

The next thing Willard said brought Wayne up short. 'You used to know Bryce Proctorr, didn't you?'

A few people knew something of the current relationship between Wayne and Bryce – Joe Katz, Detective Johnson, a few others – but Wayne hadn't gone out of his way to let people know that that particular old friendship had come back to life. Tell Willard now? But minimize it. 'Oh, I still see him from time to time.'

'You do?' Willard was surprised.

'But we don't really travel in the same circles.'

'Well, the *Review* wants an interview with him, and they wonder if you'd be the interviewer. Because you've written the same sort of novel in the past. Unless you think you're too close to him.'

Astonished, Wayne said, '*The New York Review of Books*? They want something on Bryce Proctorr?' Their having taken his piece on the American literary uses of Central American political turmoil had been somewhat surprising, though not out of character for the paper, but what did they want with Bryce?

'He's a part of the popular culture of this moment,' Willard said, 'and he has a new book coming out, his first in some time. They'd like an interview that fits him into American society now.'

'Sure,' Wayne said. 'Easy.'

'I'll have the publisher send you galleys of the book,' Willard said. 'It's called *Two Faces in the Mirror*.'

Wayne just barely managed to cover the mouthpiece before he laughed. The publisher will send him galleys! He took a deep breath, released the mouthpiece, and said, 'Good.'

'Do you have Proctorr's phone number? Apparently, he's up in Connecticut somewhere, you can call him, set up a date.'

'Sure, give me the number.'

Willard did, and said, 'I understand he used to live somewhere in the neighborhood where you've just moved. That would have been a lot more convenient.'

'Oh, well,' Wayne said.

The final Tuesday in March, and Wayne stepped off the train at ten minutes past eleven; six minutes late. Bryce was waiting for him on the platform, looking formal, as though here to meet a foreign delegation. His smile when he greeted Wayne was fitful. 'How was the trip?'

'Easy.'

This was the first Wayne had seen of Bryce since the Pegasus-Regent Christmas party, over three months ago, and he was surprised by the change. Bryce seemed to have lost a lot of weight, maybe twenty pounds or more. His face was lined, and his clothes hung loosely on him. And as he led Wayne to the little parking lot, that fitful smile kept coming and going.

Wayne still hadn't told Bryce about his move to the Central Park West apartment. Would he ever? Was it necessary? What if Bryce heard about it from somebody else? Maybe, while he was here, there'd be a way to deal with that.

Bryce stuffed Wayne's suitcase into the backseat of a good-looking black BMW. Wayne was to spend at least one night, possibly two, depending on how long he needed to complete the interview. His tape recorder and notepads were in the suitcase.

As they drove away from the station and out of the little town, they talked about the weather, and train travel, and conditions in New York, and how much Bryce enjoyed not being in all that hustle and bustle any more. There were a couple of opportunities for Wayne to mention where he lived now, but he kept silent.

Somehow, his living in Bryce's old apartment was completely different from Joe Katz moving into Wayne's former place. He felt that what he had done was more like an invasion, something that Bryce would have a right to resent, though why he felt that way he wasn't sure.

Maybe it was all about contempt. When he'd first run into Bryce in the library last year, he'd felt awkward, embarrassed, because he was at the very nadir of his life and career. Career, that was the point. They'd started out more or less even, and Bryce had become a winner, famous, rich, married to a beautiful woman, written up in *People*, while Wayne had faltered and stumbled and failed.

Even in the matter of wives: Susan was right for *Wayne*, he knew she was, but she wasn't glamorous. There would never be a photo of a triumphantly laughing Susan in *People* magazine.

So what he'd felt in that first meeting, in the library and in the bar afterward, was that what Bryce had a *right* to feel toward him was contempt. Whatever he actually felt, whatever their relationship was or would turn out to be, in Wayne's eyes Bryce had a right to be contemptuous of Wayne.

Which he must have been, to some extent, mustn't he, to even have made that offer. Had *that* shown respect, or friendship? Or had it shown contempt? 'Here's an ugly job, beneath me. *You* do it.'

Nothing Wayne had done since, certainly not the Lucie thing, not anything else, had let him believe he had risen in his right to Bryce's esteem. And now to have crept into Bryce's old apartment, live with Bryce's old furniture – Lucie's old furniture, even worse – was so servile, so hang-dog, as though he were living his life through Bryce, and not man enough to stand up and live a life of his own, that he couldn't bring himself to admit to it.

All at once, Bryce said, 'Do you think about Lucie?'

Wayne was astonished. He would have expected Bryce to stay a million miles from that topic. He knew *he* wouldn't have brought it up, didn't need the reminders, didn't need to dwell on that horrible moment. Why should Bryce? He said, 'Think *what* about her?'

'Well, what happened,' Bryce said. 'You don't think about what happened?'

'Why should I?'

Wayne watched Bryce's profile as Bryce stared fixedly at the road ahead, saying, 'Doesn't it stay with you? By God, it stays with me!'

What is this, Wayne wondered. Guilt? All this time later? He said, 'Why? Why does it have to stay with you?'

'Because I wasn't there!' This was blurted out as though it were the secret of the century, forced from him in extremis.

'You weren't there? Of course you weren't there, you weren't supposed to be there, that was the whole point, remember?'

'Yes, yes, I know.'

'That's why you sent me there,' Wayne said, and was surprised to hear a tinge of bitterness in his voice. He'd thought he'd learned to deal with that.

'But,' Bryce said, and shook his head. Wayne saw that his fingers clenched and unclenched on the steering wheel. 'But I should have been there.'

'You'd have been arrested. You'd be in jail forever.'

'I'd *know*.'

'Know what?'

'What it was like!'

Memory flashed, briefly, scoldingly, and Wayne shook his head. Suddenly hoarse, he said, 'You don't want to know what it was like.'

'Well, if it was that bad, why don't you *think* about it any more?'

'Why should I?'

'*I* have to! Why do *I* have to?'

'All right,' Wayne said. 'All right. You're obsessing on this.'

'I just want to know what it was *like*.'

'It was hell.'

'But I can't *see* it! I can't see it.'

'Oh, Jesus, Bryce, I understand what it is.' Wayne shook his head. He almost patted Bryce's arm, but thought better of it. He said, 'I'll tell you what it is. I was there, Bryce, and it was horrible, and you *can't* imagine it, but I don't have to imagine it. I was there. So what I have is a memory, and memories fade. All memories fade, Bryce, that's what they do. But you don't have the memory, all you have is imagination. And imagination never fades.'

They drove in silence for a minute or two, and then Bryce said,

'No, it doesn't. I tried to correct that for a while, but it didn't work out. It came close, but it didn't work out.'

Wayne had no idea what Bryce was talking about, but maybe that was just as well. If he explodes, he told himself, he'll blow me up with him. I'm standing next to him here, and I have no choice. I have to watch him. I have to be ready for . . . for whatever.

'There's the house,' Bryce said.

'I recognize it,' Wayne told him, 'from *People*.'

There was nobody in the house but the two of them. Bryce opened a can of soup for their lunch, and sliced some fresh local bread, and made coffee. Wayne watched him, and as they sat together at the big dining room table he said, 'Bryce, don't you have anybody working here?'

'There's a guy does the lawn.'

'No, I mean inside the house. A housekeeper. Somebody to do the meals and the laundry and the cleaning and all that.'

'There's a woman comes in once a week.'

'Bryce, you need somebody to live in, a housekeeper. You can afford it, and you should have it. Anybody in your position would have somebody like that.'

Bryce looked around, vaguely, as though for the missing house-keeper. 'I suppose you're right,' he said. 'We could never keep anybody in the house before, I used to have people, but Lucie always fought with them. Fired them, or they quit. I got used to not.'

'Well, you can do it now,' Wayne told him. 'And you should.'

Slowly, Bryce smiled. It made him look younger, and healthier. 'You're right,' he said. 'There's an agency in Danbury, I'll call them. After the interview.'

'Good.'

'You're good for me, Wayne,' Bryce said, and laughed. 'In so many ways, you're good for me.'

After lunch, Bryce showed Wayne around the house, and Wayne found it unexpectedly similar to the apartment in New York. Spacious rooms, decorated tastefully but with some flamboyance. It was funny that Bryce could see Lucie in the New York apartment and be turned off by it, but couldn't see the same influence here. Didn't want to see it, probably. Wanted to like this place because he wanted to stay cooped up here.

'That would be the housekeeper's room.'

'Very nice.'

But the way Bryce had talked in the car, though, maybe it was just as well there wasn't anybody else in the house. What if Bryce was about to go off the deep end, go running to the authorities, confess his sins so he could sleep better at night? He'd drag Wayne to hell with him. Wayne decided he'd listen very carefully over the next two days, and if there was any more of this, any further hints, it would be good to have nobody else around.

There was an airy sunporch that gleamed like satin in the weak March sunlight, and that was where they decided to sit for the interview. Wayne brought out his materials, set up the tape recorder, and was about to switch it on to *Record* when he stopped, lowered his hand, and said, 'No, wait. Something else first.'

Bryce raised a polite eyebrow.

Wayne said, 'There's a couple things you said, you got me worried, and maybe the best thing is come out with it, clear the air.'

'Things I said?'

'What I'm beginning to worry about,' Wayne told him, 'is that you might maybe suddenly get an urge to confess. Turn yourself in, for whatever reason. You'd drag me down with you, you know.'

Wayne was surprised to see Bryce smile at that, a sad kind of smile but a real one. 'Don't worry, Wayne,' he said. 'I already went through that. I already confessed once, and I won't be doing that again. Guaranteed.'

Wayne stared at him. 'You *confessed*?'

'To Ellen.'

The name meant nothing. 'You – You told somebody—'

'My first wife.'

'Oh, my God. Did she believe you?'

'Of course she believed me,' Bryce said. 'Did you think she'd think I'd make up something like that?'

'Oh, Christ on a crutch. Did you tell her about me?'

'Not by name,' Bryce said. 'Just that I, you know, arranged it.'

'What's she going to do?'

Bryce's grin was incongruous, but also real. He said, 'She chewed *me* out, I can tell you that.'

'Well, yes, of course she'd—'

'For wanting to be so selfish.'

'Yes, you could look at it—'

'For wanting to confess.'

Wayne looked at him. 'What?'

'I wasn't thinking,' Bryce explained. 'I wasn't thinking about my kids, how it would mess them up. You know, they're twenty-three, they're twenty-one, they're nineteen, this would just *destroy* their lives. You can see that, can't you?'

'Absolutely,' Wayne said. 'Sure. Ellen said that?'

'She made me promise,' Bryce said, 'never to tell anybody else about it, ever again. And I won't.'

'Because of your kids,' Wayne said.

'They're the innocent ones,' Bryce said. 'They're the victims.'

'You're right. Okay,' Wayne said, nodding. 'Okay.' He knew Bryce was sincere, he knew he was safe from Bryce in that way, there was nothing he'd have to do to defend himself from Bryce's feelings of guilt. God bless the first wife, Ellen, he thought. 'Let's uh,' he said, 'let's— Shall we start?'

'Sure.'

'This is the *New York Review of Books*, you know, so I've got some, I put together some questions.'

'Shoot.'

Wayne pushed *Record*, and began: 'Wayne Prentice interview of Bryce Proctorr, March twenty-seventh. To begin, one consistent theme in your work that the critics have remarked on is the matter of duality, that actions not only have consequences but also contain a second, altered set of consequences that might have occurred, but did not, but nevertheless haunt what really did take place. This has reminded some critics of Borges' 'The Garden of Forking Paths.' Were you influenced by Borges?'

Bryce nodded, slowly, for some time, his eyes on the tape turning in the recorder. Wayne was wondering if he should ask something further when Bryce said, 'Duality . . . is, of course, naturally it's in all of us, opposites and the movement of selves inside the skin, and the feeling that this can't be happening to me, but then what is? What *is* happening, if not what is? From that point of view, every decision has to be the right decision, every decision has to be inevitable, no way to get away from what was decided, because history then flows, you see, *flows*, history flows from each decision, and when we stand up here, you see, you see? when you stand up here on this hilltop this is where you are and you could not have been here if you hadn't decided the way you did way back *there*. Of course, naturally, of course, if you made a different decision then, *that* would be the right, the correct one, the only one, the only possible, the only way you could have gone, if only you'd *thought*, if only you'd thought it *through*, and now today, you see, you do see, don't you? today you'd be on some other hilltop looking back and you would see that you were right and that was the only possible hilltop, *that* was the only possible hilltop, if only you'd been patient, and you can't even see that hilltop from here, where you are instead, you can't get to it, you can't ever get to it, but you certainly know, you know now, you *should* have known then, you should have known, you were thinking like a madman, worse, you were thinking like a *storyteller* telling a *story*, with a *hook*, and you didn't see there were other, other, there were other, oh, let's call them *scenarios*, and the multiplicity of the scenarios, yes, forking paths, that's good, I don't know about a garden, but this multiplicity opens and then closes like stones, like giant stones closing, and all the variables, the variations, what shall we say, diversity, the multiformity narrows, constricts, strangles, until there's only the *one*, and that it is the only *one* is not the excuse, that it's the *inevitable* is not the excuse, that it's the only thing that could have happened only because it's the only thing that *did* happen is not the excuse, and we're left with a duality that is in the spirit, a remorse, a wish undone, a desire for a forking path, a garden, yes, a desire for a flower that does not grow, which is where I've always, my hand has always reached out, but the image and the reality are *wrong*, to bring us back to your question, the desire for another reality is what makes the writer of fiction, the teller of tales, to bring us back to your question, the liar, the one who forces his reality on to the world but the graft, to bring us back to your question, the graft can never survive on this new root, on this hilltop, *this* one, here. Which is I suppose what I was writing about, if I'd ever cared to pay attention. However, I've never read Borges.'

Wayne stayed just the one night, filling several hours of tape with their interview, then took the train back to New York, sat at his computer, and wrote both sides of the interview, the questions and the answers. Everybody seemed pleased by it.

Twenty-Seven

The second week in April, and Bryce was impatient for real spring to arrive. Almost every day now, he would walk up to the pool enclosure, go inside the fence, and walk around the pool with its dark green cover littered with wet clumps of last year's leaves. He always opened the pool early in May, even though the weather was usually still a little too cold then. But the pool was heated, even if the air was not, and there were always at least a few warm sunny days in May, before most of his neighbors had opened their own pools, when Bryce could swim and soak and work winter out of his body.

The second Tuesday in April, and the second day he'd eaten a lunch made by Mrs Hildebrand. A widow in her late sixties, Mrs Hildebrand had for years been a nutritionist in a private school up near the Massachusetts line. She now had a small income and no nearby family and had been living in a rather grungy apartment in Danbury. She was a quiet woman, unlikely to intrude, and she understood the job well. Cook and clean for a divorced man who worked at home, receive a small wage to supplement her Social Security, also get a room and board, have one day off a week – they'd settled on Thursday, for no particular reason – and keep to herself unless Bryce wanted company, which was unlikely to happen. She was a reader (he suspected she was a fan, though she was too discreet to gush), and there was a television set in her room, so she could fill her idle time at least as well here as in that apartment in Danbury.

There was room in the attached garage for Mrs Hildebrand's little orange Honda Civic, in which she would do the grocery shopping for the house from now on. Not the least of the benefits of his having hired Mrs Hildebrand was the fact there was no longer any chance he might actually run into Marcia Rierdon again one day. He would have to tell Wayne, next time he saw him, how grateful he was for the suggestion.

His meals were much better now, with Mrs Hildebrand in the house. Today, feeling comfortably full – feeling comfortable, in fact – he strolled up to the pool after lunch, and was roaming around it, thinking about swimming, not thinking about anything but swimming, when the cellular phone in his hip pocket rang. He stood at the end of the pool, by the brackets for the diving board he never used, but which for some reason he always had them install again every spring when they opened the pool – maybe because the brackets would be ugly without the board – and pulled the phone out of his pocket. 'Hello?'

'Bryce. Joe. How we doing?'

'Oh, well, slow, you know how it is. Getting there, I guess.'

'Okay, I didn't call to nag. I called because they sent over the interview, which I think looks terrific.'

'Oh, good.' Bryce had been a little worried about that, not at all sure he'd handled those questions well. It was a relief to hear Joe say it looked good.

'But you should go over it, too,' Joe told him. 'And I'd like an excuse to get out of the city for a day.'

'Out of the city?'

'I'm asking you to invite me up for the day tomorrow,' Joe explained. 'I'll drive up in the morning, we'll go over the interview together, and I'll drive back.'

He wants to see the work in progress, Bryce thought, but he can't see it. But even as he tried to find a way to get out of this he knew there was no way out. 'That sounds great,' he said. 'What time will you get here?'

'Around eleven, that okay?'

'Perfect,' Bryce said, and went back down to the house to tell Mrs Hildebrand there would be two for lunch tomorrow.

Bryce read the interview before lunch, while Joe chatted with Mrs Hildebrand in the kitchen. She was much more voluble with Joe than with Bryce, but of course the relationship was different.

The other things Joe had brought were the advance reviews of *Two Faces in the Mirror*, from *Publishers Weekly* and *Kirkus*. As Joe said, 'They're both very positive, very up-beat, glad to have you back, but as usual *PW* gives us more quotable quotes than *Kirkus*.'

'Just so they like it,' Bryce said, and was very pleased that both did.

He was also pleased by the interview. He was sure Wayne had edited his answers, had smoothed out some of the rambling, made the points a little clearer. At this distance, weeks later, he couldn't remember exactly which of these sentences he'd actually said and which were improved paraphrases from Wayne. In any event, he was happy with the interview and he was sure Wayne had never entirely misquoted him, which is to say he'd never changed Bryce's meaning to some opinion of his own.

He said as much to Joe, over Mrs Hildebrand's cold shrimp salad with arugula, and Joe said, 'You think he kept the tone, though.'

'Oh, sure.'

'Maybe tidied it up a little bit, here and there.'

'Well, I think that's natural,' Bryce said. 'You wouldn't want something that sounds like a police transcript.'

'No, I guess not.'

Bryce peered at Joe, who was looking grim. 'Something wrong? The salad?'

'Lunch is terrific, Bryce,' Joe assured him. 'You were smart to hire Mrs Hildebrand.'

'It was Wayne's idea.'

'Well, he was right,' Joe said. 'No point living here like a gold miner in the Yukon.'

Laughing, Bryce said, 'I was never *that* bad. I get out, I have a full social life.'

'Are you still seeing that girl Isabelle?'

'She went back to Spain,' Bryce said. 'What do you think, should we have a glass of white wine with this?'

'Not for me.' Joe put down his fork, and shook his head, and looked over at the windows, with their view up toward the pool. 'You know I don't like to nag,' he said.

'We both don't like it, Joe,' Bryce told him, smiling, hoping to deflect this.

'You've been off your feed for a long time, Bryce,' Joe said, and now he did look at Bryce, and Bryce was startled and displeased to see how concerned Joe was. 'For over a year,' Joe said. 'Maybe two years.'

'You know the divorce made me crazy,' Bryce reminded him. 'And then Lucie getting killed like that, it was a real shock.'

'I know it was. But I don't think you're getting over it.'

'Of course I am,' Bryce said. 'That was months ago, last year, for God's sake. And you know, by that point, she wasn't my favorite person.'

'Then why aren't you getting work done?'

'I am getting work done,' Bryce insisted. 'What about *Two Faces?*'

Joe shook his head. 'Bryce, you were stuck in that one for a long time and you know it, over a year.'

'I got it done, didn't I?'

'You had to call Wayne in to focus you,' Joe said, 'help you get moving, keep you on track. He had a lot to do with that book, and you know that's true.'

'Of course he did.' Bryce spread his hands. 'I never denied it, not to *you.*' Grinning, he gestured at the clippings of the reviews on the table beside them and said, 'If somebody from *PW* called and asked me about Wayne, I'd deny it, naturally, I would. But I've always told you, Wayne was a lifesaver on that book. It's just what you said, he kept me focused.'

'What about the new book? Are you focused on that?'

Mrs Hildebrand came in, hesitant, hands folded at her waist, expression worried. 'Is something wrong with the salad?'

They'd both stopped eating, some time ago. Now both hurriedly picked up their forks, assured Mrs Hildebrand the salad was delicious, they'd just been involved in their conversation, the lunch was really wonderful. When she at last stopped looking worried, and smiled instead, Bryce said, 'Actually, it's too good to have without a glass of white wine. Joe?'

'Not for me, thanks.'

'Just me, then,' Bryce said, and they went back to eating until she'd resumed, happy again, with Bryce's wine. He sipped from it, ate some more shrimp salad, and when she'd left the dining room Joe said, 'Tell me something about the new book.'

'You know I don't like to do that,' Bryce said. 'You can kill a book by talking about it before it's done.'

'I know that,' Joe agreed, 'and you know, usually, I wouldn't ask. But I just don't think you *are* in focus, Bryce. I think you're still distracted. I'm speaking as your friend now, and as your friend, I can't take vague answers any more about the book, how it's slow, but it's progressing, but it's slow. How slow is it? How much of it is done?'

'Joe, I really don't want to talk about a book I'm still—'

'How many pages?'

'Joe, you shouldn't press me on a book that—'

'I'm not asking you about plot, or setting, or characters, or title even. You can't kill a book by telling me how many pages exist.'

'Call it superstition, Joe, but—'

'I call it evasion, Bryce.'

Bryce frowned at Joe, who was looking very grim and not at all like a friend. 'Joe,' he said, 'why do you want to make an issue? We get along, I've never threatened to go anywhere else—'

'Are you threatening now?'

'Of course not.' Of course he wasn't. But he wanted to do whatever was necessary to get Joe to back off. Leave this alone. Let me work it out, leave me alone.

But Joe wouldn't. He said, 'How many pages?'

'All right,' Bryce said, 'the truth is, I'm embarrassed to tell you, because it isn't very many at all. It *has* been slow, but it's getting better and I—'

'How many pages?'

'I don't want to tell you, Joe.'

Joe sat back. Once again, they'd both forgotten their salads. Joe said, 'Is it printed out?'

'No, it's on discs. Disc.'

Joe picked up that plural: 'Discs?'

'Disc. One disc.'

'Print out the last page you've done.'

Bryce stared at him. 'Why? Why would I do that?'

'To prove to me it exists,' Joe said.

'Goddam it, Joe, now I have to prove the book exists?'

'Yes,' Joe said.

'*Why?*'

'Because we both know it doesn't.'

Bryce remained defiant a few seconds more, and then he sagged back in the chair, defeated. 'I have outlines,' he said.

'Outlines.'

'I haven't been— Yes, you're right, it's a question of focus. I haven't been able to focus, I've done some outlines, story ideas, they're on discs, I haven't been able to pick the one I want to do. *Focus* on.'

'But these really exist.'

'Oh, yes,' Bryce said. 'They're all there, they're labeled and every-thing, I just haven't felt like going back, you know, not yet, look them over, winnow them out, you know, pick the right one to do next.'

'Could I see them?'

Bryce sat up straighter. 'That's a good idea,' he said. '*You* could winnow them. I don't know how many there are, but a bunch of them. I tell you what, after lunch, why not look them over? Pick out two or three or whatever, and say, "Here, Bryce, concentrate on one of these." And then I'll get to work, I swear I will.'

'Good,' Joe said.

There was a two-person wooden bench they kept beside the pool in the summer, midway down one long side. In the winter it was kept with the other pool furniture in the pool-house, but Bryce dragged it out now, put it in its summer position, and sat there to look at the pool and think about May.

He didn't actually remember any of those story ideas, not a one of them. He hoped Joe would find a few of them useful, anyway, because he really did want to get back to work in earnest. It had been so long since he'd actually written anything, not since *Two Faces.*

Well, no. Farther back than that.

I have to do it again, he thought, I have to get started again, because that's the only person I can be. I'm just drifting around here, I'm not anybody, I'm not even the ghost of somebody, I'm just empty. I'm like a model airplane with a rubber band in it to run the propeller, and the rubber band broke. I can feel it broken in there. I've got to get it back, I've got to get it fixed.

When Joe came up to the pool, he still looked grim. Bryce had been hoping he'd have a smile on his face, he'd say, 'This one or that one is just the thing. Get *started*, Bryce!' But that wasn't going to happen.

Joe sat beside him on the bench, his feet just touching the stone walk, and gazed at the pool cover. Bryce waited for him to say something, anything at all, but Joe just sat there, so finally Bryce said. 'None of them any good, huh?'

Joe let out a long breath. He said, 'You aren't in any kind of therapy, are you.' It wasn't a question, but a statement.

Not another one, Bryce thought, thinking of his lawyer, Fred Silver, and his belief that there was a professional of some sort waiting out there to deal with whatever contingency might arise. 'No,' he said. 'I'm not.'

'I know somebody in New York—'

'No, Joe.'

Joe looked briefly at him, then stared at the pool cover again. 'May I ask why not?'

The answer was, the only way a therapist can help you is if you tell the truth, but Bryce couldn't tell the truth to anybody, not to a therapist, not to Joe, not to anybody. He said, 'I just don't want to do it. I don't see the need for it.'

Joe glanced at him again, and away. 'Wayne,' he said, 'played part of the interview tape for me.'

What was this? Some new attack, but what about? Bryce, wary, said, 'I already know what he did there isn't word for word what I said.'

'It isn't anything you said,' Joe told him. He looked at Bryce, and away. 'Wayne told me in confidence, because he's worried about you. He didn't know what to do, and he knows I'm your friend, so he played it for me.'

'And what was wrong with it?'

'It made no sense,' Joe told him. 'That entire written interview is Wayne, he wrote the whole thing.'

'No.'

'Yes.'

'But— Why?'

'Because you weren't saying anything anybody could use, or respond to, or understand. It was like the storylines on all those discs. Twenty-four discs of gibberish, Bryce.'

'I don't believe that.'

'Okay,' Joe said. 'Come on back to the house, let's look at a few of them.'

Suddenly afraid, Bryce said, 'No!'

'No?' Joe looked directly at him, tried to hold Bryce's eye. 'Why not?'

Now it was Bryce who stared at the pool cover. 'I don't feel I want to see them,' he said. 'If you don't think they're any good, what's the point in my—'

'You aren't tracking, and you don't know you aren't tracking,' Joe told him. 'You can't go on this way, Bryce, you really can't.'

'I'll be all right, Joe,' Bryce said.

'You won't see a therapist?'

'No! I don't want to, and I don't need to, and no.'

Joe nodded, then got to his feet, and moved a little away. Looking down at the gray stone walk, and the fresh grass growing beside it, he said, 'The book you aren't working on is the final one in your current contract.'

'I never pay attention to things like that, you know I don't.'

'Jerry Mossman does.'

'He's my agent, he's supposed to watch that sort of thing.'

'Because *Two Faces* was so late,' Joe told him, 'this next book, the one you aren't writing, is also late. Just over a year past the delivery date in the contract.'

'Joe, we've never worried about crap like that. You know I always—'

'Not any more,' Joe said. He turned to look at Bryce, and it occurred to Bryce that Joe had deliberately decided to stay at a safe distance. 'If you don't do something, Bryce,' he said, 'and do it *now*, something to convince me you're being helped, or you no longer need help, next Monday I'm going to inform Jerry Mossman you're in breach of contract, that we no longer have confidence in your capability to produce any more novels, and that we are canceling the contract and will demand the return of all advances.'

Bryce stood, and Joe backed a step. Bryce said, 'Joe, you can't do that, you can't mean that.'

Joe said, 'I think I'm your friend, Bryce, and I hate like hell to be such a hardnose bastard, but I'm worried about you and I think it's up to me to force you to get help. I've taken one of the discs, it's called "Kyrgyzstan," do you remember it?'

'I don't remember any of them.'

'If we have to go to court,' Joe said, 'I'll produce that, and the tape of Wayne's interview.'

'Joe, *please!*'

'Will you get help?'

Desperate, floundering, searching in this darkness for a way out, Bryce shouted, 'Wayne!'

Joe said, 'What?'

'Wayne,' Bryce said, more calmly. 'He helped me once before, didn't he? He got me on track once before. I'll call him, I'll call him today, I'll call him right now, before you leave! I'll ask him, help me again. *He'll* get me on track, you know he will. I can work if I have Wayne with me.'

Joe thought about it, then slowly nodded. 'We'll ask him,' he said. 'If he agrees, we'll try it. If he doesn't agree—'

'He'll agree!'

'All right, let's phone.'

They got the answering machine. Bryce left a message.

Twenty-Eight

When Wayne got back to the apartment after his after-lunch jog in Central Park, there was a message for him on the answering machine: 'Hi, Wayne, I'm at home in Connecticut, I'm here with Joe, we both want to talk to you as soon as possible, give us a call, okay, buddy?' Bryce sounded overly happy, manic, almost feverish. And he'd never called Wayne 'buddy' before.

Was this about the interview? Had it been a mistake after all to play the tape for Joe? It had seemed like the safest thing to do at the time.

The more Wayne had listened to that tape, trying to find something usable in it, the more he'd realized just how unstable Bryce had become. And could you count on an unstable person to do the best thing for himself? To take the best advice, even from a first wife? Bryce *knew* his Ellen was right, his public confession of Lucie's murder would be devastating for his children, but was he still sensible enough to act on that knowledge? Or would he suddenly go veering off, uncontrollable, destroying everything and everybody in spite of himself?

My only hope, Wayne had decided, is to establish ahead of time that Bryce is nuts, or going nuts, or simply no longer a reliable, stable person. *Then*, if he comes out with some wild story about paying another writer half a million dollars to kill his wife, it'll be easy to discredit him.

So Wayne had laid the groundwork, playing the tape for Joe, telling Joe he was worried about Bryce, which God knows was true

210

enough. And Joe, in confidence, had said he was becoming worried, too, he wasn't sure Bryce was actually at work on the new novel, although he claimed to be. Joe had told Wayne that he shouldn't do anything else about the problem, he shouldn't play the tape for anybody else, but give Joe time to think it over, decide what was best to do.

So had Joe decided the best thing to do was confront Bryce? Tell him what Wayne had done? How would Bryce react to that? Trying to find some clue, some forewarning, he played the message twice more, and could hear desperation in there, beneath the false cheer, but it didn't seem to him there was anything accusatory or angry in that voice. Okay; he'd call.

Supposedly, he was working on the screenplay of *Double Impact* right now, but that was seeming more and more like a waste of time. He'd written the script very fast, pleased with it as he went along, not even worried that it was a hundred fifty pages long instead of the hundred twenty the screenwriting textbooks recommended, knowing what he was doing was fast and meaty and solid, but then he showed it to Susan, and she read it and said it was wordy. Too wordy. Too much dialogue. Not letting the camera tell the story, but making the characters tell the story by talking each other's ears off.

So it wasn't quite as easy as he'd thought. But now, going through it all over again, trying to find great chunks of dialogue he could transmogrify into cunning paragraphs of instruction for the camera, he was learning to his distress that his imagination wasn't quite as visual as he'd always believed. But he refused to give up, at least not yet. I'll give it the month of April, he'd told himself, and if I can't do it by then, the hell with it.

So in a way it was an agreeable distraction to have this enigmatic message from Bryce. Telling himself he had more to worry about from the screenplay than from Bryce, he dialed the number in Connecticut, and a motherly-sounding woman answered, saying, 'Proctorr residence.'

A nurse? Had Bryce tried to kill himself? 'Oh, hi, uh . . . It's Wayne Prentice, Bryce called me.'

'One moment, please.'

He waited, not long, and then Bryce came on, still sounding manic and chipper, saying, 'Oh, damn, Wayne, Joe just left five minutes ago.'

'Who was that? The woman who answered.'

'Oh! You don't know, I took your advice. That's Mrs Hildebrand, the housekeeper.'

For some reason, that news was encouraging, as though hiring a housekeeper were such a palpably sane thing to do it suggested he needn't worry at all about Bryce any more. 'Well, I'm glad you did that,' he said.

'So am I,' Bryce assured him. 'And you'll be even more glad, the next time you come here. She knows lunch.'

'Good.'

'See, what it is,' Bryce said, his voice dropping, his manner suddenly hesitant, less sure, 'what it is, Wayne, Joe was here . . .'

'Yes, you said.'

'And he got sort of tough with me, I have to say, I didn't expect that, he was really very tough with me.'

'About what?'

'Well, he got it out of me that I haven't actually been working on the new book. I don't, uh, actually *have* a new book.'

Wayne was surprised, but then immediately he wasn't. 'What did he say?'

'Well, he wanted me to go into therapy,' Bryce said, 'but I can't do that, I mean, you know why I can't do that.'

'No, I don't,' Wayne said.

Bryce whispered, shrill and sibilant, '*You have to tell them the truth!*'

Oh, for God's sake. 'All right,' Wayne said. 'That isn't the reason you gave him, I hope.'

'No! Of course not.'

'You just said no.'

'I just said no.'

'And what did he say?'

'He said, if I didn't do something to get help, get *started*, he was going to void my contract and demand the advance back. That's a quarter, I've already got a quarter. The last time, you know, my half was really one quarter on *Two Faces* and one quarter on this next book.'

Two hundred seventy-five thousand dollars. A lot of money to have to give back. Wayne said, 'He would do that? I thought he was your pal.'

'He is. He thinks he's being my pal when he's doing this. So I had to do *something*. So I told him, "Wayne. *He'll* help me".' The voice dropping to a whisper again: '*Like last time.*'

'Ah,' Wayne said. 'Who do I kill this time?'

'*What?*" The shock in Bryce's voice was so comical that Wayne could only laugh, and then Bryce, sounding deeply offended, said, 'That's not funny.'

'Sorry,' Wayne said, 'I thought it was. So what's the idea? I already gave you *Two Faces. The Domino Doublet.*'

'I have some outlines, story treatments, Joe says they're no good, they're like the interview . . .'

'Oh, he told you about that.'

'Yes. But that's okay, I understand why you told him, it's okay. And you did a great job, fixing it up. You did a great interview, I'm only sorry I couldn't have been there.'

Again Wayne laughed, and this time he said, 'But you think there's something salvageable, right? In those outlines.'

'I *hope* there is. I haven't looked at them, I've been afraid to look at them, but you could. The deal is, if you say yes, you'll help me, Joe's gonna back off. Then you can look at these things of mine, see if we can do something with one of them, actually get *moving* at last.'

Possibilities shifted in Wayne's mind. 'I'll give it a shot, Bryce,' he said.

'Oh, Wayne, thanks, I knew I could count on you, I *knew* I could count on you.'

'You can.'

'Joe wants you to call him, tell him what you're gonna do,' Bryce said. 'Not in the office today, he's going home from here. Around five you could call him.'

'I will.'

'And you could come up, could you come up tomorrow?'

Thinking of the screenplay, not wanting to leave it because he *did* want to leave it, Wayne said, 'I've got my own stuff to do, Bryce. I could come up Saturday. Could I bring Susan?'

'Sure! Stay over, stay the weekend, I'm invited to a party Saturday night, some people up here, I'll tell them I'm bringing houseguests.'

'You don't have to do that.'

'No, that's normal up here,' Bryce explained. 'People always bring houseguests, I've always been the oddball, I never brought any extra people around, you'll be my first houseguests.'

'In that case, fine,' Wayne said. 'And Bryce, could you fax me directions? I'll rent a car and drive up.'

'Absolutely. And call Joe, okay? He's worried.'

'I'll tell him to stop worrying,' Wayne said. We'll all stop worrying, he thought, because all at once he knew what was going to happen. He was going to get to finish *The Shadowed Other*. He was going to get to see *The Shadowed Other* published. He was going to get to see *The Shadowed Other* on the best-seller list. Because he now had a secret pen name that was much better than Tim Fleet:

Bryce Proctorr.

'There it is!' Susan said. 'That's the house!' She was very excited.

'Yeah, that's it,' Wayne agreed, as they crunched slowly up the gravel drive toward the house in the rented Lexus. Eleven in the morning, sunny, cool, the columns on the front of the house gleaming white, like an old southern plantation.

'We were so close to it, weren't we?' Susan said. 'That day we looked for it.'

'You can't really see it from the road.'

'Maybe we drove past it. Did we?'

'I don't remember,' Wayne said, and parked by the garage, but just to the left, so the cars that used the garage could get in and out.

They each had packed a small overnight bag which they carried from the car, and as they neared the front door it opened and an older woman in a dark blue skirt and pink ruffled blouse smiled out at them, saying, 'Good morning. You must be the Prentices.' She looked more like a widow on a cruise ship than a housekeeper.

'And you must be Mrs Hildebrand,' Wayne said. 'We talked on the phone.'

'Yes, of course, come in.'

They entered the house, Susan looking around, her eyes sparkling, and Mrs Hildebrand said, 'Mr Proctorr is out walking, he likes to walk around the property. I'll show you to your room.'

'I know where it is,' Wayne said, 'I stayed here before.'

'Then I'll go back to doing lunch,' Mrs Hildebrand said. 'I hope you both like game hen.'

Wayne laughed, and said, 'You can count on us, Mrs Hildebrand.'

He led the way upstairs to the sunny large guest room he'd used before. When they were in the room, with the door closed, Susan said, 'It is like the apartment.'

'I told you, but he doesn't see it.'

'He's a strange man,' Susan said, and looked out the window. 'Here he comes.'

Wayne went over to stand beside her, and look out. Up-slope from here was the pool, almost at a level with this room, and beyond that a field, and beyond that thick woods leading uphill. Coming down across the field, skirting the pool, was Bryce, in a big bulky black car coat, with wood pegs instead of buttons. He wore it open and flapping, his hands in the pockets. He was bareheaded, and his expression was fixed, determined, like somebody trying to remember an important fact.

'I'll go down and talk to him,' Wayne said.

'I'll unpack,' Susan said, 'and see you at lunch.'

Wayne went downstairs and found Bryce walking toward him down the hall, still wearing the car coat, hands still in the pockets. His face brightened when he saw Wayne, and he pulled his right hand from the pocket to extend it for a shake as he came forward, saying, 'Wayne! It's great to see you.'

'And you,' Wayne said. He saw that Bryce was hyper, but controlling it.

Bryce pulled off the coat, as though not realizing till now he was wearing it, and stood there with the coat draped over his left forearm. He said, 'It's an hour till lunch, maybe more. You want to look at this stuff, or wait? I know it was a long drive.'

'No, it was easy, we rented a good car. Let's see these outlines.'

'Get the suspense over with, right?' Bryce said, and gave him a broad grin and an awkward pat on the arm.

'Right,' Wayne said.

They walked together back upstairs to Bryce's office, where he dropped the coat on the black leather sofa and said, 'You know how to operate all this stuff.'

'Sure.'

'They're in there, the outlines. Twenty-three of them. Twenty-four, but Joe took one.'

'Not the best one,' Wayne suggested.

Bryce's laugh was a little too explosive. 'He wasn't looking for the best one,' he said. 'Not by then. Listen, I'd be kind of uncomfortable in here, you reading those things. And better for you, too, if I'm not around.'

'Sure.'

'I'll see you at lunch,' Bryce said, and fled.

Wayne moved toward the desk, and Bryce appeared again, an embarrassed smile fluttering at his mouth. 'My coat,' he said, and pointed at it, and picked it up, and waved goodbye, and hurried away.

When he learns his wife had a sex-change operation years before they met, he leaves her. She pursues, and he flees into Canada, where he becomes a monk in a monastery that secretly smuggles political refugees into the United States. He falls in love with a Chinese girl who used to star in propaganda films and now wants to become a model in New York. His wife, pursuing, must disguise herself as a man.

That was the shortest of them. Some were more than three thousand words long, but most were only three or four pages. They were all hopeless.

This was not a surprise, not after he'd been told Joe's reaction to these things, but it was still depressing. What had gone wrong with

Bryce? Was it really Lucie's death, guilt feelings, the lack of closure because he hadn't been the one to do it himself?

Or was it something from earlier, maybe not even connected to Lucie at all. Maybe Lucie left him because he was turning weird, and not the other way around.

Whatever it was, and whatever profit there might be for Wayne in it, he still found the situation sad and depressing. He liked Bryce, had liked him in a casual way in the old days, had admired and envied him from afar for a long time, and had felt many different things toward him in the last six months. But he still had to identify with Bryce as another writer, another storyteller, and how horrible it has to be when the stories won't come. When this static is all you can find.

Wayne knew what should happen next, but he also knew it would be a very delicate crossing to get there. Bryce's hope, despite Joe's reaction, despite his own inner knowledge that kept him from looking at this junk himself, was that there was *something* here, some spark, some tiny slender filament of thread that could be picked up, and followed, until it led to a complete, full, valuable novel.

No. There was nothing in Bryce's mind but static, shards, jumbled wreckage. But Wayne couldn't tell Bryce that, couldn't let Bryce suspect it. He didn't want a Bryce Proctorr in despair, he'd be useless then. He needed a Bryce Proctorr who still retained hope.

Looking at the computer screen, he could sometimes see some faint reflection of himself. It wasn't until he turned away, at the end, that he spoke: 'I have to give him a reason to do what I need him to do. I have to give him his own reason.'

Mrs Hildebrand had not only transformed lunch, she'd transformed the dining room as well. The silver pieces on the sideboard gleamed from fresh polish, the spring flowers on the table seemed to sparkle with their own inner light, and even the dishes she used were a better set, more fanciful, than the utilitarian plates and bowls Bryce had provided last time for Wayne and himself.

Wayne was the last to walk into the dining room, finding the other two in awkward conversation at the table, both of them looking at him with relief when they were no longer alone. Wayne knew Bryce didn't care for Susan, and that Susan was distant to him in return, and he was sorry about that, but he didn't know what to do about it. He and Susan were going to be here a lot, if things worked out as he hoped; maybe Bryce and Susan would get used to one another, would stop making each other uncomfortable.

In addition to relief, Bryce looked at Wayne with hope in his eyes, but Wayne shook his head. 'I'm sorry,' he said, and turned away from Bryce's pained reaction.

He sat down, and Mrs Hildebrand brought in the three game hens, and the side dishes, and asked if anyone would like wine. Wayne looked to see what Bryce would do, but Bryce said, 'None for me today, Mrs Hildebrand,' so Wayne said, 'Not for me, either,' and so did Susan.

Mrs Hildebrand left the room, and Bryce said, 'Nothing? None of them?'

Wayne shook his head. 'You knew that already,' he said. 'You knew that when Joe told you. Come on, Bryce, you knew it before then, when you wouldn't even look at them.'

'This is delicious,' Susan said.

'We should eat,' Bryce said, and picked up his knife and fork.

They all ate for a little while, and then Wayne said, 'I have suggestions to make, if you want.'

'I'm grabbing at straws,' Bryce said.

'Well, I hope this isn't a straw. I think what the problem is, you're too isolated here.'

'This started before I moved up here full-time,' Bryce said.

Wayne said, 'The outlines?'

'No, you're right, I did those here.'

'Before you came up,' Wayne told him, 'you were distracted by too much stuff happening, but now you've cut yourself off, it's almost like you're in exile up here.'

'My Elba,' Bryce said, and laughed, and said, 'I can't go back, you know, I can't get that apartment back.'

'We're in it,' Susan said.

Wayne and Bryce both gave her astonished looks. Bryce said, 'You're in it?'

Calmly, Susan said, 'Didn't Wayne tell you?' Of course, she knew he hadn't. 'When we found out you were leaving,' she explained, 'we looked at it, not for ourselves, but because we needed a bigger place, and we wanted an idea about rents and space and all that. And then we fell in love with the place. We moved there, and Joe and Shelly moved into our old apartment.'

'They don't want to leave the Village,' Wayne said. He trusted Susan to know the right move to make, but this was all so tricky now, was this really the right time to add this complication?

Bryce looked from Susan to Wayne. 'Why didn't you tell me?'

Wayne said, 'It felt – I felt uncomfortable, like I was taking something that was yours.' He grinned, and shook his head, and said, 'If it was up to me, I wouldn't have done it, for that reason, but Susan just loves the place.'

'We don't feel strange,' Susan pointed out, 'about Joe and Shelly moving into our old place.'

Bryce said, 'My furniture?'

'We're getting rid of it,' Susan told him, 'replacing it, bit by bit. If there's anything you want . . .'

'No no no,' Bryce said. 'I don't want any of that, I left it there, let it stay there.' With that fitful fretful smile that had become a part of him lately, he said, 'I can come visit it. Visit the place. Visit you two. Next time I'm in the city.'

Which was, Wayne saw, his chance to get the conversation back on track. 'Bryce,' he said, 'when was the last time you were in the city?'

'What? I don't know, a while ago.'

'Some time in February, wasn't it? Early February. You left before your lease was up.'

'Around then,' Bryce agreed. 'Listen, this hen is great, if we don't eat, Mrs Hildebrand is gonna come in and ask us what's wrong.'

Again they all ate, but Wayne kept thinking about the conversation and where he needed it to go and how to get it there. At last, he said, 'You're too cut off here, Bryce, that's what it comes down to. You need input, you need to get back on track.'

'Living in New York isn't gonna—'

'That's not my idea,' Wayne told him. 'My idea is, we work

together the way you told Joe we were working together. Only this time we do it for real.'

Bryce ate hen, chewed, frowned at Wayne, and said, 'How?'

'I come up here every weekend,' Wayne said. 'We talk. You think during the week, make notes, we discuss the ideas on the weekends, shape them, focus your thinking.'

'Focus,' Bryce echoed. 'That's the word Joe used. Or maybe I did.'

'That's what we need,' Wayne said. 'Maybe Susan could come up with me sometimes.'

'Sure,' Bryce said, indifferently. 'If she won't be bored.'

Susan said, 'When do you open the pool?'

The look Bryce gave her, Wayne saw, was almost hostile. He said, 'Early in May.'

'Then that's it, then,' she said. 'I love to swim, I'm a fish.'

Wayne, needing to push his idea forward, said, 'However long it takes, Bryce, every weekend we work on it, honing your ideas. You're a very talented guy, a very successful guy, you just got derailed somewhere, the two of us can get you back on track. However long it takes.'

The repetition of that phrase finally produced the response Wayne needed. Bryce said, 'It *can't* go on and on, you know. Joe says I'm a year late already. We can't just sit here every weekend forever and talk. I need a book.'

'I have a book,' Wayne said.

Bryce peered at him. 'What?'

'Half a book,' Wayne corrected himself. 'I haven't been working on it because I've been doing all these magazine pieces, to make some money. But I could go back to it on Monday. That's what I could do during the week, while you're up here working on ideas. Then every weekend I bring up what I've done, and we go over it, and we go over your ideas, and when you're ready, you start your book.'

Bryce said, 'And yours?'

'Same as before,' Wayne said.

'That's the book we give Joe, you mean. Your book.'

'That's the only one we've got,' Wayne pointed out. 'You have to give Joe *something*, you know you do. So this is the stopgap, until you get your feet under you again.'

Bryce's face had started to crumple, as though he were a little boy, who was about to cry. But he didn't cry; he said, 'I wanted a book of mine.'

'It *will* be a book of yours,' Wayne told him. 'I haven't been working on mine for a while, because there was nothing to do with it. But now there is. It's yours, the same deal as last time, only this time, there's only half a book, you can have input from here on, that'll help you, too, getting back into the details of the characters, the plot. Every weekend, we talk about the book we're working on, and we talk about your ideas for the next one.'

'I wanted my own book,' Bryce said. 'That's why I called you, that's what I said to Joe, that's what I wanted. This time, my own book. I wanted you to help me find my own book, but *mine*.'

'I will,' Wayne said. 'I promise. We don't have time now to do a brand new novel from scratch, you know we don't, with no ideas for it, with Joe at the end of his patience, so this one is a, it's a collaboration, and—'

'It isn't mine.'

'The *next* one is yours. I promise.'

Bryce looked at him, silent, for a long time. Then he said, 'You promise?'

Twenty-Nine

Bryce said, 'He's a traveling salesman, he sells computer equipment to school systems, he travels all over the north-east. In this one school district, the Board of Education offices are in the high school, you know, consolidated high school for the whole district.'

'Uh huh,' Wayne said.

'He's coming out of there,' Bryce said, 'late afternoon, school closed, meets this woman in the parking lot, teacher, she's unhappy, recently divorced, he asks her to come have a drink, she says okay, they have dinner, wind up in his motel room.'

'Uh huh,' Wayne said.

'In the night,' Bryce said, 'she leaves, he goes on to the next town, goes back to *that* motel, she's there.'

'Ah hah,' Wayne said.

'She's attached herself to him, she's gonna follow him, she's obsessing on him, he's like her salvation,' Bryce said. 'Only he's married.'

'Uh huh,' Wayne said.

'They go out to dinner,' Bryce said, 'he tries to talk sense to her, she won't listen, they're walking back to the motel, late, dark, all at once he starts hitting her.'

'Hah,' Wayne said.

'He can't stop,' Bryce said, 'he keeps going and going, and she's dead. He goes back to the motel, showers, gets rid of those clothes, sleeps badly.'

'Uh huh,' Wayne said.

'Nobody knows he ever even met her,' Bryce said. 'Nobody knows she followed him, there's no link, they'll never catch him.'

'Right,' Wayne said.

'So it's like he has to keep going over it,' Bryce said, 'the scene itself, the killing, going over it and over it, playing it out different ways, trying to find some resolution, but there isn't any.'

'Nobody's after him,' Wayne said.

'No, that's just it,' Bryce said. 'It's *Crime and Punishment*, or it's *Les Miserables*, but there isn't any Inspector Porfiry, no Javert. He's his *own* nemesis, he tracks *himself* down.'

Wayne said, 'What does he do when he catches himself?'

Bryce knew there was mockery in that question, but he didn't care. 'He goes to the woman's family,' he said. 'He turns himself in to them.'

'Why?' Wayne asked.

'Because he can't stand it any more. But they don't want to know about it, the dead woman's sister and her brother, they don't want the whole thing opened up again, their parents upset again, her children to know she died because she was having sex with some stranger she picked up, obsessed over. So they kill him.'

Wayne said, 'Who does?'

'The brother and the sister,' Bryce said. 'They beat him to death, and that's the end. Now he knows how it feels, how it felt to her. You see?'

Wayne sat back and shook his head. 'I don't know,' he said. 'Who does he talk to?'

'It's all interior,' Bryce said. 'It's all inside him.'

'Joe would want some action, I think,' Wayne said. 'And readers, too, they expect something else from you.'

'Oh, there's action,' Bryce said. 'It's just, the main thing is, what's going on in his mind.'

'Well, okay,' Wayne said. 'It's possible. You might have something there. Only, I wish he could have somebody to talk to, get *out* of his mind sometimes.'

'I think I could do something like that,' Bryce said.

'And I'd like to know more about the action,' Wayne said. 'I tell you what. Next week, flesh that out a little more, put it down on a disc, lay it out, and we'll be able to go over it some more next week-end.'

'Okay,' Bryce said.

'And in the meantime, you could read this. *The Shadowed Other*, the first half.'

'Okay,' Bryce said.

'Did you read the manuscript?'

'Yes, it's good, all that Guatemala stuff is very good.'

'We're gonna have to switch some of that around a little,' Wayne said, 'because I used some of it for a piece I did for the *New York Review of Books*. I can show you the stuff we can't use, and you could maybe do some work in there. I mean, if you want to work on it.'

'Oh, I do want to work on it,' Bryce said. 'It's very good, but I do have some ideas.' He laughed, and rubbed his left hand over his face, and said, 'But I don't want to make another Henry-Eleanor mistake.'

'Oh, don't worry about that,' Wayne said, 'we can always discuss things and change things around. But what about the other thing? The guy that killed the woman?'

'Oh, no,' Bryce said, dismissing it. 'Not that.'

'What? You were going to add to it, write it out. The action, some-body to talk to.'

'No, forget that,' Bryce said. 'I looked it over, and you were right, it's too interior, so I've got another idea.'

'Okay, fine.'

'I want to use the same guy,' Bryce said, 'the background, selling computers to schools, traveling around, all that, but a completely different story.'

'Okay,' Wayne said. 'That's a good character, the salesman, he's very modern, with the computers and the school systems and all that, but he's classic, too, the wanderer.'

'Exactly,' Bryce said. 'And what happens is, the book opens, he's coming to in the hospital. At first, he doesn't even know who he is.'

'Uh huh,' Wayne said.

'What happened was,' Bryce said, 'somebody beat him up,

almost killed him, they got him into the hospital just in the nick of time.'

'Uh huh,' Wayne said.

'His memory comes back,' Bryce said, 'except for that. The beating. He doesn't remember anything about that.'

'Uh huh,' Wayne said.

'That's common, you know,' Bryce said. 'A traumatic experience, and people block it from their memory.'

'Yeah, I know,' Wayne said.

'So he doesn't know who did it, and he doesn't know why,' Bryce said, 'and he doesn't know if they're waiting out there to finish the job.'

'Uh huh,' Wayne said.

'So when he gets out of the hospital,' Bryce said, 'he starts searching back, trying to get to that moment of the beating, *understand* it.'

'Uh huh,' Wayne said.

Bryce looked at him. He didn't say anything.

Wayne said, 'And?'

'That's all,' Bryce said. 'I mean, that's all I have so far.'

'Well, who beat him up? Why?'

'That's what I haven't worked out,' Bryce said. 'I thought, this week, that's what I'd work on. If you thought it was a good, you know, setup.'

'Sure, it's a good setup,' Wayne said, 'but you need more than that.'

'Oh, I know.'

'And it's gotta come from you, Bryce,' Wayne said. 'You know that. If I say it was this person beat him up, or that person, for this or that reason, then it isn't your book any more. And the idea is, this is your book.'

'Oh, I know, I know,' Bryce said. He smiled and said, 'It's gonna be mine, but you're gonna help me make it happen.'

'Absolutely. And on the other . . .'

'I saw that. You brought me some more pages.'

'I mentioned it to Joe,' Wayne said.

Bryce felt a little pang. He said, 'Oh? You saw Joe?'

'He wanted to know how we were coming along,' Wayne said. 'I said you'd found something that I thought was gonna be good, gonna work out, and you were at work on it, and he wanted to know when he could see pages.'

'I don't show Joe pages,' Bryce said. 'I show him the book when it's done.'

'This time,' Wayne said, 'he's more comfortable if he sees pages. I told him, in a couple weeks you'd probably have enough to show him. You can send him a hundred pages or so, a couple weeks from now, say, the middle of May.'

Bryce didn't like this. 'That's not the way we've always done things,' he insisted.

'Once he sees you're back at work,' Wayne said, 'he'll calm down. But you know yourself, this isn't a normal situation. By the next book, *your* book, things will be back the way they were.'

'But this time,' Bryce said, 'I have to show him pages.'

'Just to keep him calm,' Wayne said.

The next Wednesday, the first week of May, they came to open the pool. Bryce went out and stood out of the way to watch them do it. The water was unappetizing when the cover was first folded back, oily-looking and gray and metallic, but he knew the chemicals would clear that up in a couple of days. When the water was clear, he'd turn the heater on. Saturday, you could swim in it, and so far, the weather prediction for Saturday was very good: sunny, low- to mid-sixties.

The story about the computer salesman in the hospital wasn't going to work. He couldn't think why the man had been beaten or what he could do to trace it back. It was a dry hole, a dead end. Before Saturday, he had to have something else, something new, something better.

What was working, and very well, was *The Shadowed Other*. He liked what Wayne was doing with the original idea, and he could see more or less where it was going, and he was very interested in making the book just as good as possible. He spent time thinking about that story, as though it actually were his own, and he liked to sit at the computer and tinker with it. He didn't do too much of that, because it was very good as it was, and also because any changes he made he'd have to clear with Wayne, and he wanted to be sure he could justify them. But those parts of his day felt good, working on that book, at that time he felt exactly the way he used to feel, at the computer, the story rolling out.

They're digging a swimming pool, he thought, and they come across ancient Indian burial mounds. Sacred Indian land, and this radical Indian group attacks the house, to burn it down.

With his left hand, he brushed cobwebs from his face.

Thirty

Wayne and Joe had lunch, late in May, to discuss the first hundred pages of *The Shadowed Other*. 'You do miracles with Bryce,' Joe commented.

'He's doing it himself,' Wayne said. 'He was just thrown off his pace for a while, that's all, things got to him, he got confused. All he needed was another writer, another novel writer, somebody who knows what it is, just to sit there and talk to him and listen to him. And now he's unblocked.'

'He certainly is.'

'This book is coming out of him, I bet it's faster than he's ever worked before.'

'It's prime Bryce Proctorr,' Joe said, 'that's all I know, and all I care, and I'm grateful to you, Wayne.'

'I'm glad I can help.'

'I have a few notes,' Joe said, 'I thought it would be easier to discuss them with you, and then you can pass them on to Bryce. I know he doesn't like to come to town these days.'

He knows, Wayne thought. He knows, and he'd rather not know. What's important to him is the brand name, keep that brand name solid and everything will be just fine. He likes Bryce, and he likes me, and if he can do this without having to admit to himself he's doing it, what's the harm? Bryce's reputation stays solid, his income remains high, and I'm a lot better off than I was before. Where's the downside? There is none.

Wayne remembered, way back when he'd first met Joe and told him about the secret pen names, Joe had said, if he had any reconstituted virgins on his list, he didn't want to know about them. So that was true. Here's one, and he doesn't want to know about it.

Susan was in the pool, and the two men sat on the terrace in the sunlight. 'So he likes it,' Bryce said.

'He's very happy,' Wayne told him, 'and he said no more pages, don't worry about it, he knows everything is fine now, just go ahead and finish the book.'

'Everything is fine now,' Bryce echoed, but his voice was flat.

This was the difficult part, keeping Bryce in line. If only the man could relax and enjoy it, if only he could say, 'What the hell, I've got a ghostwriter, I'm taking some time off, I still get half the money, and I'll get back to it when I get back to it.' But he couldn't do that, unfortunately; the thought of not working on his own novel just made him too scared, as though his not being able to work *today* meant he wouldn't be able to work *forever*.

Wayne didn't want to try to deal with that fear, because he didn't want to bring it out on the surface, where they could all look at it and Bryce could get even worse. Somehow, Wayne had to keep Bryce from losing heart, even though he wasn't really working.

He said, 'Bryce, have you figured out any more about the Indian burial mounds?'

'No, forget that, that doesn't work, that's, I don't know, juvenile. Indian raids in Connecticut, today. I'll put them in war paint, I suppose.'

'Birch-bark canoes,' Wayne suggested.

'From Sears,' Bryce said. He seemed more cheerful now.

Wayne said, 'So what've you got?'

Bryce rubbed his face. 'I think and think,' he said, 'and I don't get anything. Nothing at all this week. I like working on *your* book.'

'Is that enough for you?'

'No!'

'I didn't think it was. Can I make a suggestion?'

Bryce looked at him, hopeful but wary. 'Sure,' he said.

'First,' Wayne said, 'you remember the deal, this story is yours, it has to be yours or you won't be happy with it.'

'Yeah, sure, I know.'

'But I can make a suggestion once in a while.'

'Oh, please. Please.'

'Okay. I think you gave up too quickly on the story about the guy who murdered the woman he didn't know. I mean, nobody knew he knew her.'

Bryce cocked his head, gazing off. 'You think so?'

In fact, Wayne did not. He thought the story was suited to a paperback original published around 1954, and the woman's brother would be a gangster, probably in a gambling racket somewhere. *Kill Me Slowly*, it would be called.

But Bryce had to work on something, had to at least *believe* he was at work on something, and of all the fragments and remnants he'd come up with, *Kill Me Slowly* was the closest to coherence. It had a storyline, it had characters, it had a few scenes.

If Wayne could get Bryce to concentrate on that story, and stick with it for a while, everything would be okay. Just until *The Shadowed Other* was finished, and accepted by Joe, and paid for. Then Wayne and Susan would have a million dollars that Mark Steiner could invest for them, and Wayne could go on doing the magazine pieces, and Susan would still have her job, and they'd be set in that terrific apartment on Central Park West. He wouldn't even *start* another novel, not even if he thought of one, and if he was concentrating on the magazine pieces he doubted he'd even come up with another story.

And Bryce, after the acceptance of *The Shadowed Other*, could sink or swim on his own. All Wayne had to do was steer Bryce through these rapids. And remember never to call his idea *Kill Me Slowly*. Smooth water lay ahead.

So he said, 'I think that story has stuff in it that you can use, that can help you get into that subject you write about so often, the other possibilities besides what really did happen.'

'That's true, isn't it?' Bryce said. 'It's just – I don't see anything between when he does it and when he confesses to the brother and the sister. What you said the first time, it's all too interior, he's got nobody to talk to, nothing to *do*.'

'Well, that's where my suggestion comes in,' Wayne said. 'What if he meets the brother and the sister early on? Not long after the murder. But in a different context.'

Bryce considered that, slowly nodding. 'Seeks them out,' he said. 'Sure.'

'Wants to know more about the woman he killed. Killed her, but didn't really know her.'

'That's right.'

'Tries to learn about her through the brother and the sister.'

'It's worth fiddling with.'

'The second woman,' Bryce said.

'What second woman?'

'That's the title,' Bryce said. 'The first woman is the one he killed. The second woman is the one he's trying to find out about.'

'That's good,' Wayne said.

There was another party Saturday night, at the big weekend house of people named Hendrickson. Bryce had been right, the social life up here was varied and full. And Wayne and Susan fit into it immediately, probably better than Bryce, because it was mostly couples. Susan in particular nestled in as though the world had merely been holding a place for her here all these years, and Wayne glowed in the light of her pleasure. He loved to see Susan happy.

And everybody here was friendly, everybody was comfortably well-off, and by now most of them recognized Wayne and Susan as being a part of the group. 'You really have to get a place up here,' several people told Wayne.

On the way home, in Bryce's BMW, Susan in front, Wayne in back, Susan said, 'I really like the Hendricksons. I like them all.'

'So do I,' Wayne said.

'They're great people,' Bryce agreed.

'They kept saying,' Susan said, 'we should get a place up here.'

'They said that to me, too,' Wayne said.

Bryce said, 'You could do that. Why not?'

Susan said, 'You know, I'm taking two weeks off early in June. I could do some house-hunting then. Bryce, would it be too much if we stayed with you for part of that?'

'Stay the whole time,' Bryce offered. 'Wayne, you bring your laptop, we can both work.'

'That's perfect,' Wayne said. 'You on *The Second Woman*, me on *The Shadowed Other*.'

Three weeks later, on the Saturday, they drove up in the forest green Toyota Land Cruiser they'd just bought. Early June, bright sun, already talk in the neighborhood of drought. Mrs Hildebrand greeted them like old members of the family and helped them carry their luggage up to the guest room, where Bryce had moved in a large refectory table to serve as Wayne's desk, putting it in front of one of the windows. The view was of the pool and the hilly woods beyond. Bryce's office was on the same side of the house, just beyond the guest bathroom, with the same view.

After lunch, Susan went swimming while Wayne and Bryce sat in the living room to read each other's work for the week. *The Shadowed Other* was almost finished. Wayne believed they'd be ready to turn it in to Joe before the Fourth of July, giving him the holiday weekend to read it.

As to *The Second Woman*, progress there was more difficult to gauge. The first week, Bryce had worked with manic energy, as though something in him that had been imprisoned had finally been granted release. He'd handed Wayne thirty-two pages of finished copy that Saturday, taking Luke Parmalee from his appointment with the school board's purchaser through his meeting of Brenda Wade in the high school's parking lot, dinner, and to bed. Bryce had never been known in his novels for particularly graphic sex scenes, but this one had seemed to Wayne particularly perfunctory, as though the writer weren't entirely sure what sex was, or even if he wanted to know. Otherwise, the two characters were very good, their dialogue humorous and touching as they hesitantly revealed themselves to one another.

Wayne hadn't seen any point in negative criticism, since *The Second Woman* was very unlikely to ever be an actual completed and publishable novel. It was make-work, meant to keep Bryce happy until *The Shadowed Other* was done. So he'd merely complimented

Bryce on the positive things, the sweetness and humanity of Luke and Brenda, and let it go at that.

The second week, Bryce had produced twenty-one more pages, but they were jumpier, less polished. The transition from the first night in the motel to the later meeting outside the second motel was abrupt and awkward, badly written, with lumpy sentences. In the dialogue, while Luke remained essentially the same character as before, sweet, a little sad and unsure of himself, Brenda was almost a different person, harsh and accusative and manipulative in obvious ways. The dinner scene was awkward and stilted, and the manuscript ended as they were leaving the restaurant.

This third week should be the murder scene, but what Bryce gave Wayne was a manuscript of seventy-one pages, from page one. 'I made some changes,' he said, 'so I thought you ought to look at it from the beginning.'

'Okay, fine.'

Bryce was finished reading Wayne's eleven new pages first, of course, so he leafed through a magazine while Wayne kept reading. *The Second Woman* began as it had before, with maybe some cutting in the first scene with the buyer, but then the parking lot scene was longer and Brenda was already a little harsher than she'd been, more like the person of the second encounter. The transition to that second encounter was considerably longer and much better written, the lumpy sentences smoothed out. Dinner was also longer, and Brenda here was less harsh, so the character in this version made hardly any change at all between the two scenes. Also, in this version, Brenda talked a bit about her brother and sister, establishing who they were. The pages ended, as last week, with them leaving the restaurant.

'That's much better,' Wayne said, when he'd finished. 'You've really got Brenda consistent now, and I like bringing in the brother and sister.'

'Yeah, that felt good,' Bryce said. 'Do you, uh, have any ideas for the next part?'

'No, I think you just do what you planned to do.'

'Okay.' Bryce nodded, looking at the stack of pages Wayne had given back to him. 'I think,' he said, 'maybe I'll go do some work on it now.'

'And I might as well get my stuff set up,' Wayne said. 'Any comments on the new pages?'

'What? Oh, yours. No, it's fine, the book's just sailing.' Bryce grinned. 'You don't need me on that one.'

'Good,' Wayne said. 'That means you can concentrate on *The Second Woman*.'

And wouldn't it be strange, Wayne thought, if Bryce actually made a real novel out of this thing. He still believed that was very unlikely, but maybe not impossible. Bryce just might be able to pull it off after all. Wayne hoped he would. He didn't have faith in it, but he could hope.

They went upstairs together, and into their separate rooms, and Wayne unpacked his ThinkPad and the new small printer he'd just bought for this trip and the rest of his materials, distributing them on to the refectory table. He looked out the window, and Susan was in the pool, doing laps.

It would be great to have their own house somewhere around here, particularly if it already had a pool, but there was no hurry. This house was big and comfortable, and Mrs Hildebrand was fabulous. Wayne and Susan could stay here through this two-week vacation, and then weekend here through the summer. Susan would like that, she'd fallen in love with this house.

Thirty-One

Lucie used to swim naked in the pool; they both did. But there was no one in these rooms then, looking out the window.

Bryce sat at his desk, looking to his left at the window, and out it, at Susan doing laps in the pool. She had been doing that twice a day, after breakfast, and after lunch, for almost two weeks now. This was the second Thursday of their stay, and they'd be leaving on Sunday. But coming back, of course, next weekend.

Bryce remembered Lucie naked in the pool. He remembered how water would bead in her pubic hair when she came out of the pool, and he'd say, 'Your cunt is winking at me,' and she would laugh. Sex in the water was never totally successful, but they tried it a few times anyway, and he remembered the pale sleekness of her wet skin as she moved. He remembered the way she moved.

Susan wore a two-piece bathing suit, not quite a bikini. She had three of them, one with a design of white stars on red, one a solid royal blue, and one just swirls of color, like a kaleidoscope that had bled. Today, she wore the kaleidoscope. Every once in a while, she would climb out of the pool to use the diving board. Diving, she was efficient, made no big splash, but wasn't particularly graceful.

He closed his eyes. Time to go to work, go back to work, stop stalling, get moving here, break through that block while Wayne was still staying here. This was Bryce's last chance, and he knew it. Wayne was being very patient, urging him but not nastily, but Bryce could sense Wayne's patience wearing thin.

He couldn't get to the murder scene. Every time he approached it, the two people walking, the argument, establishing the dark, establishing the solitude, no one else around, his mind veered off and he thought about something he should do or undo in the pages that already existed. Like improve the sex scene, make it individual, make it real but not crude, he'd done that Monday. Every day he did more, he'd even tried to leapfrog to the later scene, when Luke would meet Dillon, Brenda's brother, but it didn't work. Without that experience behind him, Luke didn't yet exist in the later scenes, and Bryce had no way to write the man.

I have to do it today, he thought, and opened his eyes and looked out to see Susan toweling herself. The pattern was, she'd come in now and shower, then go down to the kitchen to chat with Mrs Hildebrand a while. She did that every day.

We all have our patterns here, he thought, we're a little community, we all have the things we do every day, but today what I have to do is the murder scene.

Susan, the towel around her, walked toward the house, moving out of sight. Bryce focused again on the screen in front of him, his fingers resting on the keyboard.

'Brenda,' he said, his hands clenching into fists

Was that right? Fists? Was it like a boxing match, punching, throwing hooks and jabs? That didn't seem right, it didn't seem violent or brutal enough. This isn't 'the fights.'

his fingers curled into claws,

No, *she* should be the one who scratches, claws and scratches. Why didn't Wayne have scratches on him?

Beyond the wall behind him, he heard the shower start. Not wanting the distraction, any distraction, he concentrated on the words on the screen.

'Brenda,' he said, his fingers curled into claws,

Her name isn't Brenda. Is that the problem? What is her name, if it isn't Brenda?

One of the reference books he kept on the shelf was a little paperback called *4000 Names for Your Baby*. He took it down now, started to leaf through it. What initial? Not *L*.

Do this later, he told himself. Push the scene through now, get past this scene, change the names later.

He put the book away, and a knock sounded at the door. When he was alone here, he kept his office door open, but with people in the house, and him being so easily distracted these days, he kept it shut.

He turned that way, called, 'Hello?'

'It's Wayne.'

'Come on in.'

Wayne opened the door as the sound of the shower stopped. 'I have to go to Danbury,' he said. 'Want to come along?'

'What do you need in Danbury?'

'A new ink cartridge for my printer.' Wayne grinned, pleased and sheepish at the same time. 'I thought I had enough till we got back to New York, but I'm working faster than I expected. Want to ride along? You haven't been in our new car yet.'

'Sure,' Bryce said, and gestured at his screen. 'Just let me—'

Shut it all down, he meant, but then he looked at the screen and saw

'Brenda,' he said, his fingers curled into claws,

and knew it was wrong. 'Wait a second,' he said.

'Sure.'

Bryce touched the keyboard.

         and his shoulders hunched. His left hand moved out, almost of its own accord, and closed painfully on her upper arm.

    She turned
      pulled back
      said,

'Bryce?'

Bryce took his fingers from the keys, looked at Wayne in the doorway. 'I think I should stay,' he said. 'I want to get through this part.'

'Oh, okay. How's it coming?'

'Oh, it's slow, you know,' Bryce said. 'There's progress, but it's slow.'

'You'll get it. See you.'

'See you,' Bryce said, and thought, I'm lying to Wayne now, exactly the way I used to lie to Joe. The same lie, the same words.

Wayne shut the office door and Bryce put his fingers on the keyboard. Faintly, he could hear the sound of the hairdryer.

> 'Claudia,' he said, and yanked at her arm. 'You're pushing me too hard.'
> 'Get your goddam hands off me,' she said, and swung at his face.

She starts it? Why would she start it? And if she starts it, doesn't that change the dynamic of the whole episode? I'm absolving him, then, if she starts it, and I'm not here to absolve him.

Claudia. That's like a joke, a stupid joke, about claws. Santa Claws, the patron saint of tough women. How tough is she?

> 'Just how tough are you, Brenda?' he said, and slapped her across the face.

A slap. A slap doesn't do anything, a slap is an insult, not a threat. He has to do . . . more. He has to *begin*.

I should go with Wayne, he thought, get out of here, go for a ride in his shiny new car, think about . . . Easier to think if I get away from this screen for a while.

Ask him. In the car. Say, 'Wayne, just theoretically, how would this violence begin? How would it start?'

He got up and went out to the hall, leaving the office door open. He crossed the hall to go into his bedroom and look out the front window there to see if the Land Cruiser was still parked in its usual place down below, but it was gone. Wayne had already left.

He went back out to the hall. He could hear the hairdryer. Today was Thursday, Mrs Hildebrand's day off, she was in Danbury, visiting friends.

Bryce walked down the hall and opened the guest room door. Susan, seated at the vanity table, wearing a gray robe, saw the movement in the mirror there and turned as Bryce walked in. She switched the hairdryer off and said, 'Bryce? What is it?'

'You see, what the problem is, Lucie,' he said, 'I just have to *know*.'

She stood. 'My name is Susan,' she said.

'Not any more,' he said.